TO HELL
& BACK

MONIQUE SINGLETON

VINCI
BOOKS

By Monique Singleton

The Dominion Series

To anyone who conquers the darkness

Vinci Books

vinci-books.com

Published by Vinci Books Ltd in 2025

1

A CIP catalogue record for this book is available from the British Library.

Paperback ISBN: 9781036705756

Chapter One

He's getting worse. Much worse.

Not just physically, but mentally too.

Jonah is paranoid. Couple that with a two-hundred-and-forty-pound physique, immense strength and a violent nature, and you have a disaster waiting to happen.

We're all tiptoeing around him, walking on eggshells to avoid him blowing up. Last time that happened—two days ago—three of Ebony's people ended up visiting doctor Patil. One came back with a cast on his arm. The other two made do with stitches.

Other days Jonah's depressed to a point where we fear for his life.

The situation is taking its toll on all of us, but most of all on Ebony. Jonah has distanced himself from everyone who cares from him including her, and it's breaking her heart.

She buries herself in work, as expected, but I can see it hurts.

The blueprints Aaliyah gave me are coming to life in the workshop: a mini re-incarnation machine. It is a completely unheard-of technology in this dimension, but common in mine. Finally, it will be used for good, if we can convince Jonah to go ahead with our plan. And that's a big "if".

Reuniting him with his old body is the only way to save him, but the outcome of the procedure is uncertain. His human body is in cryostasis, a relatively new technique here. Human medicine is able to freeze bodies but has yet to bring anyone back from the dead. Add that Jonah's essence has already been re-incarnated once before into his current —declining—alien form, and we have no way of knowing whether it can survive another procedure.

And then there's Jonah himself.

For this to work, he must want to live.

Only his tenacity will see him through. Re-incarnation is an invasive procedure, painful and disorienting. If he lacks the resolve, then all this has been for nothing.

We don't have much time.

Jonah's alien body is failing rapidly.

His blackouts are more frequent and protracted, leaving him disoriented and volatile. One of his two hearts functions on less than half-strength. We think he can live on only the second one, but the body was never designed for that. Our two hearts complement each other fully. The strain on the remaining heart is already exceptionally high and it's just a matter of time before that one gives up as well. Especially because Jonah refuses to slow down.

He complains about voices in his head that are driving him mad. And he berates me constantly for bringing him back in this new body.

In general, he hates his life.

And me.

We're running on borrowed time.

And at present, Jonah is nowhere near ready for the only thing that will save him.

Chapter Two

We were gathered together at the dinner table.

Always a difficult time.

We had to face each other and make small talk. In the past weeks, I'd found reasons not to be there, but today Ebony had specifically asked me to come.

'You have to go through this, Gabriel. You can't keep avoiding Aaliyah,' she tried to convince me.

I shrugged. 'I was doing a good job with it.' I attempted to make light of the situation.

She shook her head.

I guess that was a negative then. Bummer.

'She doesn't want me there,' I tried. Ebony stayed silent. 'Really, she doesn't.'

Still no answer.

I gave in. 'Okay. I'll be there.'

She smiled, kissed me on the cheek and turned to leave my quarters. 'Six o'clock, Gabe. No excuses.'

I'd made it on time, and it took all of five minutes before Aaliyah went for my throat. Virtually, but her words hurt me almost as much as her knife could. I felt guilty already. I didn't need her to compound the emotion.

'That's not fair, Aaliyah.' Jonah's loud voice stopped her tirade. She turned to face him, temporarily freeing me from the onslaught.

'He's not the one who killed your father.'

'It's his fault,' she shouted at the big man. 'He started this stupid quest and because of that my father is dead.'

'Actually, I started it. Gabe joined me. Not that it matters. From what I know, it was just a matter of time,' Jonah answered. 'Your families have been at each other's throats for centuries. We didn't cause this. It would have happened anyway.'

I waited. Not wanting to divert Aaliyah's attention back to me.

'Besides,' the big man continued. 'It wasn't Gabriel who killed him. It was Bashir.'

'Brainwashed by his father,' she pointed to me with an outstretched arm, her glare sending new shivers up and down my spine.

Jonah shrugged. 'Maybe. But it still wasn't Gabriel.'

She crossed her arms in front of her chest and stared at Jonah, her eyes shooting fire. 'Why are you protecting him?'

'Because he doesn't deserve this.'

I was as surprised as Aaliyah. I'd felt the brunt of Jonah's rage in the past weeks, and this was completely out of character.

'He's sacrificed everything to bring his dad down. He has no home. No family. He killed his brother for wounding me. He risked his life for every single one of us here, including you.'

Aaliyah was silenced. She looked at Jonah from under her eyebrows, sulking.

5

'He's the reason we're all here. That we're doing this. So how about we give him some slack for a change. He can't help who his dad is any more than you could.'

Jonah sat down and left it to us.

'Jonah's right,' Ebony chimed in.

Aaliyah reluctantly nodded ever so slightly.

'Maybe we should stop referring to our real enemy as "Gabriel's Father" all the time,' Jonah suggested.

He looked up at me. 'What's his name? No way I'm calling him "God" or anything like that.'

I smiled despite the situation. 'His given name in Cal-Tan, it's an old name in our dimension.'

'Not anything biblical?'

'No, it originates from before we ever came in contact with your religions.'

'Well, Cal-Tan it is then,' Jonah stated resolutely.

I was swamped with feelings of gratitude for my big friend.

I felt relief. I hoped it would distance my father from me and let me relax a bit. Jonah was right. It had felt like a personal attack every time someone referred to him as my father. My name always came first. It was depressing, and infuriating. It wasn't my fault we were related.

I despised the man, maybe more than anyone here, with the exception of Aaliyah. He'd constantly made my life a living hell. First with his never-ending manipulations and denigration tactics, and now with his relentless pursuit of me and my strange group of friends.

I needed distance, and hopefully this would give it to me.

'Now that's out of the way,' Jonah brought us back to the present in his weirdly practical way. 'Let's eat.'

His appetite was legendary, and today was no exception.

We all helped ourselves to the great meal Sly, the cook-come-bodyguard, had prepared. The man was an accomplished chef, and I enjoyed his food every single time.

We ate in relative silence. Mainly because of the good food, but still partly due to the argument and the tentative status-quo that was in effect. I glanced up from under my eyebrows at Aaliyah. She was pushing her food around on the plate, not eating like the rest of us. I felt for her. She'd been party to the brutal murder of her father. Even though she didn't agree with his practices, she'd loved the man deeply.

It showed.

Not for the first time, I wished I could turn back time.

Not one of my talents.

Regrettably.

Chapter Three

'We need to determine our next steps,' I broached the subject carefully.

After-dinner banter was over. It was time to get down to business.

We were all seated at the big round table in the dining area that doubled as an extra meeting room. The light outside was waning and subdued lamps around the perimeter offered enough illumination to be able to read the documents on electronic devices that invariably followed every meeting. The blinds were drawn and only feint pinpricks of moving headlights showed we were in a populated area. The triple glass held out any sounds.

I sat between Jonah and Ebony, I thought between friends would be comfortable, whereas the other side of the table with Aaliyah still noticeably cooler. She was coming around millimetre by millimetre, but the status quo was still very fragile.

I'd calculated badly, the air between Jonah and Ebs was almost as loaded as between Aaliyah and me, though this time it wasn't the result of anything I'd done. They were going through a difficult patch in their relationship, mainly due to Jonah's difficult disposition. He was never easy to live with, now he was downright impossible. They no longer shared a bedroom, another bad sign.

'What are our options?' Ebony asked.

Good question. We didn't have many. Not anymore.

'We've exhausted the Islamic route,' I answered.

'Unless we go to another Islamic community some-where?' Jonah suggested to my dismay, though he might have a point there.

'What if the mosque shared the information with others?' I asked.

'We have no way of knowing,' Aaliyah answered. 'We must assume they have.'

'The Christian side is actively hunting us, so I don't think we have much leeway there.' Ebony pointed out.

'Unless we can use some assets we already have.' Jonah joined the conversation.

'You have any in mind?' Aaliyah sat close by, not touching him, but still nearby. I expect it was the feeling of safety the big man gave her. No matter that he was as unstable as ever. He still exhumed a strength she needed.

'Benedict?' I asked.

Jonah shrugged. 'Maybe'

'Who's Benedict?' Aaliyah asked him.

Jonah filled her in with a brief history of our dealings with the archbishop.

'Sounds like an asset.'

'Yes, but one we don't want to endanger. Not while he may be our only way into the Inner Circle of the Estab-lishment.'

'Any success on the data side?' I asked Ebony.

'Some. I've picked up a financial stream that looks promising. If I can block that, or even better divert it, then it will be a major blow to the Ventus Dei.'

'Then what?'

'Do you have any contacts we could approach?' Jonah asked Aaliyah. 'Anyone?'

'I'd have to think,' she replied. 'Most have been lost now with the change of power, but there have always been people like me who opposed the direction Bashir wanted. Problem is most of them are still back in my dimension.'

'Is there any way you can contact them?' I added. 'Without endangering them or yourself.'

She glared at me. Still not happy with my presence. Then her eyes softened, and she let go of some of her anger. 'I'm afraid Bashir may be monitoring all communications.'

'I would, if I were him,' I agreed.

She nodded.

Okay, another dead end then.

'If we could find a way, 'Ebony suggested. 'Would you be open to it?'

'Maybe.'

Chapter Four

After the attack on the ranch, we'd decided to hide in plain sight.

Or more appropriately, hide in the masses.

We still didn't know how they'd found us at the ranch. We ruled out a traitor. The only ones who knew Jonah had been there were Ebony's men—none of whom were suspect —and the doctor. I had no idea what the hold was Ebony had on him, but it garnered absolute loyalty. So he was also not a candidate.

Our big friend had reluctantly been very careful after Michael found him in San Diego on the beach. Plus, he'd been closely monitored. Jonah hadn't let anything slip. No clues there.

So how had they found us?

It would stay a mystery. Luck, coincidence, if there were such a thing. A one-time thing.

We hoped.

We were back in Los Angeles.

In a massive office building in the centre of the financial

district. I had no idea what our new digs must have cost, but it was our new home.

The top floors housed the living quarters and the computer lab. Under that was a medical centre that rivalled the best private hospital in the country. Unlimited funds were definitely a benefit. I didn't care how and where Ebony got them. I was even resigned to it being less than legal.

The first thirty-odd floors of the building were legitimate offices, inhabited by "real" businesses. They were the front to our operation. Ebony hinted this legitimate area funded the slightly grey operation up top. Whatever, I was just happy we had a new base of operations.

It made sense.

This place was a bastion of security.

No one went in or out without a retina- and hand scan. In addition, x-ray functionality identified aliens from my dimension by their physiology. Electronics and digital security ruled out any tracking devices or hacking attempts. Nothing was left to chance. Ebony was thorough.

The living quarters were lavish. Mini apartments for all of us. Also, a master kitchen that a three-Michelin star restaurant would be jealous of, a fully stocked gym, sauna, everything.

My apartment was on the shadow side of the building. I'd asked for it, I liked the shade. Besides, it caught the evening sun, and I enjoyed sitting on the balcony with a good glass of whisky, watching the sunset. There was a living room, fully equipped bathroom and a more than adequate bedroom with a walk-in wardrobe. Like all the other apartments, it came with a small kitchen and every comfort you could wish for.

It felt like home. Kind of.

And of course there was the computer stuff.

That took up a whole floor.

I didn't pretend to know what the equipment was, or what it did, but it was extensive and state-of-the-art. I'm sure some of it wasn't even mainline available. Some of it was newly invented, created by Ebony using a mixture of human and Taxore technology. It was light years ahead of anything else on earth.

Ebony's geeks had enthusiastically reverse-engineered everything they'd recovered from my dimension. Everything Aaliyah and I brought, the blueprints, what we'd recovered from the attackers, everything.

Ebs was at the forefront of it all. Her technical genius was unparalleled, and she outshone everyone.

Her main focus in the past weeks had been the reincarnation technology. Ever since we acquired the blueprints, she'd been submerged in the technology day and night.

I was worried for her. She wasn't sleeping much. Too little really. Sly made sure she ate well, but rest had no place in her agenda. I think she felt responsible. That she was the only one who would be able to put it together and ultimately reunite Jonah with his old self.

No pressure, right?

Chapter Five

'I'm not sure I can do it again,' Jonah stated softly.

'Reincarnation?'

He nodded.

'Talk to me. Please, Jonah.' Ebony took his hand.

He looked at her and his features softened. His lips curled up in a small smile that failed to reach his eyes. The purple capillaries around his irises stood out brightly against what was left of the white in his eyes. The inflamed veins were rapidly taking over and gave him a sickly countenance. His cheeks were pronounced, the pale-grey skin pulled tightly over the bone and sparce muscle. Even the hair of his beard looked flat and shabby, streaks of grey now more prominent. My big friend was losing his battle to stay alive, and it was killing us all.

'It was bad. Worse than dying itself,' he concluded as he pushed himself deeper into the sofa.

We were seated in the living room of Ebony's apartment, a cosy space with lots of soft colours and muted lighting. The lights from the city streamed past the tall windows in a never-ending snake of red taillights and neon signs, slightly blurred by the coating on the windows.

Words eluded me. There was nothing I could say.

'I don't want to do it again.'

'I understand that,' I tried.

'How could you? Have you ever experienced it?' There was venom in his voice and a hint of reproach.

I shook my head.

'Then you don't know.' Jonah's eyes shot daggers.

'No. You're right. I don't. But I do know you have a lot to live for. You're not done yet. And we need you.'

'For your quest?' His tone was sarcastic. There was no use reminding him it had initially been his crusade.

'For our family,' I answered moving my arms around to add everyone in the room. That shut him up. He lowered his gaze to the floor.

'This.' I gestured to the collection of misfits in the room. 'This is the closest I've ever come to having a real family. And I don't want you to lose it. I don't want to lose you. Sure, you're a pain sometimes to be around, literally. But you're my pain. One that I need to keep me focussed and on the right path. You changed my life. Like your nun did for you. You've opened my eyes to what I was doing and that made me a better man. You're more a brother to me than any of my kin. So, no. I don't want to lose you.'

I sat down, emotionally drained.

Jonah looked up at me. He cocked his head and smiled, this time extending it to his eyes that shone for just a moment.

'Thanks.'

I shrugged.

'We need you, big man,' Ebony agreed. 'We can't do this without you.'

He nodded slowly.

The creases returned to his brow. 'Yeah, but what are the odds of it working?'

Ebony glanced at me, I nodded to urge her onwards.

'We don't know. Not really. I can give you tons of statistics, but those are just conjecture. Bottom line: it's never been done before so no-one knows.'

'That's reassuring,' he half joked.

'The technology is sound,' Ebony continued. 'It works in Gabe's dimension on new recruits. But it's never been tested here, or on human bodies. And we have no way of knowing whether your old form will accept you back, or what state it will be in.'

Jonah cocked his head and shrugged. 'Well, at least you're honest about it.'

'You won't survive for long with this body,' Aaliyah chimed in, continuing the tough love trend we had going. 'It's dying. But you don't have to.'

'Sugar-coating isn't one of your kind's qualities, is it?' he asked her.

'It wouldn't help.'

She had a point.

'I have to think about it,' Jonah tried.

'You don't have much time. You must decide soon, or there will be no chance anymore.' Ebony's voice was almost a whisper. 'We're running out of time, big man.'

The next day still saw no resolution, though he was able to express his doubts when we convened in Ebony's lab.

'How do you know I won't be reincarnated in your father's facility, or Bashir's?' Jonah asked. 'It's happened before.' He aimed his question at me.

'This body doesn't have their nanos. Those were in your old body, and we flushed them out. We'll administer new ones to you that we built and will show up on this computer.'

'How do you administer them this time?'

At least he was asking more detailed questions, that gave me a slight glimmer of hope that he would go through with the procedure.

Ebony picked up the explanation. 'Not like last time. This time we'll inject them in your blood stream over the course of two days. That will allow them to permeate this body and we can test whether the link is correct.'

'Have you tested anything?' He was tentative again, his fingers pushing a paperclip around on the table.

'We tested the nanos on one of the alien bodies we have on ice.' Ebony continued unfazed. 'We flushed all the existing ones out of the body, then hooked it up to a heart-lung machine and made sure there was circulation. Then we injected the new ones and waited. They show up. So we know that works.'

'But you couldn't test whether the soul is captured?'

She shook her head. 'No. The body was empty.'

'You would need a live guinea pig?'

'Yes.'

'And that's me.'

We refrained from answering.

'Unless of course we could capture someone from your dimension.' His suggestion was offered softly as he glanced at me. But he had a point. Only, how could we do that? And would it be ethical to test on a live subject? More dilemmas. Just what I needed.

'Just for argument's sake,' I continued the line of

thought despite my reservations. 'How could we get someone?'

'We'd need to set up a trap.'

'It might be worth looking into. Just to make sure we've covered all bases,' Ebony chimed in.

Chapter Six

Ebony's brow was creased as she absentmindedly pushed loose strands of hair into the clip on the back of her head. Sleep had eluded her for the past thirty-six hours and I was worried about her. She was living off energy drinks, protein shakes and possibly supplements I didn't want to know about, working non-stop to get this alien reincarnation technology working.

The blueprints Aaliyah procured were strewn over the surface of the large desk, spilling onto the floor. Red letters highlighted the parts where Ebony had questions. We'd gone over them again and again in the past three hours, searching for alternatives if the technology was unavailable here on earth.

'We need to test the technology on live subjects. There's no way we can be sure it will even recognise the tagged soul,' she stated.

The slight tremble in her voice was not lost on me. I wished I could help her more, but my knowledge was exhausted and there were still open questions. One in particular.

She looked up at me from the calculations she'd just written on the iPad and projected them onto the screen in front of the massive desk. 'We have to.' There was determination in her tone, but underneath a desperation I wasn't used to encountering in my tiny friend.

She was right though.

We had to test the machine she'd created on something alive. There was nothing more she could do without real live data. Ebony had followed the blueprint to the letter as far as possible, it should work. It had to.

Jonah's life depended on it.

'How do we do that?' I asked, dreading the answer. We couldn't just kill someone in an attempt to capture the soul. It was unethical and went against everything we stood for. We were trying to save mankind, not kill them, and we'd ruled out someone from my dimension, because of the difference in physiology and essence density.

'We'll have to start on an animal,' she relieved me from my dread. 'Not that I want to, I hate animal testing, but we have no choice. I've run all the computer simulations, and they point to success, but we need to be sure.'

Yes, I thought. As sure as we can get.

There were so many variables in play here. Even if we did manage to secure the soul, there was the next hurdle, getting it back into Jonah's old body. Never mind resurrecting that one from Cryo.

'What kind of animal?' I asked.

'Mice, I think,' she answered, her head once again buried in the papers. 'They share ninety-five percent of our DNA. Enough to validate the simulations.'

'But is DNA relevant in what we're doing?' I had to ask.

She looked up at me, her head cocked in question.

'We're not going after the body,' I explained further.

'No,' she answered contemplating my words. 'The soul.'

We were silent for a few minutes. The only sound the soft whirring of the computer's fans.

'What do you call it in your dimension?' Ebony broke the silence.

'What? The soul?'

She nodded.

'It differs. People like my brother or my father are so immersed in the scam that they've started to believe it themselves, they call it the soul. Our scientists call it the Life Essence.'

'And is that present in all living creatures?'

'Yes. It's the life force. Everything that lives, has it in some form.'

'So we could test this part of the procedure out on mice?' She deduced.

I shrugged. 'It should be possible.' I couldn't make it any more definite. This was unknown territory for me too.

'How did your scientists test the reincarnation process when you started reaping Life Essence from this dimension?'

'You don't want to know,' I answered avoiding her gaze.

'They experimented on humans.' It wasn't a question anymore.

I nodded. 'Humans were animals to them. Like mice and monkeys to your scientists. They've never seen humans as peers or anything more than a commodity.'

I felt ashamed. Tainted by the actions of my kind--my own actions until I met Jonah. Ebony lay a hand on my arm in support.

'You didn't know.'

'I do now.'

'And you're working on setting it right.'

I smiled and suddenly felt childish, not to mention egotistical. Once again, I'd made this all about me. Inside, I admonished myself and turned back to the present issue. The one that really mattered.

'How will we test the process?' I asked.

'We'll need to use multiple mice. Some have to be trained to do certain actions while the others aren't.'

Ebony was back in scientist mode. It warmed my hearts to see her dedication and steadfastness. I pitted strength from her.

'From what you told me, the essence will remember things from the previous life, right?'

I nodded.

'So, theoretically, if we transplant the essence of a mouse that learned a specific action into one that hasn't, we should see that mouse performing what the first one learned,' she mused.

I shrugged, it sounded logical. 'I'm not sure it works that fast, but it sounds plausible.'

'Then that's what we'll do to start off with.'

Ebony turned her attention back to the computer screens. I know she didn't do it on purpose, but I felt dismissed. Again, I admonished myself for being such a wimp.

I squeezed her shoulder, she absentmindedly touched my hand, and I turned and walked out of the lab.

The facility she'd set up was state-of-the-art, not that I'd expected anything less from her. Ebony was a perfectionist, and in her mind, perfection came with the right tools.

It must have been frustrating for her to be restricted by

what she could get here on Earth. The blueprints referred to our technology on Taxore, and some things were just not reproducible with earthen materials. But Ebony was resourceful. After all, she'd managed to put the machine together.

Chapter Seven

The first test results were in only ten days later.

They were not very encouraging.

It had taken a few days and many attempts for the technology to recognise the rodent's essence. The group of trained mice slunk fast without any conclusive results. Ebony and her team tweaked the software, replaced nanos in the test subjects and finally traces of the life essence were picked up by the technology.

'Thankfully we know the blueprint of the nanos we've made, so we can recognise the exact moment when the essence is released, and the essence itself,' she explained to Aaliyah and me.

'We've been able to capture it and move it to the final stage, but that's where we stumble. We place the essence into the new mouse, but it won't take hold. There's something missing.'

Ebony looked even more stressed than the past weeks. Her normally vivacious nature was drawn and morose. She snapped at the scientists and Doctor Patil when they tried to help her and isolated herself in the lab as much as possible. Sly all but force-fed her to get her nourishment.

We were worried. All of us.

'I followed the blueprints,' she mused. 'It should all be there. It should work.'

No one needed to add the rest of the sentence. It didn't work. This one vital step brought everything to a halt.

'Walk me through what you made,' Aaliyah encouraged Ebony. 'Maybe I can help.'

I wasn't sure how. I mean, I knew more about technology than she did, but every extra mind and set of eyes would help.

Aaliyah and Ebony were hunched over the blueprints, with my little friend gesturing to where she'd been forced to change the design and what was authentic.

I was no longer a help here, so I left the room in search of Jonah.

My best bet was one of two places. The gym for his daily workout, or the fridge in the main kitchen, on the rampage to still his enormous appetite.

I found him in the kitchen. He'd raided the fridge and the enormous plate of sub sandwiches and fruit in front of him was enough to feed a small army. Or in this case; one person with an infinite appetite.

'Pull up a chair,' he beckoned me. 'Want a sandwich?'

'No thanks, I'm good.' I smiled. 'How was the workout?'

He shrugged his shoulders as he took another mouthful of the well-filled steak roll. 'Okay,' he commented between bites.

His lack of enthusiasm hinted at disappointment. Jonah pushed himself to the absolute edge of what his body could take. It was his way of relieving stress, and he had enough of that with everything going on.

But his waning strength was also an indicator of his general failing health. He hated weakness in himself and just pushed harder, resulting in even more disappointment. It was a vicious circle he couldn't break. We'd tried to talk sense into him, but he just shrugged it off. He still underestimated the criticality of the situation with his borrowed body.

To be fair, none of us knew what the prognosis really was. Sure, it was deteriorating fast, but how long he could hold out was anyone's guess. So, he did his best to ignore the degradation and get on with life.

Jonah pushed one of the soda cans my way and I took it, holding it up in a silent thank you. I sipped the cool drink and contemplated Ebony's last results again. Not good. Not good at all. But she would get there. No doubt in my mind. If anyone could, it would be Ebs and her team.

We sat in silence; the only sound was Jonah chewing on the last sandwich.

Finally, he pushed the plate away, took a swig of his own soda and sat back in the chair, a big smile on his face. 'Nothing like a snack to get you in a good mood.'

I laughed. 'You call that a snack?'

'What would you call it?' he asked in mock indignation.

I enjoyed our little barter sessions. It brought back the real Jonah. The one I'd known before he died.

'A family meal maybe?'

His lips pulled into a big smile that lit up his face. His eyes full of mischief and promises of more to come.

'One thing I have to say,' he continued. 'Sly does keep the fridge stocked.'

'You might have just eaten dinner for the whole group,' I taunted.

'Then they should have gotten here quicker. First come, first served.'

We drank our sodas, comfortable in each other's company. Quite a difference from a month ago.

'How are the tests going?' Jonah broke the silence, bringing me back down to earth.

'They're coming along well,' I tried.

'You know, you're a lousy liar, Gabe,' he replied. 'You really have to work on your poker face.'

I looked at him. The happy go-lucky Jonah of a few minutes ago was gone. In his place I saw someone haunted by stress and worry. The lines in his brow were more pronounced and the shine had left his eyes.

'The first part is ok, Ebony can intercept the essence—the soul, if you like.'

'But…?'

'She hasn't been able to put it back into a body yet.'

The silence was heavy and loaded.

'But she's working on it,' I added with a feeble attempt at enthusiasm. 'With Aaliyah.'

That raised his eyebrow. 'They're working on it together?'

'Yep.'

He laughed. 'Who knew they could get along.'

'Well, get along might be stretching it,' I joked. 'But they are cooperating.'

The smile slipped away, anxiety once again clouding his features.

'It'll work, Jonah.' I assured him.

'Yeah. I know.'

He pushed his chair away from the table and stood up, gathering his plate and the pitiful remnants of the steak Sly had stashed away. 'It has to.'

I had no answer to that. He was right. The alternative wasn't acceptable.

I racked my brain to think of what I could do to help speed up the process. Even if I chanced everything to go back to my dimension, what good would it do? I had no one who could help. No knowledge of what it was I would be looking for, if—no, when—Ebony found what was wrong, But I could suggest that I try to retrieve what was missing. I could at least try.

My line of thought was broken by the sound of shattering crockery as Jonah's plate smashed onto the stone tiles of the kitchen floor.

I looked up in surprise and saw Jonah reach for his chest. The skin of his face was ashen and grey. His lips had a blue sheen to them, and his breath came in gasps.

He clutched his chest as he slowly slid down the kitchen cabinet door until he sat on the floor with his back to the hard wood.

I jumped up, knocking my own chair over in my haste.

'Jonah!' I shouted.

I ran over to him and knelt beside him. Slowly he turned his head to face me, the bloodshot eyes fixing on mine.

'I'm not feeling very well, Gabe,' he whispered. 'Real shitty.' His eyes closed slowly, and his hand slid down his chest to lie limp in his lap. His head fell forward and came to rest on his chest. I pulled him upright and held on.

I looked around, grabbed my phone that had fallen to the floor when I stood up, and speed dialled Sly.

'Get doctor Patil to the kitchen,' I shouted into the phone. 'Jonah has collapsed.'

I dropped the phone and held my fingers on the jugulars in Jonah's neck. I felt a weak pulse in one, but nothing in the other. Dread filled me and sent tingles up my spine. It was happening. Now. Jonah's hearts were giving up. At least one of them was.

'Hang in there, big man,' I urged him, not sure whether he could hear me or not. 'Don't leave us. Fight. You have to. We're not ready to let you go. Not yet. We haven't tried everything.'

I was talking gibberish, but it didn't matter. As long as he held on.

A commotion at the door heralded Doctor Patil's arrival, flanked by Sly and an anxious Ebony. Just behind her I spotted Aaliyah, the same distress on her features.

Doctor Patil pushed me to the side and together with Sly he lay the big man flat on his back. He proceeded to check Jonah's vitals, working methodically. I stood up and held on to Ebony. She leaned into me and stared at the scene that unfolded before us.

Doctor Patil's assistant pushed past us with a wheeled stretcher he collapsed next to Jonah. They carefully loaded him on and—under constant observation—sped him out of the kitchen to the temporary infirmary Ebony had installed for just this kind of circumstance. We trudged on behind them and waited impatiently outside the open door. We understood the only thing we could do now was stay out of the way and leave it to the professionals.

Half an hour later, Jonah was hooked up to a heart monitor and lay sleeping with an oxygen mask covering the biggest part of his face.

Doctor Patil came out to speak with us.

'He's experienced catastrophic cardiac arrest in the weak heart, causing it to stop functioning. His other heart is still working, but it's strained. It has to pump the blood for both of them now. Thankfully they are both linked to the full cardiovascular system, so he should not experience a breakdown of functionality to one side of his body.'

'Will his remaining heart be able to endure the strain?' I asked.

'We have no way of knowing,' he answered truthfully. 'As yet, it's pumping sufficiently to enable blood and oxygen to reach the vital organs.'

'How long will you keep him asleep?'

'Just until he's stable. Then we'll slowly bring him out of it.'

'To assess the damage?'

'Yes.'

The way he said it was ominous. Regrettably, it was also accurate. We wouldn't know the extent of the damage from the heart attack until Jonah woke up.

Chapter Eight

It took another three days for him to come back to us, two of which he was kept in a coma by Doctor Patil. We felt every minute as though they were weeks or even months. During the whole time there was always one of us sitting by his bedside, just in case he regained consciousness.

When he finally did, he was groggy and flustered.

His first reaction was to lash out, but the energy wasn't there. He retreated into his own world, wherever that was, and we couldn't reach him. The walls he put up were impenetrable. Even Ebony couldn't make him react to her.

Another three days later and we were slowly allowed to engage with him. First, he acknowledged our presence, but didn't speak. Then gradually he reacted to our questions with short, abrupt answers. We were happy with everything we could get.

'What happened?' he finally asked Doctor Patil.

'One of your hearts stopped working.'

He looked at me and Aaliyah. 'Has anything like that ever happened to anyone in your dimension?'

'Sometimes,' I answered, trying to avoid a more detailed reply.

'Mostly it's with the reincarnated bodies.' Aaliyah had no reserve like me. 'It happens.'

'And what do you do when it does?'

Aaliyah and I looked at each other. I raised an eyebrow. She wanted to be frank, well then, she could answer this one.

'The grunt is terminated.'

'Killed?'

She nodded, then turned her face to the side, out of Jonah's piercing gaze.

'It doesn't happen to any of you?'

'Not that I know of,' I answered.

In truth, we are a particularly healthy race. Most of the ails that plagued our kind were eradicated centuries ago. We have nothing like cancer, heart disease, diabetes or anything like that. Not because we live so healthily, just all the bad genetic code was removed from the gene pool long ago.

We have been basically immortal since all the natural diseases had been conquered. There on Taxore, and here on Earth. Maybe that was why we became so violent? There was no danger anymore. Nothing to confront us with death. Nothing other than ourselves.

In my part of Taxore, our most common cause of death was my father.

'So, any cardiac issues are restricted to the reincarnated bodies.'

I didn't react. It wasn't a question.

'And because it doesn't affect you, there's no cure or medicine?'

'Right,' Aaliyah confirmed.

'You don't know if a body can live on one heart?'

'One of my uncles lived with one heart,' I offered. 'His second one was damaged during a fight.'

'And he lived?'

'For a while. Yes.' I tried to trivialise the answer, but it sounded weak, even to me.

After that Jonah stopped asking questions on the subject. The answers were just too depressing.

We were silent. All of us lost for words.

'What am I going to be able to do?' Jonah asked Doctor Patil.

'Not much, I'm afraid.' There was no sugar-coating it. Jonah knew even before he asked.

'Bed ridden?'

'That depends on you. On how long you want to live.'

Ebony gasped, almost imperceptibly.

The truth was hard. Very hard.

'How long do I have?'

'It's conjecture. But I expect a month, something like that.'

'If I stay immobile?'

'Yes.'

'Well,' Jonah stated. 'Looks like we'll have to revisit the reincarnation crap.'

His last comment said it all.

'What do you need?' I asked.

Ebony, Aaliyah and I were back in the lab. With Jonah's tentative decision and the horrific health predictions, there was even more urgency in getting the machines to work. We had to get results. Jonah's life depended on it. And our sanity, I expect.

'There are a few parts in the blueprint that are not

detailed out, so I had to guess at the composition,' Ebony answered.

She'd narrowed the issues down to three separate components. Two she could repair. The third was a bigger issue.

Ebony showed me the technical design of the missing object. It was projected as a complete component you purchase in our dimension as a product, no details.

'You need either the blueprints for those, or the actual objects themselves?' I asked.

'Exactly.'

'Is there any way you can bypass these components?'

Ebony stared at me and raised an eyebrow, her features a compilation of accusatory traits.

'Sorry,' I mumbled. If there had been a way, Ebony would have found it.

'We need to get the parts,' Aaliyah said softly.

'I'll go back,' I stated resolutely.'

Aaliyah stared at me. She sighed audibly. I felt like a child, reprimanded by my elders. There was a lot of that going around lately.

'And how would you find them?' she asked cynically.

'There must be a way,' I tried half-heartedly.

'There is,' she replied. 'But you're not in it.'

She dismissed me.

Anger filled my gut, warming me, urging me onwards. 'I can try,' I attempted.

She folded her arms and looked at me. The snub was clear. Her eyes and her posture said it all.

Sure, she was right. I had no idea where I would get the parts. Or the blueprints. But at least I could try. I could do something. This hanging around and watching the big man die was eating away at me. I needed to act. Do something. Whatever I could.

'You wouldn't be able to acquire the parts,' Aaliyah stated simply as she seemed to soften her approach a bit. 'You don't have the contacts. It would be a waste of your life.'

She was right. But I wasn't ready to concede yet.

'And you do?' I asked, my tone harsher that I wanted.

She stared at me for what felt like a long time before she answered. 'As a matter of fact, yes I do.'

That shut me up very effectively.

I thought back to previous conversations and quickly landed on the memory of my last visit to Taxore, when I found her in the tavern. There had been a man there. A friend of hers. Someone she confided in. Maybe he was the contact. Maybe she had more.

But it would come at a cost. She'd left Taxore in a hurry and her return would be as perilous as mine.

'Are you going back?' I asked softly.

'No.'

I let out my pent-up breath.

'I don't have to,' she added much to my surprise. 'We're in contact.'

'What?' Ebony was vexed. 'You are in contact with someone in your dimension and you didn't let us know?'

'It's a secure communication.'

'You still should have told us.' Ebony's voice had an edge.

'I'm telling you now.' Aaliyah's tone mirrored that of our tech wizard as she squared her shoulders at the obvious anger Ebony portrayed.

Tensions were high, anything could set off a major conflict. We were all on edge.

'Let's just concentrate on getting it, shall we?' I tried to pacify them.

It backfired. They both looked at me as though I were the new enemy. I wilted under their glares. So much so, that I held up my hands in defence and backed away. I would leave it up to them.

I wanted to ask when Aaliyah could procure the parts but decided it wouldn't be prudent given the current circumstances.

Chapter Nine

Time is a funny thing.

On the one hand, hours sitting beside a sleeping Jonah seemed endless. But when it came to solutions for our problems, we never had enough hours in a day.

Aaliyah had been gone for more than a day, twenty-five hours and thirty-six minutes to be exact.

Ridiculous. My impatience wasn't helping anyone. Least of all me.

I sat in the half dark looking at the big man. He'd been reasonably compliant—for his doing—and stayed in bed all day. Early this evening he'd had enough and attempted to walk out of the room. He made it three steps before he collapsed. We carried him back to the bed where he descended into a deep depression.

Through the anger I could see his fear. He tried to camouflage it under his stern exterior and piercing stare, daring me to mention anything remotely resembling anxiety. I didn't, not because I was afraid, but to spare him. He hated being dependent. His strength was his rock. He fiercely defended it, so being restricted to bed like this felt like the ultimate betrayal. He didn't need me to point that out.

I stepped back to rest my back against the wall and just stayed there. Words wouldn't have helped. He wouldn't have heard them; besides how do I comfort someone who doesn't want to know.

The status quo lasted for twenty minutes.

'Have you heard anything from Aaliyah?' His voice, though soft, resonated in the silence of the room.

I shook my head.

Jonah shrugged. Nothing more to say. He knew the score. We needed that part. Without it we would run out of time, that was assuming Ebony could eventually make a replacement for the whole component. Aaliyah was our only hope. Jonah's only chance of survival.

And that was all it was; a chance.

There were no guarantees. It could all go horribly wrong. The only definite was what would happen if we didn't attempt the impossible.

And there was still one major hurdle. It only worked if the big man completely committed to the procedure.

He still hadn't. Not really.

And time was running out.

Fast.

Chapter Ten

Two days later Aaliyah finally showed up with the missing part and an unexpected guest.

Security sounded the alarm as soon as they saw she had a companion. The CCTV picked them up three streets from the building and followed the twosome all the way to the front door.

I rushed to the control room and peered into the security feed. From behind, the visitor looked generic. I shook my head. Nope, didn't look familiar.

They walked on to the restricted lift area and new cameras picked them up. The man--we'd deduced that--walked closely behind Aaliyah. He wore a dark grey hoody that obscured most of his features. His hands were tucked in the bands of his rucksack, but I could see his skin was a light coffee colour. Like mine.

Dread started its merry way up my spine and nested in the already tense muscles of my neck. I felt he was from my dimension and that rang more alarm bells than I was comfortable with. It threw up questions too. Had they found us again? Had Aaliyah been captured, and was she being forced to betray us? No, she wouldn't. Of that, I was sure. No matter what they threatened her with, she wouldn't cave. So, we could rule that out.

The lift doors opened, and Aaliyah and the man entered the tastefully panelled space. Aaliyah glanced up at the camera as she turned around to face the door. The man stood beside her. Aaliyah nudged him and cocked her head in the direction of the camera. He pulled the hood up and let it fall onto his back, uncovering his features.

I recognised his face. This was the man from the tavern. From when I'd gone back to warn Aaliyah about Ibrahim.

I felt the tension decrease to a more manageable level. It didn't disappear, we still had no idea why he was here.

'I know him,' I informed Sly who raised an eyebrow and looked at me totally unimpressed. 'He's a confidant. One of the Taxorian underground.'

'From your dimension?'

'Yes.'

He looked only slightly convinced and turned back to the screens. He gestured to one of the guards to join us as we walked out of the control room towards the lift.

We waited in silence three metres from the doors and watched the number on the display increase.

The doors opened with a soft whooshing sound.

Aaliyah stared at us defiantly. The guy was as timid as I remembered him, though he did seem very impressed by the "welcoming" committee. He took an involuntary step backwards and glanced at Aaliyah.

'Hi,' I tried. She looked at me as though I'd insulted her, and I swallowed my questions. They would come later.

Sly has no such reservations. 'We need to search him.'

'No, you don't,' she answered coldly. 'He's here on my invitation. I vouch for him. So does Gabriel.'

What? I looked at her, my eyes open in surprise. Leave me out of this. Besides, I'd just seen the guy once. I didn't know him.

'With all due respect,' Sly was unimpressed. 'Lady E's rules.'

Aaliyah stared at him, something that would have clearly intimidated most people. Not Sly. He stood his ground, calm and collected. The air shivered with the tension between the two, until Aaliyah glanced at her companion and cocked her head.

Sly proceeded to give the mousy man a tap down, something he was clearly not used to. He kept glancing at Aaliyah, his body trembling slightly, but he complied. Sly was efficient and quickly completed the search. He held his hand out for the rucksack. Again, the small man required Aaliyah's agreement before he handed it over.

Sly opened the bag, took a look inside and closed it again. He moved backwards to allow Aaliyah and her companion to walk down the short hallway into the apartment but held on to the rucksack.

She brushed past us with a look of contempt. Okay, we'd clearly not made any friends here. Stupid really, she knew the drill. She knew why security was so tight. She knew who were after us.

I followed the small procession into the big living room. Our visitor looked around the massive space, his mouth open in surprise as he scanned what must be foreign for him.

The room spanned the width of the penthouse, giving it a double-aspect, very open feel. The dark blue, wrap-around sofa--that sat at least ten--broke the almost stark white format predominant in the rest of the room. The art adorning the walls followed the same line. White backgrounds, with one splash of colour, mostly tones of blue.

The colour scheme continued into the dining area and the big clean lines of the kitchen against the right wall.

The small man's eyes lingered on the vast expanse of balcony and the vista beyond. From this vantage point you could see the blue sea in the background between the high rises. It was a prime location, and this penthouse made the best use of it.

Aaliyah nudged him and pointed to the sofa. He followed her and sat down on the edge of the furniture, clearly not comfortable in the company or with the situation.

Ebony walked up to us and joined our merry group. She glanced at the small man, then at me. I shrugged and cocked my head at Aaliyah, who remained silent.

'Were you able to get the parts?' Ebony asked her, ignoring our new visitor.

'We were,' she answered, immediately setting down the guy's position. So, he'd helped her. I'd gathered that.

Sly handed over the rucksack and Ebony peered into it. Her face immediately lit up when she spied what she was looking for. She reached in and pulled out what to me looked like a small battery. Ebony placed it on the table in front of the sofa and reached back for another.

'He brought two,' Aaliyah explained. 'In case one got damaged by the transportation.

Ebony smiled her thanks at the small man, which caused him to blush uncontrollably.

'There's more,' Aaliyah added.

Ebs pulled out more parts, some I recognised, others I

had no idea what they were for. The creases in Ebony's brow told me she was at a loss with some of them too.

'Tajan is here to help us.' Aaliyah remarked noticing our confusion. 'He was instrumental in the design of the reincarnation equipment.'

'You are an engineer?' Ebony asked him directly,

'What is an engineer?' he answered in the soft, slightly trembling voice I remembered. He spoke English with a heavy accent, rolling the words as was common in our dimension. It had an endearing effect and Ebs smiled again.

'An engineer is someone who designs and builds machines,' she replied.

Tajan glanced at Aaliyah who nodded almost imperceptibly before he answered Ebony's original question.

'Yes. I think I am.'

'Thank you. This can't be easy for you.' Ebony continued. 'And it is also dangerous.'

He nodded nervously, continuously glancing sideways at Aaliyah.

'Tajan is part of what you would call the resistance. The freedom fighters. They have been undermining Bashir and Cal-Tan's tyranny for years. He knows what danger is.' Aaliyah was protective.

'No doubt.' I answered trying to ease the tension.

'We appreciate your help,' Ebony chimed in.

Slowly we all started to relax.

Sly placed a tray of soda and water bottles with glasses on the table. 'Anyone thirsty?'

Tajan studied the for him unfamiliar beverages and was relieved when Aaliyah pushed one his way. He must have been dehydrated after his transportation.

Aaliyah, Tajan and Ebony left the room with the parts and their drinks.

I settled into the sofa, my mind mulling over the new developments.

Chapter Eleven

All eyes were glued to the monitor. Would the technology work with the new parts?

The essence of the mouse had been harvested. We knew that. The moment of truth would be if—no, when—it was inserted into the second rodent.

Those were the animal's vitals we were observing. It had been dead. Very dead. No pulse, no heartbeat, nothing. It was now on life support, a machine pumping the blood around the small body and pushing air into its lungs. The essence transfer should, in theory, jumpstart the autonomic nervous system, allowing the body to breath by itself.

'I'm turning off the life support,' Ebony said to no one in particular.

The ensuing silence was oppressive.

I glanced to the right where Tajan and Ebony sat hunched over the keyboards feeding the machine with prompts and commands. They worked well together, each complementing the other.

Turned out Tajan was a genius in his own right. He'd

been instrumental in the development of the revolutionary technology Aaliyah's family used to mobilise reincarnation. The mousey little man had been a vital element in putting the last pieces of the puzzle together.

The minutes dragged by. I sipped on my tenth cup of coffee. Not helpful, the caffeine made me even more impatient and jittery.

Glancing to the side I saw Jonah was in no better state. He fidgeted constantly, pulling at invisible dust bugs on his clothes, and pushing the blanket away doctor Patil demanded he use. He'd insisted on coming down to the lab. I guess neither of us was good at waiting.

The concentrated silence was broken by a faint beep. Then another one.

We all held our breath.

The sounds became stronger. More regular.

I put the cup down and made my way to where I had a better view of the computer screens.

There it was. The heartbeat. The dead mouse had been brought back to life. At least part of the process was a success.

No one dared to talk. It all seemed so fragile. I looked through the glass partitions to the rodent laying on the table. The technician in the sterile glass box was dressed head-to-toe in a white hazmat suit. I couldn't see if it was a woman or a man, but it didn't matter anyway. Whoever it was, they softly placed a mirror in front of the mouse's snout as an extra check that it was breathing. It was.

The animal moved one of its front legs. Not a massive movement, but one none-the-less, and an epic event under the circumstances.

I saw smiles on Ebony and Tajan's faces and dared to

believe they'd done it. They'd resurrected an animal from a cryogenic state. It was massive.

Ebony turned to us, and we echoed her smiles.

'We don't know whether the essence is still intact,' she cautioned us. For that we will need to wait a day or two. Then we can test whether it remembers the actions we taught the previous animal.'

We nodded in unison. But it didn't dampen the excitement. Another hurdle had been successfully scaled. We were on the right track. The only one who stayed reserved was Jonah. Understandable, he had the most at stake here. This was potentially his next journey.

It actually took three days before there was conclusive proof of the transfer.

The mouse, now thriving, though quite quickly tired, was presented with a brain teaser it had learned in its old body. Ebony shooed us all out of the room to give the animal some space and peace to work its magic.

We reluctantly left. To be honest I think she didn't want to jinx it. Our super intelligent technical wizard was still a bit superstitious. I smiled at the thought. It made her human.

So we all sat in the sofas and chairs staring at some stupid program on TV that none of us really wanted to watch.

Jonah was relegated to a wheelchair.

His energy level was deteriorating even quicker than Doctor Patel had anticipated. Prolonged walks were out of the question, just staying upright was a chore. Patel insisted he either stay in bed or at least not walk. His one remaining heart was doing overtime as it was just keeping him alive.

Jonah was not the man to be restricted. His abhorrence for weakness wouldn't let him, but even he was quiet now after his last collapse yesterday. He'd pushed his deteriorating body too far and it rebelled, shutting him down. He couldn't ignore it anymore. Something had to be done, quickly.

Ebony joined us after three agonising hours, followed by a very tired looking Tajan. The smiles on their faces stretched from ear to ear. there was hardly a need to ask the question anymore.

'It worked,' she said softly to Jonah. 'The essence has been transferred and its memory still works.'

The collective sigh of relief was audible over the noise of the TV. I took the remote and turned off the reality series.

'It took an hour for the mouse to really perform the test successfully, but it did,' Ebony explained.

'We wanted to be sure,' Tajan added. 'So, we repeated the test. Then let the animal rest and repeated it again.'

'And it's conclusive?' I asked completely redundantly.

Ebony smiled and nodded. 'Decisively.'

Jonah took her hand and squeezed it, even his lips pulled into a careful smile. It was short lived, but it had been there.

Another hurdle taken.

Another step closer to our goal.

Chapter Twelve

Would Ebony and Tajan be able to harness Jonah's essence before it left this world for good? The question was foremost in everyone's mind.

And to achieve it, he would have to die again.

That was a given.

After his death, everything was on thin ice.

Oh sure, all the tests were positive. But that was exactly what they were, just tests. Relative. Never attempted on humans.

I understood Jonah's reluctance. At least part of it. I think even Ebony did.

But we had to convince him to proceed with the reincarnation.

It hadn't been easy. Sure, he'd seen the results. Ebony had repeated the process three more times with new mice. All with the same outcome. All were successful.

The mice were slow to recover, at least in Jonah's mind. In reality, they took to their new bodies with gusto. But the energy was short lived. Like every reincarnation, the new body needed a lot of sustenance to renew its energy reserves on a more permanent basis.

On Ebony's insistence, they'd tried the procedure on a monkey. It went against many of our ethics, but we saw the need. The big man was not a mouse, he needed more convincing.

It took another ten days.

Days I was afraid he didn't have. Days I woke up wondering if he was still alive.

Jonah was bedridden now all the time. He was barely able to sit upright. Even his appetite had dissipated to a point where Patel had to threaten to tube-feed him.

His eyes were sunken in his face and the skin looked almost translucent with its dull, grey pallor. The normally full muscles were wasting away, and he looked small in the bed. Insignificant. Something I'd never thought would be possible.

Ebony and Tajan were completely focussed on the reincarnation. There was no room for anything else. All our missions were on hold. Eb's team still monitored the dark web and gathered all the information they could, but Ebony had no time to look at it.

Aaliyah and I tried to fill the gap, but only partially succeeded. Together we identified possible recruiters and analysed the attacks that were becoming more and more frequent. In the past weeks the violence had escalated exponentially, both sides secure in their moral righteousness. Both as bad as the other.

There was a lot of collateral damage. Innocent people caught in the middle of the fight my family had instigated. Their numbers ran into the tens of thousands.

Urged on by the mounting tension between the religions, the conflict spread. Countries became involved. The

Middle East, still unsettled after the fight for Gaza, once again became a hot spot. There were demonstrations in all major cities around the world. There was no safe place anymore. Polarisation had taken root and was multiplying like a malignant cancer.

We kept hunting for new leads. Anything to get a foothold back in the Establishment. And to keep our mind off what was happening closer to home.

There was an abundance of information, making it difficult to find what we were looking for. For now, we made do with aggregating the data.

Ebony's team monitored it all.

Thank goodness for the geeks.

And AI.

Chapter Thirteen

This was it.

Today Jonah would pass through the reincarnation process.

Again.

At least, that was the theory.

I hadn't slept all night, in contrast to my big friend. His body had shut itself down, too weak to stay awake. He hadn't even needed any assistance from Doctor Patel to fall into a deep dreamless sleep.

His body was done. There was nothing left.

Jonah had agreed it would be today.

It had to be. Patel had been exceptionally clear on that.

'You won't live another twenty-four hours,' he stated clearly yesterday evening. 'It's now or never.'

'Please Jonah,' Ebony begged him. 'You have to do this. I know it's terrifying, but it's the only option. Without this you'll die.'

'Stay dead, you mean?' Jonah's voice wasn't much more than a whisper. We had to lean in to hear him.

There were three of us there. Ebony, the doctor and me. Aaliyah had disappeared, unable to handle the wasting-away anymore. I think she truly cared for Jonah, and to see him descend into a vegetative state like this was too much.

'Yes,' the good doctor answered for us.

Silence descended on us once more.

It was all up to Jonah now. He had to agree to fight. He had to want to come through the procedure.

'What if I'm too weak?' he'd asked Ebony earlier. 'I don't have the energy. I can't even lift my hand anymore.'

'It's not physical strength,' she answered gently stroking his fingers. 'It's your mental strength. Emotional strength.'

'I'm beat.'

'I know. But this will bring you back as you were. Not in this,' she gestured the almost still form under the sheets. 'In your real body.'

He nodded almost imperceptibly.

'You have to try, Jonah.' Her voice was shaky. 'Please. We can't lose you.'

He looked at her and attempted a smile. It didn't reach his sunken eyes.

'I need you.' Ebony begged.

A tear formed at the edge of Jonah's eye and made its way down his cheek. Ebony reached out and took him in her arms, holding him close to her chest. I glanced up and saw her tears drop and mingle with his on the bed sheets. I felt the same constriction in my throat and the tingle behind my eyes, we were all emotionally drained by the situation.

I swallowed hard and looked away.

It was such an intimate moment between them that I stepped back. I would leave them to their emotions.

This was a goodbye, and we all knew it.

There was no guarantee he would make it. No certainty

that his old body would accept the essence back again. At most, we were talking about a twenty percent chance of success—for the level of success we wanted. Our big man back, as we knew him.

Reincarnation is a fickle thing.

Risky.

I'd never seen it that way, not until this happened. It was so common in Taxore, that I never gave it a second thought. I took for granted that every time we reincarnated, or transported for that matter, we would come out of it perfectly. No side effects, other than maybe a heightened appetite and a mild headache.

All I could do now was hope. And stay out of the way. I would observe from a distance, in the hallway from outside the room, through the large window.

The image in front of me sent shivers up my spine.

The room had been effectively split in two using the privacy curtains around the hospital beds. They'd been pulled closed just beyond the end of the beds. From my vantage point at the big window, I could see both sides.

On the left, the bed was occupied by the almost still form of Jonah in his second body. He was sleeping, his body on the brink of giving up. His features were calm, the brow relaxed and no longer crunched. His breathing regular, thanks to the machines surrounding the bed. I hadn't seen him so peaceful for a long time.

The right bed was surrounded by even more machines and the form beneath the covers was very recognisable as the old Jonah. His heavily tattooed body was in a lot better state than the withered, wasted form on the left bed. The difference was extremely striking. This form was artificially alive thanks to the heart and lung machines hooked up to his chest. His breathing was deep and full, adding colour to the body. I had to remind myself it was just a shell at this time, and that the essence was still in the form on the left.

My throat constricted as I contemplated what was about to happen.

What if it didn't work? How would we, and especially Ebony, continue?

Turning my attention back to the scene in front of me, I observed the machine that would actually capture the essence, if it worked. It was stationed between the two beds, on the left side of the curtains. To me it looked like a computer, maybe even a game computer with a line of lights on the top.

I'd asked yesterday how it worked, as it wasn't physically connected to either body.

Tajan and Ebony tried to explain it to me, but the technology went way over my head.

'Just think of it as a kind of sender that uses a frequency to transport the essence,' Ebony attempted to summarise the technology.

'How does it know where to go?'

'We've injected receptors into Jonah's old body,' she answered. 'They will connect to the frequency and basically show the essence the way.'

'Receptors?' I asked. 'More nano tech?'

'Exactly,' Tajan joined in. 'Just a different kind, with a different task.'

'And that's how it's done on Taxore?'

'In principle, yes. Most times an extra step is needed where the essence is stored until it can be inserted into the body.'

My brain hurt with the effort, but some of the explanations stuck and I more or less understood the fundamentals of what they were saying.

'Is the essence an actual physical entity?' I asked. 'Something you can touch.'

Tajan shook his head and creased his brow. 'Yes, and no,' he continued. 'We don't actually know what it is, and it's not something you can actually hold in your hands. But it can be contained.'

'And if it isn't?'

He shrugged. 'We have no idea. It dissipates into the air and disappears.'

'And we don't know where it goes to then?'

'No.'

I liked to think that maybe the escaped essence—the soul—did continue its intended journey to whatever heaven might be out there.

Jonah had asked yesterday to see his old body.

It had been moved to the room in preparation of the procedure.

The moment had been emotional. More than I'd expected, and I thought I'd contemplated the worst.

Tears had run down Jonah's face as he observed his old form. His hand reached out under the covers but stopped when he became aware of his action. He pulled it back and just stared at the familiar form. I cannot imagine the amount of turmoil his mind must have been in. The shaking of his body and elevated heart rate hinted, but he kept it inside, choosing not to share, not even with Ebony.

I had to leave then.

I couldn't take it any longer.

When I returned an hour later the curtains were closed around his old body and Jonah himself was sleeping.

'It was too much for him,' Ebony confirmed. 'He's locked himself behind a wall and I can't get through.'

I squeezed her small body against me and held her tight,

as much for me as for her. We needed physical contact, just to continue our vigil.

'He'll come through,' I tried to console her.

'He has to.'

And so there we were.

Ready to pull the plug on Jonah's borrowed body.

My gut clenched in spasms at the thought, the emotional pain resonating physically. I had to believe in the collaboration between Ebony and Tajan. That it was enough to see Jonah through. And that he had the strength and the resolve to go through hell one more time.

He lay in the big bed, still in his deep sleep. His face at ease. His body still. He hadn't regained consciousness, just descended deeper into his isolation.

Doctor Patel said something to Ebony. She glanced at Tajan and then back to Patel.

She nodded.

My heart sank. This was it. The point of no return.

Tajan sat behind the computer ready to catch the essence in the machine they'd built. He nodded too.

Doctor Patel pressed a switch on the machines keeping Jonah alive.

It was done.

I don't know what I'd expected.

Maybe that his body would fight and spasm. That there would be great gasps and his eyes would fly open, his hand would grip the air to stay alive.

But there was nothing.

No sound, other than a soft continuous beep signalling there was no pulse.

We all looked at the monitors.

Then Tajan diverted his attention to his screen. Ebony

left the left bedside and stood next to him examining the data on the screen.

I stopped breathing.

I think we all did.

I felt a presence next to me. A hand slipped softly into mine. I glanced to the side momentarily and squeezed Aaliyah's fingers. We were united in our concern for the big man, and I was glad she'd showed up after all.

Her eyes glanced from one form to the other, her body trembling in anxiety. I put my arm around her shoulder and pulled her close. Her left hand snaked behind my back, holding on to her right hand that circled the front of my waist.

Words wouldn't have added any value, so we stayed silent, our eyes glued to the scene in front of us.

It was clinical, all the people in the infirmary room dressed in blue disposable medical PPE. A silly thought crossed my mind and I almost smiled; they looked more alien that we did.

One of Patil's assistants pulled the covers over the left body and turned off the monitors, bringing home how definite the procedure had now become.

This body was gone. We'd passed the point of no return.

Tajan was hunched over the keyboard, his fingers flying over the black keys. Pearls of sweat on his exposed brow showed the strain he was under. In the short time he'd been here, he'd become invested in this endeavour. He was just as anxious to bring Jonah back as we were.

Doctor Patel stood calmly beside the right Jonah's heart monitor; his gaze locked to the flat red line that cut through the otherwise midnight-blue screen.

The lights in the room were subdued. Most of the

bright illumination came from the computer screens Tajan sat behind and the monitors hooked to Jonah's old body. Ebony moved to that bedside and stood by Jonah's still form, holding his hand in hers and gently stroking his fingers.

The strain on her face was clear. It mirrored ours.

Time stood still.

Nothing moved.

Chapter Fourteen

Jonah's first heartbeat in his old body shocked us all.

We'd been waiting for it, hoping for it, anxiously listening for that beep on the heart monitor, but I still jumped at the sound when it finally happened, clearly audible in the absolute silence even through the glass.

My eyes were glued to the now blue line that jumped up in regular spikes. His heart was strong. It beat in a steady rhythm.

Step one achieved.

Aaliyah and I moved closer to the open doorway.

I glanced sideways at Ebony. A small tear hung at the edge of her eye. I wanted to wipe it away, hold her in this moment, but she was too concentrated.

Besides this was just the beginning.

'He's not out of the woods yet,' Doctor Patil brought us down to earth ten minutes later. 'His body is reacting well, and his heartbeat is steady and strong, but we have no way of knowing yet whether the essence has taken root further than his autonomous nervous system.'

He was right.

Of course he was. I just didn't want to think about it. We couldn't fail. Not now. Not after we'd talked him into doing this.

Again.

'When will we know?' Aaliyah asked, her features now the colour of hope and relief.

'If, and when, he wakes up.'

'And when will that be?' Her tone was laced with venom.

The good doctor was unimpressed. 'We have no way of knowing. It's a waiting game now. We'll continue to monitor him and make sure his body is nourished and functioning as required.'

He was so clinical. Distanced. But I guess that was necessary. The rest of us would do the hoping, we'd leave the medical part to the doctor. He would be calm. We'd be the emotional wreaks.

'There is no use in you all staying here,' he continued. 'I will contact you if there are any developments.'

With the exception of Ebony, we all filed away from the room further into the corridor.

As one, we looked lost.

I desperately wanted to do something. Anything. Just as long as I was contributing to the reincarnation, but there was nothing I could do.

'Now what?' Aaliyah asked.

I shrugged. 'Now we wait. Again.'

I returned to the command centre. We still had a quest here.

There was a message from Benedict.

Chapter Fifteen

I noticed the tail after I left Starbucks.

It was a big black SUV, the kind you see the bad guys drive in all the car chase films. So cliche. But still very real.

They were three cars behind me, keeping a steady distance, but still close enough to keep up.

Traffic was slow but the roads were packed and didn't allow for strange manoeuvres; there was no option to race through the red light at the last moment. I had to try other ways to get rid of them. I took a right, then a left, but they stayed steadily behind me, now only one car separating us. They weren't even trying to disguise their presence. Arrogant bastards.

I called Sly on speed dial.

'I have a tail.' I stated simply.

'Where are you?'

'Los Angeles Street, between Little Tokyo and Union Station.'

I heard the keys as he struck them. 'Which one is the tail?'

Black SUV, Dark windows. I think three or four occupants including the driver.'

'Traffic?'

'Heavy.'

He was silent for a minute. I glanced in the rear-view mirror. It was still there. I could see the SUV clearly over a small city car that separated us.

Despite the tinted windows, I could make out that the driver and his passenger both had short, cropped hair. They looked Caucasian or light skinned and wore dark sunglasses. Their stern visages completed the cliche tough guy look.

Traffic crept forward. From my vantage point I could see a van parked in the right-hand lane, the same lane I was in. The driver was unloading pallets which caused the hold up. It blocked the flow.

I looked around me, searching for a way I could change lanes and pass the van. Initially no-one was inclined to offer any space but finally someone let me in, and I switched to the left, which brought me to the middle lane of the road. The SUV was struggling to do the same, with less success. Must be their stern image.

'Take a left turn on Templestreet.' I heard Sly say.

The corner was only thirty metres away, so I turned on the indicator and charmed my way to the left lane. As I turned the corner I glanced back. The SUV was still in the same place, the driver angrily gesturing to the cars beside him and the truck driver in equal measures.

I smiled internally, doubled back, thanked Sly for his help and continued on my way. Traffic picked up quickly and before long I was on the Pacific Coast highway outside of Los Angeles in the direction of San Diego, enjoying the beautiful view.

It was an uneventful trip, no black SUV's, no more

suspicious cars tailing behind me. I was lulled into a sense of security.

Sure, I was rattled that they'd found me. I'd have to stay out of L.A for a while. Just as well we had another safe house in San Diego. Sly had already given me the entry code and prepared the caretaker for my arrival. It was an unexpected trip, not one I was happy about, but I had to evade possible search parties and keep the rest safe.

A nagging voice at the back of my mind kept wondering how they'd found me, and whether I really was safe? Even if they had the licence plate number—which they must have —it wouldn't do them any good. I'd switched to another set at a diner I passed just before the highway. This car was one of Ebony's and it was nondescript, common, and blended in with the traffic easily.

Still the hairs on the back of my neck refused to lie still.

I'd been careful, we all were. None of us ventured out into the city much, or anywhere for that matter. The cars were in the underground parking. We didn't go out for food, it was delivered. Nothing. I thought back to the route I'd taken today. Where had I messed up?

The garage, nothing strange there. It was hermetically sealed off and no one could access it. Visitors for the offices had a separate parking level, so did the employees. No. Not that. Then what?

A thought struck me: Starbucks. I hadn't left the car. The one on 6th street had a drive-in. I'd waited in the long line of cars that snaked around the block. Nothing out-of-the ordinary came to mind. But it had to have been there. There were no other options. Unless the Establishment had found a way to identify us on the move.

Face recognition came to mind. I added that to all the surveillance cameras in that part of the city and the feeling of dread resurfaced. Goosebumps ran up and down my arms, joining the hairs on my neck in their merry nervous dance.

Could they hack into the traffic cams? And the surveillance cameras? Of course they could. Ebony's team did it all the time. Sly had no doubt been watching a live feed when he advised me on my route.

Shit. Now what? Cameras could have picked me up when I turned the corner. Maybe even seen me change the plates.

My earlier relaxed attitude dissipated. I sat up straight in my seat and anxiously glanced from left to right, scrutinising the people in the cars around me. None of them seemed to match what I expected the Establishment guys to look like. No big SUVs anymore. No burly guys packed in a car.

I admonished myself for my paranoia and tried to calm my nerves, succeeding up to a point and continued my uneventful drive to the safe house. By the time I exited the Pacific Highway after Newport Beach and took the 1-5 at Santa Ana, I'd convinced myself again that all was well.

Boy, was I wrong.

Chapter Sixteen

Two guys in an old rusty pickup came out of a ramp from a small side road and drove parallel to me on my right.

The way they avoided any kind of eye contact and didn't even glance my way sent up the well-known alarm bells. People are inherently curious and will always observe the inhabitants of the car next to them, even if just for a glance. Unless of course, they already knew who the driver was.

I put my indicator out and started to move to the left when another car, this time a battered white van with faded letters on the side, pulled up on my left. The driver refused to give me the space to change lanes and slowly boxed me in.

I'd seen a sign for the offramp up ahead and decided in that instant to race for the exit and try to lose them that way. I floored the gas, but my escape attempt was thwarted when a relatively new black Ford F150 swerved from the right lane in front of me, effectively blocking that flight route. A flash of red in my rear-view mirror completed the trap as a big semi pulled up behind me, quickly filling my view with its threatening massive chrome grill.

I was truly and completely boxed in.

Dread took hold of my gut, and I felt tingles race up my spine. I alternated looking in the rear-view mirror with anxious glances to the sides. My breath came in bursts, and I felt my hearts rapid beatings in my temples. Panic was taking hold.

The driver of the rusty pickup looked at me and smiled —not in a nice way. The passenger in the van echoed the sentiment.

Shit. Now what?

The off-ramp was coming up on the right and I did my best to force the cars around me to give me space. They stayed in formation, not allowing me even an inch of respite. I scanned the surroundings for anything that could give me an advantage.

Nothing.

Suddenly, the van on my left rammed the side of my car and pushed me hard to the right. The pickup made room and together they drove me off the road onto the off-ramp. The semi followed and the Ford stayed on point. We moved in formation onto the highway, all of us hogging the two lanes of the off-ramp. I was completely hemmed in, with nowhere to escape to. Cars in front of us moved quickly to the shoulder as the close-knit group of vehicles approached. The F150 honked its horn at any stragglers, quickly pushing them off the road.

As we came onto the highway, I speed dialled Sly again and just managed to scream that I was under attack when the van blindsided my car again and I was jolted to the side.

I swerved to the right, but the pick-up was in my way, and I collided with it hard, rocking my vehicle back into the van. They alternated in battering the car until I felt the structure give and the left back wheel buckle. The car tilted to the left and I was pushed into the door.

The imbalance of the broken axel caused my car to swerve heavily to the right and crash into the old pickup which made way for me to career onto the grass shoulder of the road. I fought the wheel and tried to keep the car straight, but the steering was heavily damaged and wouldn't respond. The tires slipped on the wet grass, then snagged on something solid, flipping the car. It tumbled over and over until it came to rest on its roof in a dry ditch.

The airbags had deployed at the first tumble, and I was pinned to the seat upside down hanging from the seat belt.

My head was spinning, and my vision was badly blurred from the impact. I shook my head to try and focus, but the only result was a sharp stab to the back of my skull. I felt blood trickle down my face. Nothing bad, but a hindrance. I closed my eyes and did a mental inventory of the damage to my body. Any broken bones? Nope. Bruises? Tons. Cuts? A few, one of which on my head. Not bad for the crash I'd just survived.

There was a distinct high-pitched whine in my ears, probably the result of my head being impacted when the side airbag deployed. Through the noise I heard a car stop and doors close. Running feet made their way to where I was.

Dazed, I struggled unsuccessfully to get out of the seat belt. I was completely helpless, strung up and incapacitated against the seat by the airbag. I punched the bag repeatedly, finally depleting it so I could move my hand to the seatbelt buckle and click it open.

I fell a short distance onto my shoulder as the restraint gave way. I struggled to upright myself when I heard the voices outside my upturned vehicle. I managed to get my legs under me and was about to crawl out of the broken window on my side when I felt a sharp prick to the side of my neck. I pulled back, but it was too late.

My hand went to my neck and pulled out the syringe. The spot had already gone numb. A sensation of warmth travelled quickly up my veins from the spot where the needle had entered my neck and before it reached my temple I felt my body tremble uncontrollably.

'It's ok, he's alive. We got this. I'm a doctor.' I heard voices say to the bystanders in what to me seemed like a fluffy cloud of cotton wool before everything went black.

Chapter Seventeen

I was home again.

Back in my own dimension.

I knew it. I felt it.

The smells, the sounds. Everything. All so familiar, but in such a bad way.

This was not how I'd envisioned returning.

To be frank, I'd more or less given up on the idea or ever seeing my home dimension again. At least until we'd overthrown the Establishment and everything my father stood for. That had been my dream. To return as some kind of conquering hero.

Instead, I was unceremoniously dragged over the floor from the transporter pad to the door: incapacitated, in chains, with a bag over my head.

Rough hands grabbed me under my armpits and pulled me to my feet. The sudden movement and disorientation compounded my nausea, and I almost threw up in the bag. I gagged and swallowed the vile liquid, forcing it back into my protesting stomach. Transportation always played havoc with my digestive system and this time was no different.

They callously pulled me forward and I stumbled, trying to find my feet. I admonished myself and forced my body to get a grip on the movement. Slowly I found my feet and propelled myself forward. I wouldn't give them the satisfaction of dragging me like a dog. I would keep my dignity. No matter what.

I'd lost any sense of direction. The bag over my head effectively blocked out all light and left me completely unhinged. I reasoned they would take me to my father's palace. That meant a vehicle of some sort.

Sure enough, a few minutes later I was bundled, face down, onto a hard metal surface and a booted foot was placed squarely on my back, pinning me to the floor. A door was slammed shut and we took off.

A short time later the vehicle stopped, and the process was reversed. Strong hands pulled me out and set me on my feet again. According to my calculations, we'd arrived at the palace.

A hard push in the centre of my back propelled me forward and I stumbled to stay upright. They hooked my arms again and steered me up the stairs to the entrance. It was the palace, of that, I was sure. I knew this place blindfolded, which was more accurate than I wanted. I envisioned the stairs to the ornate Earth-oak doors, the vast cavernous hallway behind it. The long walk to my father's office.

I counted the steps, like I had so many times before.

This was home. The place where I'd lived for thousands of earth years. The place I loathed. And the place I always returned to. There was no escaping it. Not even now.

My forward momentum halted abruptly.

We were in my father's office. And he was here. I felt it.

The hairs on my neck stood on end. Dread crept up my body and threatened to overwhelm me, like it had so many times before.

He had that effect on me.

Not just me, on all of us.

A hard blow to the back of my knees broke the terror, and I fell to the floor. I was roughly pulled back up until I was on my knees.

The bag was pulled off my head and bright light tortured my eyes as I pulled back involuntarily, squinting them shut tightly. The man behind me pushed me roughly back to my previous position.

No one spoke.

Slowly, I opened my eyes, still squinting until my vision adapted.

A pair of leather boots came into view and my father's trademark red and gold flowing coat over black silk pants. I raised my head slowly and looked up past his arms, crossed over his chest, to the stern face accentuated by his dark beard and thick eyebrows.

'Hi, dad. Good to see you too.' I couldn't help myself, and my sarcastic remark was rewarded with a hard slap to the back of my head from the guy behind me. My father just stared at me, allowing his henchmen to bully me, again.

I righted myself and glared back at the man who was biologically my father but fit more in the tormenter category.

He raised an eyebrow in his classic show of disdain. An emotion I was all too familiar with. His piercing eyes looked through me, daring me to say something. For once, I declined.

He finally broke the silence.

'You are a disgrace.'

Wow, how original. Never heard that from him before. I bit my tongue to keep my cynical remarks inside.

'I don't believe you are my son. You have no morals, no loyalty.'

I wanted to shout out that he was the one who missed those traits and any kind of empathy. Instead, I just stared at him, refusing to lower my eyes.

'I had hopes for you. But you continue to force my hand. Now.' He waved his hand over me and the situation. 'Now, you are here in chains. Like the common criminal you have become.'

He waited for me to contradict him.

I didn't.

He pulled his mouth into a thin line, his upper lip trembled slightly echoing his rising anger. Internally, I was laughing, Who knew that not answering angered him more than talking back?

He changed tactics.

He smiled. That eerie, frightening smile that said something very bad was coming.

'You must be wondering how we found you?' He was enjoying this immensely.

I stayed silent. Yes, I did want to know, but I'd never give him the satisfaction of asking.

'I'll tell you anyway.'

I lowered my head and stared at the floor in front of me, not trusting myself to keep my emotions under control.

'We've always known where you were,' he continued, unfazed by my stubbornness. 'Ever since your human partner visited Arand's facility.'

I couldn't help myself. I looked up.

'Did you really think we hadn't intercepted him?' His grin was vicious, pushing home the futility of our cause.

A large block of concrete dropped into my gut, cramping my muscles with dread. They knew? They'd known while Jonah was here? What had they done to him?

My father's laughter was mirthless. It chilled me to the bone and sent goosebumps up and down my arms.

He had a knack for knowing exactly what I was thinking.

'You must be desperate to know what happened to Jonah while he was here,' he walked up to me and stared down into my eyes.

I felt like the small ten-year-old boy from so many years ago when I'd done something he disapproved of. That in itself wasn't difficult, he disapproved of everything I did.

He'd installed a great fear in me from my very first recollection. My childhood was a continuous bombardment of his criticism and disparagement. I was destined to disappoint him in everything I did. All these feelings swamped me as I stared up into the eyes of this terrible man. They threatened to overwhelm me and send me reeling from his silent onslaught.

But I wasn't that child anymore. I saw through the facade and recognised the narcissist. The small man with a massive chip on his shoulder. A megalomaniac, an abuser, and a pathetic excuse for a parent.

I squared my shoulders, pulled my lips into a thin, determined line and stared back at him. I refused to flinch or look away.

'Well, well, well.' He cocked his head in amusement then turned to Michael. 'It seems your brother has grown a pair of balls.'

Michael, as usual, had no idea what dad was talking about.

'You surprise me, Gabriel,' he continued as he slowly walked around me. I stared straight ahead, my back straight and my re-found resolve not allowing me to react to his incessant posturing.

'In a good way, this time. It seems you have finally matured into a man.' He returned to face me. 'Too bad it's too late.'

He walked back to his desk, there he turned to face me again and leant against the big wooden furniture.

'I will tell you. You have earned that.'

Who hoo, I thought to myself.

'Before you die, I will answer your unspoken questions.'

It was no surprise.

I knew he wouldn't let this rebellion slide. I had defied him. Multiple times. And I'd evaded his best for so long that it was reflecting on him. His ego wouldn't let that go. No matter that we were related. Or maybe, because we were. He wanted to make an example. To his people, and probably most of all to the rest of the family. He would show everyone how ruthless he was.

I'd resigned myself to my fate as soon as I woke up. This would be my last day in either dimension.

And he was right about one thing. I did want to know. Not that I would give him the satisfaction of asking. I stayed silent.

'We intercepted your human partner the moment his essence entered the system. Bashir was alerted that an unknown soul had entered the process. It's standard procedure. And naturally he informed me.'

His condescending tone was getting to me, but I swallowed my irritation and continued to stare at him. He was enjoying this too much. I wouldn't give him the satisfaction of knowing how his words affected me.

'The DNA was confusing, so we decided to create the body and see what happened. Lo-and-behold, the body resembled your rogue priest. We figured out what had happened and how you'd tried to save his life with the nanos and that you would possibly attempt to bring him back to earth.'

Shit.

They'd known from the start.

It was becoming harder to stay in character.

'You did us a favour, Gabriel.' Again, that vicious grin, the one I hated so, so, much.

'Your frantic action played into my long-term plan perfectly.'

I couldn't help myself; I scrunched my brow in question. What long-term plan? What was the old man concocting now? It couldn't be good. Not for Earth.

'We decided to use Jonah as our first field-test subject. We have been preparing reincarnated bodies to potentially be returned to Earth. Your action speeded up our process. I suppose I should thank you for that.'

An experiment? Why would he want to return grunts to earth. There was no market for them there. It would be ridiculous to kidnap them first then return them. So why?

'Naturally, we wanted to monitor him.' He continued.

The tingles up my spine sent sharp tendrils of pain into my brain. What was he talking about? Monitor Jonah?

'We implanted an agent in his brain. It has been transmitting data back to us from the moment he set foot in the Twelfth dimension. We have known where he was, and what he was doing all the time.'

My heart sank.

'And you.'

I dropped my gaze to the floor, dumbfounded at my father's revelations.

'I'm surprised you were so gullible to think we wouldn't have intercepted him. Did you really think it was that simple for Aaliyah to break him out of the facility and bring him back to Earth? We made sure she was successful.'

They'd known all the time. About Jonah, about Aaliyah even. In hindsight, it explained a lot about how Jonah had escaped. We'd been so relieved; we hadn't questioned the ease with which Aaliyah transported him back home. And I hadn't dared to ask her. Our attention was quickly diverted to how to deal with this new version of our friend.

In my wildest nightmares I'd never contemplated my father would have let Jonah go. We'd been afraid he would identify Jonah and torture the big man to find us. This insidious twist came completely out of the blue. Again, I'd underestimated the man and his deviousness.

I was devastated. Everything I thought I'd achieved was just a scam. He had known all along where I was and what we were doing. There were no secrets. It was history repeating itself. There was no way I could escape my father's influence. He had played me like a puppet. My earlier strength dissipated, and I felt deflated. My body sank in on itself as my self respect melted.

'So, you see, Gabriel. Your earlier resolve to stay silent and loyal to your friends is meaningless. It is based on thin air. On delusions. You cannot escape my control.' He voiced my conclusions.

'And now that his new body is dead, there was no reason anymore to let you stay alive like a louse in my hair.'

I was lost in my desolation. There was no light at the

end of the tunnel. Just a black hole where all my emotions and self-respect were sucked out of me.

This was what he did. He broke even the strongest man.

Chapter Eighteen

'And now that you see how pathetic your dissent is, you will tell me about your little group of misfits and your allies,' he continued, acutely aware of my disposition. 'You do realise we will find and kill them. Not answering me only prolongs their nervous wait. Their time has come.'

I stubbornly stayed silent. Determined to keep at least a semblance of control.

I wanted to cry out my pain and devastation. Drop down to the floor and curl up in a foetal position. I needed to block out the world, whichever one I was in. It was too much. I couldn't take it anymore. Everything we had done, everything we'd achieved had been for nothing. All our careful secrecy was moot. My father had been able to follow each step we'd taken.

A voice at the back of my head attempted to break through the tirade of self-pity. It pushed at the feelings of helplessness. I tried to push it back, ignore it, and wallow in my misery.

The voice was relentless, it pushed and pushed itself to the foreground.

'It's a lie,' it repeated endlessly.

I took a deep breath and concentrated on the silent inner voice.

'If he knows everything, why does he still need to interrogate you?' The voice resonated in my head.

'Why do you have to tell him about your allies?'

Slowly, a realisation started to take hold. He didn't know. My father didn't know everything. He hadn't been partial to Jonah's thoughts. He hadn't been able to listen in on our conversations. Otherwise, he wouldn't need me.

'He doesn't know.' I kept repeating this to myself silently. 'He doesn't know. He's bluffing.'

I forced myself to keep the smile from my lips.

Straightening my back again, I pulled myself together.

Yes, a setback. But not nearly as bad as he would like me to believe. My friends were still safe. If he'd known they would be here with me right now, or dead. Our cause was still alive. They would keep up the pressure. Then realisation of his words hit me, Jonah was dead. He had no idea that Ebony was attempting to reunite Jonah's essence to his old body. He only knew about the grunt body. The data his implant had transmitted was restricted to what the body registered. Not the mind. He hadn't been able to control Jonah's mind.

He didn't know.

I took a deep breath.

'What's it all for?' I asked, finally breaking my silence.

My father turned around and stared at me.

'What?'

I shrugged. 'What is all this for? What's your long-term

plan? Why did you have Arand killed? You've been enemies in a status quo for centuries. Why now?'

His smile was eerie. Like a bad horror villain in a b-movie.

'Oh Gabriel. I'd expected more vision from you. You, who were destined to follow in my footsteps.'

I glanced at Michael who visibly tensed. He swallowed his anger and attempted to push his frustration at my father's barely veiled rejection away. He failed miserably. That made me smile internally. Up yours, Michael.

'You resemble Arand in that.' My father continued, oblivious to the effect his words had on his eldest son. 'He was small minded. He lacked ambition. Arand was satisfied with his business. But as you no doubt know, stagnation means decline. A company needs to evolve. To grow. There's an enormous untapped market out there and he refused to investigate it.'

I was intrigued, despite my predicament.

'There is so much more we can do. So many profitable markets out there.'

'Like what?' I pushed at his narcissism. He wanted to boast about his plans to prove his superiority.

'Other dimensions,' he answered, so pleased with himself. 'Why should we stop here? We have the technology to transport products to countless worlds. Many of which share the same need for cheap labour.'

'Slaves, you mean.'

He looked at me with amusement. 'They are a commodity, Gabriel. That is your one true Achilles heel. You view them as people. Not as assets. A serious flaw for this line of work.'

I pushed my resentment down and encouraged him to spill the beans on his plans. Not that it would help much. I couldn't see a way out of the situation, so maybe it was just morbid curiosity. But never give up hope, right?

'I'm expanding the business,' he answered. 'Arand stood in my way.'

'You needed his technology,' I concluded. 'Again.'

That hit a nerve. His eyes shot knives at me, and my smile probably didn't help to placate him. From the corner of my eye, I saw Michael step forward to hit me for my insolence. A wave of our father's hand stopped him.

'Yes. I needed his technology,' he said slowly, pronouncing the words in an exaggerated manner, only barely masking his anger. 'So, I took it. End of story.'

'And then you conquer more dimensions?'

'Not conquer, not yet. I see them more as market potential than a short-term annexation.'

Ice cold fingers gripped my gut. 'You want to sell slaves to other dimensions?' I surmised.

He nodded.

'Where will you get the slaves from?' I asked, though I knew the answer.

'Where do you think?' His amusement had returned. 'Your precious humans. There is an almost inexhaustible supply on Earth. With all the religions under my control, I can harvest as many as I like.'

'All the religions? You're going to attack the other families.' Apprehension once again my main emotion.

'Attack? Not necessarily, if they accept my terms. I would prefer diplomacy, but if they cannot abide by the new status quo, then they will force my hand.'

'Diplomacy, like you did with Arand?'

The edges of his lips curled up in a vicious grin.

'Arand wasn't only about business, was it?' I asked. 'You enjoyed killing him.'

He didn't answer verbally, but I knew I was right. Cal-Tan, my father, was a class act psychopath. A narcissist with a love for blood. Anyone's blood. No one was exempt. By the look of my predicament, not even blood relatives.

'What about mother's family?' I asked. My grandparents ruled the Sixth dimension.

'What about them? They can fold or they can die.'

I'd heard enough. 'What are you trying to prove?' I threw all caution to the wind.

'I have nothing to prove.'

'Seems to me like it's the only thing you're doing. Showing how big you think you are. How important.'

He glared at me as he approached.

'It won't work, you know. You won't get the acknowledgement and recognition you crave. They will never see you as an equal. Never.' I alluded to the Council and the reigning class of our world. 'You are, and always will be a pirate. A criminal.'

Before I knew it, I was thrown backward by a hard kick to the side of my head. My head reeled. I struggled to stay conscious. A searing pain radiated from my ear and my temple into my brain. I shook my head, trying to release myself from the agony: to no avail. My eyes were shut tight, but lightning bolts still flashed on the inside of my lids. I'd bitten my own tongue with the force of the blow and blood filled my mouth, threatening to choke me. I spat it out.

'Get him up.' I heard my father order Michael.

Hands grabbed me under the armpits. I felt Michael's hot breath in my neck as he bent to pull me back to my kneeling position.

'You really screwed up now,' he whispered. 'Bye, bye brother. This is the end for you.'

He sounded so smug, but he was probably right. This

had been one insult too many. It had been a good one though. Almost worth it. Who was I kidding? I was a dead man anyway. It had definitely been worth a headache to stick it to the old man. He never lost control. Never—until now.

I opened my eyes and looked up. The room was still spinning slightly, but I willed myself to make it stop. I concentrated on one spot to the side of my father's head.

He glared down at me. I'd seen this side of him before. It chilled me to the bone, despite my earlier elation. He'd made a decision.

Cal-Tan's voice was cold, void of any emotion.

'You are stubborn, Gabriel. I had hoped we could avoid this unnecessary messiness. But you continue your disrespect. I cannot allow that. Not from anyone. What happens now is on your head.'

He waved his hand in dismissal.

The door opened and I heard a struggle behind me. My mother's voice mingled with that of the guards. It cut me to the bone. I hadn't expected to see her. I desperately wanted to, just not like this, bloody and defeated.

'Let me in,' she shouted at the guards. 'Take your hands off me.'

'My lady, please. You cannot enter without an invitation, you know that,' the guard pleaded with her.

I stared at the floor. I didn't trust my emotions, not with my mother. Her presence had broken my resolve. She was the one person I'd missed the whole time I was on Earth. And now, the last time she would see me was under these circumstances.

'Let her in,' Cal-Tan's booming voice stopped the scuffle.

I could imagine my mother pulling herself loose and I

heard her footsteps as she rushed over to me. She knelt on the floor next to me and softly placed her hands either side of my face. She lifted my face to look at her.

The tears trickled over her cheeks and dropped to the floor as she looked at me. 'Gabriel,' she whispered. 'Gabriel.'

She didn't have to ask what had happened. She knew. Hundreds of years of marriage to this monster had taught her not to question his actions or be surprised by them. She'd wiped the blood off all her children's faces after confrontations with their father. Unable to stand up to him, she had consoled us, healed us and tried to put us back together again after each episode. Any attempts she'd made to intervene had resulted in battery. My father had no qualms about violence towards her. Bruises and cuts were a given to anyone if they thwarted him. Anyone. Including the woman who had stayed by his side no matter what he had done.

Her helplessness and pain constricted my breath and almost brought tears to my own eyes. I swallowed hard and pushed the anguish back. I would not cry in my father's presence. Never.

Cal-Tan cocked his head and Michael softly pulled our mother's embrace from me. He helped her up and held her close, reluctant to leave her to my father's wrath.

'Take her away,' he dismissed her so easily. So callously. 'I will deal with her later.'

Anger replaced my grief again and I glared at him.

I wanted to shout threats, make him leave her alone, but I knew how hollow that would be.

I heard my mother's stifled sniffles as Michael coached her out of the room.

Despite his cool exterior, my mother's actions had had

an effect on Cal-Tan. He walked behind the immense desk and sat down on what I had always joked was his throne.

He placed both hands on the cool surface and spread his fingers in contemplation.

I waited.

There wasn't a chance in hell this would end well. I knew that, and I'd resigned myself to it.

My only regret was the pain it would inflict on my mother. I loved her with a fervour that shocked even me. With my upbringing I never thought I was capable of such an emotion. But I realised that was exactly why I was. It was wholly thanks to her. She was the Yin to my father's Yang. His callousness and indifference were compensated by her warmth and empathy.

And now it would all end in this messed up manner.

She didn't deserve this.

Chapter Nineteen

'Let him in.' My father broke the silence.

His words brought me out of my depressive musings. Now what? Let who in?

The door opened behind me again and I heard strong, booted steps. I resisted the temptation to turn around and see who had come in. I didn't want to give my father that pleasure.

'Consolidating the two religions has given me a lot of advantages, one of which you are about to encounter. This will, I believe, be a reunion of sorts.'

The vicious tone had returned to Cal-Tan's voice. The psychopath was showing through again.

I stared at the legs of the man who'd moved to stand in front of me. The gilded black cloak and stiff leather boots of the Hashta sent shivers of fear up my spine. My worst nightmare had come true.

'Hello Gabriel, or should I call you Karief?'

His heinous tone resembled Cal-Tan's. I knew the barbaric character would too.

I straightened my back, pushed my shoulders back and slowly raised my head to look Ibrahim in the eye. I would not fold. He wouldn't have the pleasure of seeing my despair. Neither of them would. No matter what happened, my last rebellious action would be to keep my dignity.

'So good to see you again. I lived, or should I say, re-lived for this moment,' Ibrahim added.

His thin, mirthless lips were curled in a vicious grimace, eyes blazing with expected brutality, I could see why my father would easily navigate towards someone like Ibrahim. They were like-minded. Bonded in a bloodthirsty, psycho-pathic need.

'When your father informed me of your capture I rejoiced. Finally, I would take my revenge.'

'Whatever.' I shrugged and rolled my eyes.

Ibrahim laughed. The tone cold and vicious. It dropped a block of concrete in my gut. I struggled to stay upright. I knew what was coming. Maybe not the details, but it would be bloody, prolonged and excruciating.

'My new friends have been very informative.' Ibrahim continued, unfazed by my supposed indifference. 'I have learnt new ways of torture that will extend your pain expo-nentially. I will keep you alive so much longer, with more agony than you could imagine.'

Oh, I could imagine it, I was doing just that, and it almost sent me into a panic. But I wasn't about to react to him. I continued to stare at a point in front of me.

'You will beg for death, Gabriel. And I will not give it to you. Not until I am ready.'

I shivered inside.

'And then I will bring you back and do it all over again.'

I'm not a hero. I don't do well with pain. Just the thought of what was to come terrified me. Images of the

Hashta's work on my cousins so long ago resurfaced and enhanced my dread.

His hollow laugh didn't help either.

'You will give me what I want before I finally kill you, Gabriel. That is a given. The only thing you can control is how much pain you will endure before you die. Personally, I hope you withstand the torture for a long time. It will enhance my pleasure. But I expect you are a coward without a spine, and your pampered upbringing will cause you to crumble very quickly.'

Pampered upbringing? You've got to be kidding me. My hellish childhood and adolescence were the reason I would endure. It was why I was much stronger than he could know.

From the corner of my eye, I saw Michael had re-joined our merry little reunion.

He looked rattled, though he tried to hide it. I figured our mother's grief was the reason. He loved her as much as I did. All of us did. She was our rock.

Ibrahim continued his litany of creative ways to inflict mind-blowing pain. I tried to block it out. Shreds of his sentences half-registered, but I pushed them away. There was nothing I could do now anyway. What would happen was out of my hands, no matter what he said. There was no way I would betray my friends. Not even if they skinned me alive.

I started to turn my mind in on myself, a survival trick I'd developed during my childhood. Michael had bullied me endlessly during my younger years, terrorised was probably more accurate. I'd blocked it out then. I could do it now.

Despite his hatred for me, Michael looked decidedly sick due to Ibrahim's graphic descriptions. Internally, I laughed.

Who had the spine now, brother? When it actually mattered.

'The first torture I will leave up to you,' I heard Ibrahim say. It made no sense to me, so I discarded the comment.

'You will have time to contemplate and comprehend what is waiting for you. It will eat you up: the apprehension, knowing what pain awaits when the sun rises tomorrow morning. You will live through the anticipation of terror and endless pain this night. I will leave you with your nightmares. They will eat you alive.'

Oh great. Thanks.

I knew what he was doing. He would let me live another night in complete dread to hollow out my resolve. He knew I was strong now, and gambled I would lose most of that during the night to the trepidation of what I knew was coming. Even though I'd zoned out as much as possible, the general gist of what he would do to me had registered.

I actually would have preferred him to just get it over with, but he wanted to extend my agony, increase my fear. It was psychological torture.

'Bring him to the dungeon,' Ibrahim ordered the guards. They glanced at Cal-Tan before obeying.

Dungeon? Wasn't that just a bit too dramatic? Come on.

The guards pulled me to my feet and stood me up. I felt queasy. The sudden change in posture reminded me of how much my head still hurt. I probably had a concussion, not that it mattered. It was the least of my worries.

I locked eyes with Michael on my way out of the room. His brow was creased, and he bit his top lip. Michael was rattled. Something I'd never imagined seeing. But then again, I guess it was quite confronting to realise that even Cal-Tan's sons were not exempt of his bloodthirsty wrath.

I was marched out of the room and down the hallway.

Out in the courtyard, the guards and servants stopped to watch me being manoeuvred forward. I pulled my arm free from the guard beside me, righted my back and strode confidently onwards. Whatever happened, I would keep my dignity. It was the only thing I had left.

We walked past the living lodgings, to the soldiers' quarters. Still, we continued. We were in a part of the palace I was less familiar with. It had been out-of-bounds for us during our childhood and once mature, it had no attraction because of my supposed superiority.

A door was opened, and I was led inside and down a flight of stairs I didn't even know existed, onwards into the bowels of the palace. Ok, maybe I had been a bit premature discarding the idea of dungeons.

There were long underground corridors that changed direction often. I had to concede I was completely lost. I had no idea where I was or what was above us.

Our trip ended when we took a sharp right into a collection of cells. They were bare rooms hewn out of the rock. No windows. No furniture, just a bucket in the corner. All I saw was hard rock and stark white light from an artificial source overhead. The whole thing was frankly a hole in the ground.

The walls of each cell were rough stone and reached up to nine feet where they effortlessly morphed into the stone ceiling. It was cold. Cold and damp. Not exactly the five-star accommodation I was used to in the palace.

A hand pushed the small of my back and I stumbled into what would be the place where I was to live my last night. My hands were still bound, and no one made an effort to remedy that. I assumed this was how I would stay. How I was supposed to use the bucket alluded me, but that again was an attempt at intimidation.

I moved to the back of the cell, turned to face the guards and tried what I hoped was my most determined face.

None of them would look me in the eye.

I knew them. All of them. We'd worked together in my previous life. I'd laughed with them; we'd partied long and hard. And now they were doing their best to distance themselves from me. I understood; they felt uneasy. I could see that. They felt conflicted. Torn between old allegiances and current safety.

'Leave the light on,' the battalion leader said. 'Ibrahim's orders.'

There was disdain in the last sentence. No love lost there then.

I slowly lowered myself into a seated position with my legs crossed. It was reasonably comfortable. And I prepared to wait for what was inevitable.

I vowed to think of the good things in my life, instead of dwelling on what Ibrahim had in store for me. I would not fold.

I was determined.

Yeah. Right.

I hoped I really believed that.

Chapter Twenty

I lost all sense of time.

Sitting on the hard floor in the cold cell, time had no meaning. The underground location, without any natural illumination, robbed me of any indication of the light level outside. It could have been midnight, or morning. I had no idea.

My initial resolve to think only of good thing lasted for a while, but inevitably led to a haunting realisation of loss. All those good friends, I would lose them. Everything I'd tried to achieve in the past two years was for nothing. No, not nothing, I admonished myself. But I would not be able to see it through.

It saddened me. I'd wasted my life. Thousands of years. And only really lived since I met Jonah. A drop in the ocean of my existence.

And why?

Because I finally had a reason to live. And now, it was a reason to die apparently.

I descend into a deep state of self-pity. Woe is me, and all that crap. It didn't help. I felt even worse.

So, change of plans. I'd have to steel myself some way for what was coming tomorrow.

I would have to meditate. Call on all the lessons my mother gave me so long ago. She was a master in managing pain. She'd had enough practice with dad.

I closed my eyes and let myself glide on the wave of silence in my head. My shoulders relaxed, my arms, even with the binds still on my wrists, followed suite. The incessant light dimmed in my mind, and I found at least a semblance of peace.

I had no idea how long it had been, all context of time was lost in the meditative state, but at one point I noticed differences. The light outside my closed lids faltered.

I opened my eyes and the flickering continued until the overhead lights faded entirely. It was a welcome development. The bright light had been stark and ultimately painful. But this darkness had its own questions and potential dangers.

Why was the light out?

I'd expected Ibrahim to leave it on all night to torment me. Keep me awake to contemplate the immense horror that awaited. Why the change of heart?

It wasn't pitch black. There turned out to be small faint lights dotted around the underground complex, they cast deep shadows into every corner. I could barely make out the shapes of the cells and the corridor.

There was no sound.

The hairs on the back of my neck stood on end. This wasn't right. Where were the guards?

I pushed myself up off the floor and stood upright, all senses on high alert. I scanned the dark recesses, listened for any sounds. Nothing.

There, a soft footfall.

Coming this way.

I stared at the corridor in front of the cell.

The footsteps drew closer, and a long shadow filled the hallway. I waited.

Michael walked up to the bars of the cell.

He was the last person I'd expected to see.

He wasn't gloating, not as I had expected. He was angry, sure, but not elated at my predicament.

'What are you doing here?' I couldn't stop myself from asking.

'Getting you out.'

He surprised me again. Michael opened the cell door and approached me.

'I still hate your guts,' he continued. 'I want you dead. But not this way. Not trussed as some sacrificial pig in a slaughterhouse. And not by that butcher.' He spat out the last words.

I stayed silent; a glimmer of hope planted in my heart.

'You will die. Be assured of that. But not as a piece of meat for the psychotic bastards to get off on. I've seen their work and I have no desire to see more.'

Plural. Ibrahim and dad?

The dying part was not exactly what I wanted to hear, but okay, at this point I would take whatever I could get.

'You will die in a hunt, I will kill you, or you go by your own hand. I will let you out of this cell. Go into the city or whatever and we will hunt you. You will not be able to transport back to your precious Earth. But you will be able to die with some dignity. Even you deserve that.'

'This is for mother, isn't it?

I'd hit a nerve. He glared at me. For a moment I thought he would strike me, but instead he roughly turned me around and cut the bonds around my wrists with a short sword.

I stepped back, still not sure about my brother's resolve.

We stared at each other. A stand-off. Born of hundreds of years of sibling conflict, and—if I'm honest—an endless need to gain our father's approval. He'd trained us well.

Michael finally turned and walked out of the cell. He put the sword on the chair outside and turned back to me.

'This is all you get,' he stated. 'Make your ancestors proud. Die like a man.'

With that he left.

Chapter Twenty-One

I stood in the cool darkness reeling from what had just happened. I remembered the expression I'd seen on his face in my father's office. I guess our father's level of brutality was too much even for my brother. Not surprising. It scared the shit out of me as well. It also proved no one was safe. Not even me, and I was his self-professed "favourite".

But now I had a possible way out. Maybe not from death, but at least from the endless torture Ibrahim had in store for me.

I had hope. No matter how small. It was something.

Now all I had to do was get out of the palace.

Oh yeah, and then find a way of transporting back to Earth without leaving a trail. Chances were about zero. But not quite. And I had a knack of getting out of difficult situations.

At least that was what I tried to convince myself of.

It felt strange to leave the cell. I'd resigned myself to the end of my life happening there. This would be the last place. This and the torture room.

I pushed myself forward, dread still my companion. Picking up the sword I made my way after Michael, out to whatever awaited me there.

He'd given me more than I could have expected: a chance. Not much more than that. But it was enough to ignite the fire of survival in my core. I would get out of this. I would get back to what I now called home. Earth.

I passed a dead guard on the way out. Probably best. Come morning, he would have felt my father's wrath if he'd still been alive.

I crept along the corridor, hugging the shadows. The sounds of the palace all around me both terrified and reassured me. I was alive and they would mask my presence, but they were also potential threats. I had to move. It would be light soon. Any chance of escape dwindled with the darkness.

Thirty minutes later I was still in the palace. I'd circumvented the busier parts and did my best to stay out of site. I wasn't making much progress, but vigilance was more important at that moment. The expected alarms were still silent. No one had found out I was gone yet, but it was just a matter of time.

Moving in the shadows I navigated to where I knew there was a gateway out of the palace. It would put me in the middle of the narrow back streets in the bad side of town. The best place I could be under the circumstances, I deduced, as long as I wasn't recognised. I was thankful for my thick beard and long hair and hardly resembled the arrogant clean-shaven, vain man I'd been before.

My only issue was my clothes. They were distinctly earthen and covered in blood. I had to find something more appropriate for this dimension.

I walked down a dark corridor listening for any sounds that would indicate people nearby. Nothing. Yet.

In front of me was a small courtyard I would have to cross to get to the exit. There was no avoiding that, it was the only way out. I studied the space. There was a gardener working on the shrubs in the far-right corner. A scullery maid emerged from a door on my left and crossed over to an opposite corridor. The gardener didn't react. His full attention was on his work. I waited until she'd disappeared out of sight then took my first steps out into the open.

I was suddenly lifted off my feet and pulled backward into the shadows by strong hands. One grabbed my right hand and pushed the blade away, encircling my waist. The other effectively closed over my mouth, silencing me immediately. I kicked with my feet but whoever had me in his grip took no notice and dragged me back effortlessly. I dropped the sword and clawed at his hand over my mouth, to no avail.

'Quiet, my lord. If you want to live,' he whispered in my ear.

I stopped flailing and let myself be pulled deeper into the corridor and through a door into a small room.

He set me down on my feet and I turned to face a giant of a man towering over me. He would have given Jonah a run for his money in size. The giant was dressed in the modest clothes of a servant, but his soft-spoken language belied a simple upbringing.

I didn't recognise him and had no idea whether he was trustworthy or not. He'd found me. If he wanted to hand me over to the authorities, there would be precious little I could do about it. I glanced at the suddenly very ineffective looking short sword lying on the floor where I'd discarded it just outside the door. His calm and unfazed gaze followed mine and I realised I had no choice but to comply.

'Your brother is waiting for you behind the door you were aiming for,' he stated resolutely. 'He will take your head and claim his reward from your father. You need to escape; we will help you. We are on the same side here. We will get you out of the city where you can transport back to Earth. But there is someone who wants to speak to you first. Follow me.'

He turned, exited the room and walked down the corridor into the dark recesses of the palace.

I was confused. Could I trust this guy? If he'd wanted to kill me, he'd had ample time. I decided to follow him. What did I have to lose, except my life, that is. I picked up the sword on my way out of the room, just as a safeguard, and trailed my would-be saviour.

We walked deeper into the maze of corridors, and I was quickly lost. He finally stopped and opened a door into a dark box-like room. The only light was the faint glow from the corridor. I turned around in the room, dread once again sending goosebumps up and down my arms. Was it a trap after all? The voice in my head screamed at me to run.

A sound from behind me made me turn. Someone moved out of the shadows. It was a small figure clothed in a long hooded cloak that obscured all its features. I deduced by the size and gait that it was a woman.

I was confused. Who was this and why would she want to speak to me?

The figure raised her hands to the hood and pushed it slowly over her hair to free her face. Even in the dim light I recognised those soft features.

'Mother?'

'My beautiful, brave son.' She took my face in her hands again and pulled me close.

I hugged her tightly. Tears pricked at the edges of my eyes. I'd resigned myself to never seeing her again, and now she was there, in my arms.

I pulled back softly and held her at arm's length.

The black eye and bruised cheek were clear, even in this soft light. I cocked my head in question, though I already knew the answer.

'No matter, Gabriel. It is a small price to pay.'

'What are you doing here? It's dangerous for you.'

'We're helping you escape. You must get back to Earth and continue your rebellion. You must expose the Establishment. Cal-Tan's plans can never come to fruition. He needs to be stopped.' She surprised me with her fervour.

'Come with me,' I blurted out. 'I will keep you safe on Earth.'

She smiled and shook her head slowly.

'No Gabriel. I have work to do here. You attack Cal-Tan from the outside, we,' she indicated the giant behind me. 'We undermine him from the inside.'

I was flabbergasted. My demure, silent, almost invisible mother was in fact rebelling against my father? I stared at her, then at the man who moved more into view and stood protectively behind my mother.

She smiled at my surprise.

'I have fought against him in secret for centuries, Gabriel. All this time, it was my only goal. To stop his tyranny and save my children. That and your safety were the only reasons I stayed with him. I found like-minded people, like Maron.' She placed her hand on the big man's muscled arm. 'And together we do what we can to thwart his plans.'

I smiled. I should have known. I resembled my mother in so many ways, it seemed I got my rebellious streak from her too.

'You have allies here, my boy. For years we've been sabotaging your father's goals. In small ways. Never overt. But we are here, and we will continue to resist his expansion. He must be stopped.'

Her brow creased and there was a hardness in her eyes I had never seen before.

'Your father plans to take over all the families. He will monopolise the trade in souls and slaves.'

I nodded. I'd figured that out.

'And then he will expand it to other dimensions and universes,' I added.

'If that happens, he will take more drastic measures to accumulate the resources.' My mother looked down at the floor and took a deep breath.

'He has been experimenting on people from Earth,' she whispered. 'He abducted some young men and brought them back to this dimension to monitor their adaptability to our world again.'

I cocked my head in question.

'He wants to cut out the costly process of reincarnation,' my mother's friend chimed in. 'Go directly to the source and bring the slaves back in great numbers.'

'But the trials are not going well,' my mother continued. 'The bodies are too frail for this dimension. Their one heart is insufficient to allow them to work or do any strenuous activities.'

'He now sends them to other dimensions to see if the atmospheres there are more beneficial to his business model.'

My unspoken question resonated in the silence.

'There are promising results,' my mother uttered the dreaded words.

This was a massive blow. If my father was able to cut out the reincarnation process and supply slaves directly from Earth to other worlds, there was nothing to stop him from abducting humans in large numbers. If they no longer required the resolve—the belief in a better life—to survive the reincarnation, then the acquisition process would be much quicker and easier. He would no longer need the Establishment; he could send troops to gather slaves any time and transport them directly to their new worlds.

Our strategy had been geared around exposing the Establishment and stopping the harvest of souls. That would be moot if my father had his way.

'So you see the stakes are high,' my mother whispered. 'For all of us.'

I nodded. There wasn't much more to say. It was much worse than I'd imagined. We would have to rethink our next steps. If, that is, I could get back to Earth.

'Do you remember how we used to send secret messages when you were a child?' My mother pulled me out of my dark reverie.

I nodded. 'Hide in plain sight.'

'Exactly. We have someone in the Establishment, he can hide messages in something called a podcast. Read the rendering of the podcast every Friday and use the sequence we had before. If you want to answer, or initiate a communication, answer in the comments. But make sure it is untraceable.'

I nodded.

'Should we have a key word that will let you recognise that it's me?'

'Let's use "weariness" Find a way to incorporate that in the first two sentences. Then I will know it's you.'

'Take this,' she pushed a small device into my hands. 'If you ever come back again it will allow us a rudimentary form of untraceable communication in this dimension.'

I looked down at the ancient gadget.

'It will stay off their radar, as long as you use it correctly,' Maron explained. 'Only open it once every two days, on the uneven calendar dates. Around this time. And keep it live for no more than two minutes. If you don't hear the reply tone, close it immediately.'

I nodded. I was familiar with the communicator. We'd used them as children for play. Mother nodded at the giant. He put his hand in his tunic and came out with a small transporter, not a type I'd ever seen before.

'There are positives to your father's expansion efforts,' Maron explained. 'We now have access to Arand's technology. It is far more advanced than ours. This is the newest transporter our allies have been able to create. It will not leave a trace. Nothing for anyone to link you to any destination or source.'

'This will send you back to Earth. It has been programmed more or less with the coordinates of your last vector. You will materialise in a secluded spot where no one should see you. Turn the transporter off immediately. It cannot be traced, but we need to stay vigilant. Just in case.'

'And you need something else to wear,' my mother added. 'These clothes will stand out in the streets here.'

She gave me a bundle of clothes. I started to undress and heard her sharp intake of breath from the bruises all over my body. The kidnapping had been rough, it would leave some scars. But I couldn't linger on pain now. Not unless I wanted more of the same.

I pushed the communicator deep into the pockets of my borrowed pants and turned back to my mother.

'You must leave now,' she said. 'Maron will lead you out of the palace.'

'Be careful, mother.' I feared for her life. If my father ever found out, his wrath would be legendary.

'I will, Gabriel. You do the same.' She smiled, rose on her tiptoes and kissed my cheek. 'I am so proud of you, son.' A small tear gathered at the edge of her eyes.

I felt the corresponding tightness in my throat and the pin pricks behind my own eyes. I didn't know if I would ever see her again.

Reluctantly I let her go and nodded softly. She turned and disappeared back into the shadows.

Chapter Twenty-Two

The giant addressed me again and brought my full attention back to my current situation.

'I'll take you out of town into the wastes, you're on your own then. I can't risk exposure.'

I nodded. It made sense.

We proceeded down the tunnel, circumventing most of the filth that had accumulated there. This was the less attractive side of the city. The sewers. Necessary, but dirty. I'd never consciously thought about it before, but I was thankful now that it was there, and it offered concealment.

I saw a light around a corner and other noises started to over stem the constant rushing of water underfoot. Before we turned, I took Maron's arm and stopped him.

He turned to me, his brow creased and worried at the interruption.

'Will my mother be safe?' I asked.

'She never was,' he answered. 'She's lived with the danger of your father's wrath for centuries, and still, she continues her work.'

'I never knew.' I felt so overwhelmed. So guilty that I never thought about my mother's pain. Her dedication towards us. It had always been there. Taken for granted, even by me, and I thought I had a good relationship with her. I only now saw how egotistical I had been. How much she'd given. And of course, how much I'd taken.

'No, and that is how it should be. She is a master of misdirection. Of hiding in plain sight.' He must have seen my worried features in the dim light. 'She will be all right. We will protect her with our lives.'

His words soothed my anxious mind and brought me some relief.

'Thank you, Maron. I will not forget.'

'Just make sure your side of the battle is won,' he answered. 'We will take care of here. It's time the tyrant was deposed. For that we will need all the help we can get.'

I nodded.

'What will happen when he finds out I'm gone?'

'He'll go ballistic.' I couldn't see his face, but I heard the amusement in his tone.

I smiled. I would have liked to see that. From a safe distance.

'Won't he go after my mother? After she came up for me last night?' Worry pushed away any thoughts of mirth.

'No. He has punished her for that. His ego won't let him consider she could do anything more than complain. To him, your mother is a nobody. Not a threat. She is the mother of his progeny, so he has a basic respect that keeps her here with him. He underestimates her strength. Her resolve.'

'What about the others?'

'We have covered our tracks. And if anyone is exposed, we have a death pact. We cannot be caught and interrogated. Most of our teams do not know of your mother's involvement. Only a few. She keeps it that way.'

'That's why you have the pact?' I'd concluded.

He nodded. 'If any of us were linked to your disappearance, they would have been turned over to the Hashta or even worse; the psycho.'

'Ibrahim.'

'Yes.' His voice was softer. 'Suicide is preferable.'

As hard as it was, I agreed with him.

We continued, him leading the way and me hot on his heels.

I still couldn't get my head around what had happened in the past twenty-four hours. Abducted, sentenced to a terrible death, busted out by my biggest enemy and then the revelation that my mother was as much a rebel as I was.

I was humbled at her centuries of dedication to her cause. I'd often wondered why she stayed with a man who so systematically and nonchalantly abused her. It had never crossed my mind that she had been undermining him all this time. I felt a great warmth for her. Love and pride. And trepidation. She had to stay safe. She had to. Not just for the cause, for me too. I knew it was egotistical, but she was my mother.

We stopped suddenly in a small courtyard doorway. The awning and dark interior of the corridor still hid us from view.

There was a vehicle parked to the left, a transporter stacked with empty produce cases. This was the supply chain for the extensive kitchens in the palace. The hundred strong staff and guards—and of course my family—had to be fed and catered for. This was the delivery hub of the goods. Daily runs to the artificial growing pods made sure everything was fresh, especially for my father.

'You will hide in one of the empty containers,' Maron informed me. I will take you out of the palace to a place where you can slip out of the container and make your way to where you can transport safely. Wait for my sign before you make yourself known. There are many dangers.'

I nodded.

It was dark and extremely uncomfortable in the small space. I felt every bump and movement of the vehicle as I banged against the hard metal wall when the vehicle braked. A small hole near my head allowed me to catch glimpses of the scenery passing by as Maron navigated the busy city streets.

After what was probably ten minutes but felt like hours in my confined space, we left the heavily populated area and moved into the suburbs. There was less noise here, less traffic. The roads were the same, but Maron could drive in a more constant manner, not having to stop and accelerate all the time.

I lost track of time as the motion of the vehicle rocked me into a state of meditation. I mulled over what had happened in the past hours.

My mother! Who knew?

Actually, I shouldn't be so surprised, she'd always taken my side and slipped me small advantages that gave me a slight edge over my brothers. She'd been my supporter. Never overtly, I understood that now. She couldn't officially contradict my father. He wouldn't accept that. And she had to keep her cover. But she had always been there, my rock, my support.

Miles outside of town, the vehicle slowed down and rumbled over the edge of the road where it settled to a stop at a slant, with the wheels on one side in the verge. Maron killed the engine, and I heard the door open with a soft whooshing sound. His footsteps moved around the wagon, closer to where I was. I readied myself for movement.

The hood of the container was opened, and I saw the worried face of my rescuer.

'You must hurry up. Get into the ditch. I can't stay here long.'

I nodded and pushed myself out of the small space onto the vegetation. I crouched down and quickly made my way to the ditch, where I dropped out of sight of anyone on the road.

'Good luck, my lord.' Maron closed the hood and moved back to the cockpit.

From my hiding place I heard him argue with dispatch. 'For fuck's sake, I had to pee.' The wagons were constantly monitored, and every stop was registered. 'What do you want me to do? Piss all over the console?'

The engine purred into life, and I lost the rest of the heated conversation as he pulled back onto the road.

I stayed put for ten minutes, listening attentively to the noises around me. There was the soft sound of the wind in the undergrowth, ours is much like the grass on earth, though of a different colour. Occasionally I would hear an animal call out far in the background. What was left of our wildlife steered clear of roads and people. Though not a highway as such, there was regular traffic going by that scared them away.

I started to move.

The shoulder deep ditch ran parallel to the road for another fifty metres, then continued straight onwards where the road bent off sharply to the left. I decided to follow it as much as possible and let it lead me out into the uninhabited wasteland.

This area had exhausted its natural resources many centuries ago, or more accurately we had. With toxic ground covering the open wind-ravaged spaces there was little we could cultivate, which made us completely dependent on the irrigation slopes on the other side of the city or the artificial pods near the mountains. This place was a cross between your arid deserts and a tundra, but then with poisonous grass and tall spiked constructions, some of which were six metres high. Only the toughest of animals were able to live here. People had deserted it long ago.

It was the ideal place for me to disappear. I was counting on Michael expecting me to remain in the city. He had no reason to think anyone would have helped me escape. It bought me some time, but I had to be quick. His impatience would get the better of him soon, and he would expand his search. And of course he wasn't the only one looking for me. I imagined Ibrahim would have mobilised his fellow Hashta by now, and I desperately wanted to steer clear of them.

My back bent, I crouched forward along the ditch and quickly put more than a mile between me and the road. I found a copse of raggedy tree-like plants that would shield me from a highly unlikely observer while I took the transporter out of my pocket.

It was different from the one I was used to. Different even from Aaliyah's. Compact and light in my hand, it felt almost like a toy.

The principles thankfully were the same, so I would be able to use it. Besides it was already pre-programmed. I had no idea where I would be landing, but everywhere was better than here.

I looked around one last time, to make sure I was alone and unobserved. And as a farewell, I suppose. No matter the circumstances, this dimension was still my original home. It pulled at me.

I swallowed hard, took a deep breath and turned the dial on the transporter.

The strange tingling sensation engulfed me almost immediately and the view of my home dimension blurred and disappeared.

Chapter Twenty-Three

I opened my eyes slowly and waited for the scenery to stop spinning around my head.

The new age transporter did nothing for the actual experience and I was very nauseous. My legs felt like jelly, and I doubted whether they would hold my weight if I tried to take a step.

I took deep breaths and forced my rebellious body to relax. The smells told me I was back on Earth. The deep tang of the living undergrowth, the smell of water on the breeze. All things I didn't link to my dimension.

I was in a grassland between low rolling hills to my back and mountains in the distance. Trees lined the small stream that meandered between the grasslands and the rise of the landscape. Another thing we'd mostly killed off in our dimension; trees.

My gaze travelled over the hills to the long expanse of grass that led off to a hard-top road completely void of any traffic on the horizon.

I estimated it to be early in the morning. The smell of dew was still in the air and the sun had not reached its apex.

I listened intently for any sounds of human habitation. Nothing. Just birds and some occasional scuffling in the tall grass. Probably some kind of ground hog or gopher. I stayed silent and immobile.

Nothing.

Wait. There. A machine of some kind, coming from the other side of the hill to my left.

I carefully picked my way through the tall grass. I still didn't trust my balance though the frailty of my leg muscles was waning. Take it slow. I told myself.

I hated transportation. It played havoc on my body, every single time. The new transporter hadn't changed that.

My legs were back to normal by the time I reached the top of the hill. I concealed myself behind a shrub under a tree and peered over the rise.

In the distance to the left, about five hundred metres from the hill, I saw a farmhouse with outbuildings. Two horses grazed in a paddock to the left of the building and a doghouse identified there was at least one canine defender there.

I had no explanation why I was out here in the middle of nowhere—wherever it was—so I decided to avoid the farm. I'd have to think of an excuse before I encountered anyone.

Turning my head to the right I saw the road I'd identified earlier. It snaked in an almost straight line past the side road to the farm and continued onto the horizon where I could make out a town. From my vantage point, I could see a collection of houses and what looked like a busy truck stop on the outskirts.

I reasoned that would be a good place to find some kind

of transport, maybe hitch a ride with one of the eighteen wheelers. I had to find out where I was and get a message to Ebony and the gang.

My father's words—that he'd tagged Jonah's body— rang constantly in my ears. Were they all okay? Had another team been sent to take them out? Was Jonah still alive?

Worry pushed me on, and I started the long walk to the truck stop.

The sun was at its zenith when I finally trudged into the parking lot. There were eight fully loaded trucks and two small pick-ups parked in the area in front and to the left side of the diner. A single dented pickup stood to the right of the one-story building.

The diner itself was a throwback from the fifties, a metallic rounded form like an elongated aluminium Airstream caravan. The three steps leading up to the door on the left of the building were worn and coated with fading metal paint. The awnings that decked most of the windows, in what would at some time have been bright yellow and white, was now a faded sickly cream. At least they would offer some respite from the burning sun.

I needed to get to a phone. And preferably get some-thing to drink. But I had no money or identification on me. So, on my long walk I'd concocted a story about a prank I hoped was believable. My weathered and dust-covered, dirty clothes upheld the image.

I opened the door and was immediately engulfed by the coolness of the air conditioning. After the relentless sun, it was a very welcome change of temperature.

There were five customers and two staff at the counter,

and a family of three sitting in the nearest booth. No one turned to look at me.

I glanced to the right, walked slowly to one of the booths and sat down on the bright red plastic bench.

The small friendly looking waitress approached me within minutes.

'You look like you're parched,' she said in a soft sing-song voice.

I smiled my best smile. 'I am.'

'Like you've walked the desert,' she added as I glanced down at my dusty clothes and raised an eyebrow.

'Not by choice,' I replied with a smile.

She cocked her head in question.

'What brings you here then?'

I laughed softly. 'A prank,' I explained. 'I'm getting married next week, and my best man and the goon squad thought it would be a good idea to give me one more lesson in survival skills. I'd need them for married life, they said.'

That brought a smile to her pretty lips.

'So, they left you out in the desert to fend for yourself?' she asked incredulously.

'Yes. With friends like that, who needs enemies, right?'

She shook her head. 'How long have you been walking?'

'About three hours or so. I came from over the hills there.' I pointed to the outcrop. 'They dropped me off, took my phone and wallet and wished me well.'

She frowned.

'I'm afraid I don't have any money.' I added sheepishly, my brow creased and offering my best puppy-eyes.

She stayed silent.

'But if you could possibly let me use a phone, I can get one of my buddies to pick me up and bring some cash.'

'Same buddies that left you out there?' she asked with a chuckle.

I laughed. 'No, definitely not them. A colleague. He wasn't part of the prank.'

'What do you do for work?'

'Security. I design security systems, mainly for big companies and government buildings.' I hoped this would sound convincing and she would think I was reliable.

'So, you need a phone?'

I nodded.

She looked me hard in the eyes, then seemed to decide I was genuine and reached into the pocket of her checked apron. She keyed in the password and handed me the phone.

'Thank you,' I said sincerely. 'I'll pay you for the call as soon as my friend comes.'

'By the way,' I asked just before she left. 'Where are we exactly?'

She laughed and answered: 'Pahrump. Vegas is that way' she pointed in the general direction of the town. 'This is highway 160.' With that she left to help another customer.

I keyed in the alarm number Ebony had made me memorise. I vowed to kiss her for that once I got back.

'It's me,' I said into the borrowed phone.

'Gabe?' I was so happy to hear Sly's voice, I almost lost it and dropped the phone.

'Yep.'

'Where are you?

'In a town called Pahrump, west of Vegas, on the 160. Could you send someone for me?'

'Get me the exact address.' Ever the professional. I passed on the information printed on the back of the menu and heard the sound of fingers on a keyboard in the background.

'I see it,' he came back. 'Make sure you stay at the diner for the next two hours. You'll be picked up there.'

My shoulders sagged with relief, the tense muscles now finally relaxing a bit. The real reprieve would come once I was back in one of the safe houses.

'They tagged the big man.' I added.

'We know.'

With that parting message, Sly hung up.

I returned the phone back to its rightful owner and thanked her once again profusely.

'They're coming to get you?'

'Yes, ma'am.' I smiled my biggest smile at her.

'Good, this is no place to get stranded.'

'Very true.' I laughed.

'And no more of those stupid pranks,' she admonished me.

'I'm cured for life,' I joked.

She replaced her phone in her apron and walked back to the counter.

Just shy of two hours later, a big black SUV cruised softly into the parking lot. Sly stepped out of the driver's side and looked around, his dark sunglasses obscuring his eyes. His gaze stopped momentarily when he saw me through the window, then continued until he was satisfied all was well.

He stepped up to the entrance of the diner, took off his sunglasses and opened the door. Once inside he made a beeline for the booth I was in and sat down opposite me.

The waitress came back and eyed him suspiciously. 'This is your friend?' she asked.

I smiled and nodded.

Sly turned on the charm and smiled at her. 'Thank you for taking care of him.' He cocked his head at me.

She nodded, still not completely reassured. 'What'll it be?'

'Coffee please and what would you recommend?'

'The pie is good, fresh this morning.'

'That would be great. Thank you, ma'am.'

'And you?' She turned to me.

'No thanks. I couldn't eat another bite,' I joked. But seriously, she'd fed me just about everything on the menu in the past two hours.

She chuckled and left.

Sly took a small lead-lined box out of his bag.

'Put your transporter in there, please.'

'It's turned off,' I stated.

He raised an eyebrow and cocked his head slightly, waiting for me to comply.

'Lady E's orders,' he explained.

Okay, no getting around that then. I knew Sly wouldn't relent.

'Will I get it back?'

'Once she's satisfied it's not been tagged.'

'It hasn't.'

'We'll see, won't we.'

A few minutes later the waitress returned with Sly's order. He thanked her, once again flashing his winning smile. She left to help new customers who'd just entered and taken up residence at the counter.

'We thought you'd be dead by now.' Sly was direct.

'So did I.'

'We'll discuss the details once we get back.'

I nodded. 'You found the tag?'

'Dr Patil did.'

'And you moved.'

Another nod.

I asked the question that had been haunting me since I got back. The one thing I had to know, but dreaded hearing. 'How's the big man?'

'Same as when you left.'

'Okay.' At least he wasn't worse. 'Still in a coma?'

He nodded as he forked a piece of pie into his mouth. He put down the utensil and took a swig of the coffee.

'Dr Patil is keeping him that way for a few more days until he's confident the body can function independently.'

It made sense.

He bent sideways and pulled a small package of clothes out of the bag at his feet.

'Change your clothes. We'll burn the ones you're wearing once we get out of town.'

Ebony and Sly were being paranoid. But I couldn't blame them. I couldn't imagine anything my mother had given me would contain a tracking device, but then again, we'd been surprised by the one in Jonah. And they didn't know where I'd acquired these threads.

We'd seriously underestimated my father and Michael. Something we wouldn't do again.

I left Sly to his meal, took the clothes and proceeded to the restrooms where I changed into the more appropriate and comfortable jeans and a rugby shirt. I splashed water on my face and hair and tried to coax the shoulder length tresses into something resembling a civilised style.

The waitress gave me an appreciative smile as I re-joined Sly. She was right. I had looked like a bum. This was a distinct improvement.

Sly finished his meal, cleaning off even the last piece of pie with a satisfied sigh. He signalled the waitress, complimented her and the cook on the fantastic meal, and asked for the bill.

He paid cash, adding a significant tip, and gave her an extra fifty dollars for the use of the phone.

'Not necessary,' she tried. 'The tip has covered the phone costs.'

'No. I insist,' he countered. 'There aren't many people now-a-days who would help a stranger like that.' He looked at me and added, 'especially not the way he looked.'

We all laughed at that, though I could feel the blush colouring my cheeks.

Chapter Twenty-Four

We passed Las Vegas thirty minutes later and drove onwards. Okay, so not the penthouse in Vegas.

I had no idea where Sly was taking me, not that it mattered. I trusted him completely, so I rested my head against the door frame and closed my eyes.

I was exhausted. The past twenty-four hours had drained me. Both physically and mentally. My muscles ached in places I didn't even know I had them. Even with my healing abilities, I was bruised and sore over most of my body, courtesy my father and his goons. My legs felt as though I'd just completed a triathlon and my back simply gave up on supporting me anymore. I felt weak and beaten.

My mind closed in on me. I recognised this as the survival mechanism I'd cultivated as a child. So many things vied for my attention that I couldn't handle it anymore. To avoid choosing, I closed myself off for everything. No decision needed. My mind threw up walls, virtual ones I could see in my mind's eye and almost touch. Ones that protected me. From my brother, my father, anything that threatened to overpower me. I descended into my safe place. Momentarily unable to face any- and everything that was happening.

I drifted off to a dreamless sleep, finally giving in to what my body and mind hunkered for.

Peace. Rest.

A dark void of nothingness.

Slowly I registered a voice that pulled me out of my deep restfulness.

'We're here,' Sly repeated. The first comment, whatever it had been, opened the door in my self-imposed isolation, and this one actually came through and made sense.

Reluctantly, I tried to open my eyes. I felt a sense of loss for the past hour's peace. My mind rebelled, not allowing my body to acknowledge Sly. It wanted me to stay in the dark. Not face everything that was ganging up on me.

But the voice of reason intervened to gently coax my reluctant side to allow me to wake up and join the land of the living again.

I stretched my aching muscles and turned to face Sly.

'Thanks.'

He just cocked his head and his lips turned up slightly in what was almost a smile.

I looked out of the window as we slowly made our way up a secluded driveway.

I never ceased to be surprised at the locations Ebony seemed to have the use of. I didn't know whether she owned them all, rented or maybe even just used them. It didn't matter. We would be safe here. Whoever owned it.

Normally, I would be distressed if I didn't know where I

was. Here, with Sly, I just trusted it would be safe. I'd come a long way since I'd left my father's employ.

The dark driveway gave way to an open clearing with on one side a well-tended grass area, bordered with California-native flower beds. Opposite that was a colonial style white building. The large stone pillars holding up a balcony over the entrance were impressive to say the least. Tall windows hinted that the rooms would be airy and light.

The big oak door opened as Sly stopped the car at the two steps leading up to the entrance. Ebony stood in the opening, her face radiant in her relief.

I opened the car door and—on slightly unstable legs—made my way up the two steps to her.

'We thought we'd lost you,' she almost whispered, as she threw her arms around my waist.

'Nope. I'm tougher than I look,' I joked as I embraced her.

'Thank goodness for that,' she added. 'I'm getting used to having you around.'

I smiled, my heart brimming with this feeling of belonging. Something I'd never had back home. It registered once again, how this—these humans—had become my new family. My new home.

We hugged. Both relieved we still could.

It had been close this time. Dangerously close.

Scary.

Ebony linked her arm in mine and steered me inside. The building immediately engulfed me, the soft earthen colours offering warmth despite the vast size of the rooms. Cream coloured rugs broke up the dark oak floor. Caramel tinted drapes softened the bright light from outside. Deep, cushioned sofas and natural wood-and-stone furniture completed the look. A vast modern art collection adorned the walls, this time the focus was on works with the same earthen tones.

We sat down on the cream sofa and half turned to face each other. Ebony seemed reluctant to surrender the physical contact and held on to my hand, softly stroking my fingers.

'How are you?' She locked eyes with me.

'Better, now that I'm home again,' I answered truthfully. The word "home" registering with both of us.

Her smile was warming.

'But how is Jonah?' I asked. 'Still in the coma?'

Sly nodded. 'Stable.'

'Any idea when he could wake up?'

'Probably within the next two days.' The relief was visible in her features, though there was still an undertone.

We didn't know how he would awaken. Who he would be. What he would be like.

'Doctor Patil is monitoring his brainwaves, and everything looks normal. Nothing stands out.' She answered my unspoken question.

'Then we have to believe he will be all right.' I answered squeezing her hands in support and fervently hoping I could believe what I'd just said myself.

'I do hope so.'

I heard footfalls from the hall and turned to see Aaliyah in the vast doorway.

'Good to have you back,' she said in an unexpected show of concern. She even smiled, for a second.

My smile was genuine, and I felt even better. 'Thanks, I'm happy to be back.'

She sat down in the armchair opposite us. 'How was it?'

'Bad.'

She nodded. No sarcastic comments. Nothing. It made

me think we might have started a new chapter in our relationship.

Sly joined us, placed a tray of glasses and three decanters of liquor on the salon table and sat in the second armchair.

'What would you like?' Ebony asked.

'As long as there's alcohol in it,' I answered. 'I'm not fussy.'

I needed a drink. I knew what was coming. We had to discuss what had happened. But I wasn't looking forward to reliving it.

She took the decanter of what I presumed was whisky, poured me a more than generous amount in a cut crystal glass and handed over.

My hand was shaking so much that she had to have noticed, but she didn't comment. Aaliyah and Ebony settled back in their seats with their own drinks, while Sly nursed his ever-present soda. I'd never seen him drink alcohol; ever the professional.

I rested my back against the plush sofa and took a long haul from my glass. The alcohol burned a welcome path down my throat. It focussed my attention on something other than my fear.

The relief was short lived.

'We need to debrief,' Sly reminded us.

They all looked at me. The goosebumps returned with a vengeance. I had to hold the glass with both hands. And even then, the trembles continued as the memories resurfaced.

I took another deep gulp of the whisky and concentrated on the burn. Then, after a deep breath, I leaned forward with my elbows on my knees and stared into the rest of the amber liquid in my glass.

I exhaled hard. Hoping my nerves would leave my body the same way. No chance. If only it were that simple.

I looked up and made eye contact with each of them. They waited patiently until I was ready, even Aaliyah.

'My family tagged Jonah when he was in the reincarnation facility. They knew he was there all along. Bashir intercepted his essence and informed Michael and Cal-Tan. They decided to allow the reincarnation and use it to their advantage.'

Ebony only just managed to swallow a gasp. Sly and Aaliyah took the news relatively well.

'That's why the reincarnation took longer than normal,' Aaliyah commented. 'And why it was so difficult for me to find him.'

'Yes. They kept him in limbo while they implanted a chip in his brain.'

'The voices in his head?' Ebony asked.

'Most likely.'

'Why?' Ebony asked.

'To infiltrate our group,' I answered. They nodded; it made sense. 'There's more,' I added.

I took another deep glug and emptied the glass. Ebony leaned over and refilled it. I nodded my thanks.

'Cal-Tan wanted to know how a reincarnated body would perform here on Earth.'

That comment resulted in creased brows all around. All except Aaliyah.

'Why?' Her voice was full of dread. She must have realised what was going on.

I took another deep breath, straightened my back. 'I think he might want to invade Earth.'

'What?' Sly's unconventional outburst said it all. I didn't have to repeat myself.

'They're going to invade with an army of reincarnated souls?' Aaliyah connected the dots.

I was grateful she didn't put it all on my family.

'It's the worst-case scenario.' I tried to settle the panic. 'It could be something else.'

'This quest has just risen to a whole other level,' Ebony concluded, her voice dark and low with concern. 'How do you know?'

'My father,' I explained. 'One thing I can always count on is his narcissism. He couldn't help himself and gloated about it.'

'Why?'

'He was going to kill me anyway, so I guess he thought I wouldn't be able to use the information.'

'He's your father.' Ebony exclaimed: her eyes wide open in shock.

'That makes no difference to him,' I answered. 'Me, my siblings, we're expendable. He has no love for his prodigy. Besides, I betrayed him.'

'And so he spilled the beans?'

I nodded.

'How do you know he isn't playing you again?' Aaliyah planted the seeds of doubt.

I hesitated before I answered.

'I don't. But he was going to kill me. I don't believe it crossed his mind that I might escape. My father doesn't suffer betrayal well. He kept telling me he'd expected me to be his heir. His successor.'

'Bullshit.'

'Probably.' I took another deep haul of the liquor. 'I think it was more for my siblings than for me. If he kills me, his so-called favourite, then it will send a message to my family that treason is not accepted. He wanted me to suffer. As much as possible.'

My mouth was so dry I had a problem forming the words. The edges of my vision clouded and shook as I felt feint. Holding on to the glass for dear life, I sat back in the sofa. I didn't trust myself to stay upright without the support of the backrest.

I closed my eyes and took a deep breath, actively forcing my hearts to slow their erratic thumping. The lights still sparkled on the inside of my eye lids, but their brilliance diminished with the slowing of my heartbeat. I pushed myself deeper into the plush of the seat, admonishing myself for my weakness.

It didn't help. Ibrahim's sadistic face was plastered on the inside of my lids.

I opened my eyes.

They were all looking at me. Ebony with a mixture of curiosity and sympathy. Aaliyah echoed the curiosity but mixed it with impatience. Sly was his regular stoic self.

'My father handed me over to Ibrahim,' I whispered.

Ebony's hand shot up to her mouth. Even Aaliyah's eyes opened wide in shock.

'He told Ibrahim to make it count.'

They all lowered their gaze. It was clear they knew what would have happened.

'Ibrahim is Hashta, like we surmised,' I continued. 'My father has pulled him into his own personal circle. I guess they have a lot in common.'

'How is that possible?' Ebony couldn't get her head around my father's cruelty.

I just shrugged, unable to talk.

'How did you escape?' Aaliyah's suspicion returned.

'Now that's a funny story.' I almost smiled.

She cocked her head.

'Michael,' I said to everyone's surprise.

'What?' Aaliyah almost shouted.

'Michael let me go. He said he wanted to hunt me. But frankly, I think the image of how Ibrahim would go to town on me was too much, even for him.'

'That sounds uncharacteristic. I'd have thought he would be happy to see you dead.'

I nodded. 'He would. Just not like that.'

The silence returned.

'So how do we stop Cal-Tan?' Aaliyah asked.

I shrugged. 'Good question. I don't know. But we'll think of something.'

I tried to relieve the enormous tension in the room. 'And it's just conjecture, I don't know for sure that he wants to invade us. I just can't think of anything else.'

I turned to Ebony. I wanted to change the subject to sooth the cramp that knotted the muscles in my back.

'How did you find the tag?'

'Doctor Patil did an autopsy on Jonah's alien body,' Ebony explained. 'The reincarnated one. Straight after the transfer he noticed there were still electrical impulses in the corpse's' brain. He monitored them and once it was clear the body was no longer needed, he investigated it. There was an implant in the brain, between the frontal and the limbic lobes. He removed it and placed it in a metal container until my people could take a closer look.'

My surprise must have been visible in my face.

'We disassembled it in a safe environment. It looked like a tracker with some kind of transmitter. We made sure it was deactivated.'

'And you left the base.'

She nodded. `

130

Sly joined the conversation. 'We packed up as soon as we found the tracker and assumed all locations had been compromised.'

'That's when we came here.'

'The tracker?'

'Not here. It's in a hundred small pieces in a lead-lined stone box. It won't transmit anymore.'

'What now?' Aaliyah brought us back to our main problem.

'We have to regroup,' Ebony stated. 'Assume that a lot of what we have done since Jonah returned is compromised and go from there.'

'We must warn Benedict. Jonah met him in that body.'

'Won't they know now anyway? If they listened in on everything Jonah did?' Aaliyah asked.

'I don't think they could,' I contended. 'My father pretended he knew our every step, but he didn't. Ibrahim was going to torture me to tell him who was in our group. He might have been able to follow Jonah around, but he didn't know his thoughts or what he saw or did.'

'That's a relief. But we still shouldn't underestimate him. Or what the technology is capable of,' Ebony stated.

We agreed.

The silence was heavy as we all sat back and contemplated our predicament.

Chapter Twenty-Five

Time for some good news.

Though slightly censured.

'We have allies.' I said. That got their attention.

'What allies?'

'Friends back in my dimension.' I divulged. 'They helped me escape.'

'I think you should fill us in on all the details,' Ebony suggested.

I don't know why, but I didn't want to divulge all the specifics. Not yet. Call me paranoid, but I wasn't ready. Not after uncovering the way my father tagged Jonah. Nothing was a given anymore. I didn't know who was listening in, who I could trust.

I gave them the abbreviated version. Without the names.

'So there's a rebellion?' Ebony asked.

I nodded.

'Didn't you know?' Aaliyah surprised me.

'No.' I felt challenged. Then admonished myself. 'I

knew there were occasional issues. Things went wrong with shipment of parts for the re-incarnators. People disappeared. I guess I was used to that happening to my father's competitors, I never gave it another thought. In hindsight, I should have known, but I never connected the dots.' I felt stupid. Of course I should have been aware. I'd been so full of myself, embroiled in my own petty rebellion that I never even considered anyone else would do the same. How's that for arrogance?

Then Aaliyah surprised us even more.

'Your father's rebels and ours are in contact.'

The silence was loaded. I saw my surprise mirrored in everyone's faces.

'That's very significant. When were you going to inform us?' There was an edge to Sly's words.

'When the time was right,' Aaliyah answered, on the defensive. Her cold, hard features dared him to push the subject or question her again. Thankfully, he declined, though he didn't back off.

'What exactly do you mean by in contact?' I asked. There was no end to the surprises today.

'The underground groups have started communicating to each other. They are careful, so it's just baby steps. They're low on trust, but agree they have a common enemy: slavery.'

'They oppose the practice, not necessarily the leaders?'

She shook her head. 'Both. Cal-Tan is the most hated man in our dimension. So, his adversaries are prevalent in the underground, just because of that. But the realisation that slavery is abhorrent grows more and more in all layers of the population. We see what the families are doing. We know we have to bring them down to stop the practice.'

'We?' I asked what the others were thinking. 'You're part of the underground?'

'Yes. I have been for a long time.'

'And you just thought it wasn't prudent to tell us?'

My temper was showing in the tone of my voice. Everything from the past twenty-four hours bubbled close to a breakdown. Aaliyah's secrecy threatened to be the last drop in the overflowing bucket.

'Need to know basis.' She dismissed it so easily.

'We needed to know,' I pushed on, the volume of my voice almost at shouting level.

'No. You didn't.' She dared me.

Realisation hit me like a brick wall. 'You still don't trust me.'

'Would you?' Her voice was raised. 'Your family has been at our throats for centuries, for as long as I can remember. Your father repeatedly tried to kill us. Why would I trust you? And this lot.' She waved her hand at the rest of the people gathered. 'These humans. They haven't proven themselves. Not to me.'

'What do we need to do to win your trust?' I shouted, exasperated. It was just too much.

'Not screw things up.'

She made it sound so simple.

'Cool down. Both of you.' Ebony was forceful.

'Fighting amongst ourselves is not what we need now. Do you really want to play into Cal-Tan's cards?'

I stared at her, angry that she hadn't taken my side. But understanding quickly set in; she was right. I glanced at Aaliyah and saw the same reasoning in her features.

We may have been pushed together through no choice of our own. But we were all we had.

We were it.

Chapter Twenty-Six

Two days later Jonah opened his eyes.

I'd almost given up on him, but he beat the odds again.

This was never-before executed technology. Mind blowing stuff. First the Cryo, then catching his essence, and finally putting it all together.

But we were still at the very start of the process, as we quickly found out.

He'd lost his memory.

At least, the part pertaining to the last six months or so.

He had no idea what had happened to him or where he was.

Doctor Patil called Ebony to the infirmary just as we sat down to dinner. She dropped everything and stormed out of the room, shouting something about waking up.

I stared at Sly, who quickly pushed his chair back and stood up.' Jonah,' he concluded, never one to mince words.

My fork clattered to the plate as realisation hit me. Jonah had woken up? He was alive. Really alive?

Was he?

I joined the mass rush out of the dining room, through the long hallway to the make-shift infirmary.

The nurse stopped us before we charged into the room. 'Please wait here. You can see him through the window. He needs rest.'

'How is he?'

'Confused.' She looked worried; her brow creased.

Aaliyah, Sly and I took up positions at the large window that separated the infirmary from the hallway.

The scene was as I'd seen it earlier that day. It looked and felt like something out of an A&E series. Blue clad people, including Ebony, standing around a hospital bed. Standards with equipment making the mandatory beeping sounds and drips positioned like sentries around the head of the bed. I glanced at the monitors.

A steady heartbeat.

Just the one.

My eyes moved slowly to the right to where Jonah sat up in his bed. He looked pale in the places where I could see his skin colour. The familiar tattoos and scars brought a rush of gratitude to me I hadn't expected.

It was him. At least on the outside.

His eyes flitted from one side to another nervously as he scanned the room and the window. Jonah's breath came in spurts, his nostrils flaring as he struggled to calm himself. Doctor Patil talked to him, but he wasn't paying attention. The monitor showed an increased heart rate and his flushed face validated that.

Ebony sat beside him, her face and form hidden in the blue scrubs. Jonah's glance kept returning to Ebony, but he looked confused, not sure who she was or what she was doing there.

Ebony said something to doctor Patil, who shook his

head, but she was adamant and pulled the mask off her face as she took Jonah's hand.

He flinched, pulled his hand back, but she held on as she softly spoke to him.

Slowly he concentrated on her. On what she said, and the tension in his muscled form relaxed slightly. He let his hand rest in hers and she continued to softly stroke the top of his fingers. His features softened and I could see what I hoped was recognition.

He said something.

We couldn't hear the words, not from outside the room, but I could lip read Ebony's name. Tears started to form in her eyes. Jonah's right hand lifted from the bed and softly traced them down her face. He smiled and said her name again.

I felt the sting of tears in my own eyes and glanced to the others in the hallway. Aaliyah was silently and very uncharacteristically crying. Sly was his normal stoic self, but for the wide smile that adorned his face. We were all feeling the relief.

Jonah's hand left her face and moved to his chest to where Raphael's sword had pierced his body. He looked down at the new scar, a thick ridge of tissue a memory of when he had died. Understanding hit him and he looked confused again, pulling his left hand free from Ebony's grasp to pull the hospital gown away from his body. The drips prevented him from throwing the garment away and he pulled at the tubes in his arm. Ebony frantically tried to comfort him and prevent him from ripping them out.

Doctor Patil called something out to the nurse who ran to a table to the right of the bed. Sly pushed the door open and rushed to help the doctor and Ebony struggle to keep the big man restrained to the bed.

Aaliyah and I stayed where we were. We would only hinder them, and probably scare Jonah even more. His terror was clear in the way he fought them to leave the bed, feeling strength he shouldn't have had yet.

The nurse inserted the needle of the syringe into the drip that led to Jonah's right arm and quickly pushed the plunger.

The effect was almost instantaneous. I saw Jonah's eyes cloud over as his body relaxed back into the bed.

I breathed a sigh of relief.

Yes, it was Jonah.

But he had a long way to go.

Half an hour later we were all seated in the living area, the remnants of the re-heated dinner on the table. No one had much of an appetite.

'He has no recollection of the past months, or his other body. His last memory was the fight where he was killed,' Doctor Patil filled us in.

'Naturally, that was a very traumatic experience and confusing. I expect he realises he couldn't have survived that ordeal, and that frightens him. I'll keep him under a light sedation for the coming days so he can acclimatise to the new situation.'

'Will he get his memory back?' Aaliyah asked what we were all wondering.

'I don't know. This is an unprecedented scenario. No one has ever come back from the dead and to tell you the truth, I'm winging it.'

Though understandable, it sounded ominous coming from a man of science who was usually so calm and professional. Dread had taken its place again in my gut. Had we done the right thing? Again?

'Only time will tell,' the doctor continued. 'He's sleeping now. Ebony will stay with him.'

'With one of our team too,' Sly cut in. 'In case he wakes up confused again.'

I nodded. No one knew what to expect.

'What about his body?' I asked. 'How is that doing?'

'Remarkably well, considering it was frozen for an elongated period of time.'

'Strong?'

'Maybe not physically in the way Jonah was used to. But his organs are working well, and his heart is powerful. All in all, it looks as though the procedures were successful, though it's still too early to say for sure.'

We held on to that spark of optimism. He was alive. His body was working, taking in nutrition, converting that to energy.

We had hope.

Chapter Twenty-Seven

'Are you bullshitting me?' Jonah's booming voice carried into the corridor of the infirmary. He was clearly awake.

He sat up straight in the bed, the tint of his skin now resembled what I expected from him. All paleness from yesterday was gone. He looked in good health, and clearly felt that way too.

'Why do I have to stay here like this?' He confronted the poor nurse who attempted to keep him immobile in the bed.

'Please sir, you need to rest.'

'I've rested more than enough. I feel good. No need to stay in bed.'

I walked into the room with a smile on my face. My big friend certainly was back. He was his old obnoxious self, not giving an inch.

'Gabe. You tell her I'm ok. I wanna get up.' He recognised me.

'To do what?'

'Anything, as long as it's out of this bed. I've been stuck here for ages.'

I laughed.

'You've been in that bed for exactly one day since you woke up. And no, you're in no state to go anywhere else. What did Doctor Patil say?'

He sulked, looking at me from under his creased brow. This was not what he wanted me to say. I took up position next to the bed, ignoring his dark looks.

He tried a different tactic. 'Oh, come on, Gabe. I need some exercise, even Patil agrees with that.'

'Yes. That's why the physiotherapist is coming tomorrow,' I answered to his dismay.

'Fuck that. I feel good. What is everyone pussy footing around for anyway? You're all exaggerating. I'll rest if I need to. Just get me out of here.'

I raised my right eyebrow. 'Exaggerating?'

'Yeah,' he sounded less convinced.

'Let me think. Two days ago, you were in an induced coma to allow your body to recuperate from being frozen solid—actually dead—for months and to see if your essence had found the way home. You have been the subject of never before attempted—let alone successful—medical procedures. Procedures that most specialists still banish to the realms of fantasy.'

He stared at the bed covers, his hand curling the material into a ball.

'What part of that is an exaggeration?'

Jonah sighed and for an instant I saw vulnerability creep into his face.

'You're allowed to rest, Jonah. It will take time.' I said in a much softer voice.

'I know. Patience has never been my strongest point.'

'Nope. I'll agree with that.'

He smiled, for all of ten seconds.

'How are you really doing?' I asked him softly.

He looked up at me. 'I don't know.' He shrugged.

I nodded to urge him on.

'I don't know how to feel.' His bed covers had become interesting again. 'Like you said, no precedent.'

His smile didn't reach his lips.

'Ebony told me I died.' He looked up for validation. I nodded.

'Twice.' Another nod.

'Something about a host body. Me, but not me.'

He took a deep breath. 'I don't remember anything about that. Nothing at all. Just a shitload of pain.'

I pulled up a chair and sat down next to the bed. 'What is the last thing you recall?'

'The fight.' His brow creased in concentration. 'We'd won. You were lying on the floor. I reached down to help you up. Then pain. Immeasurable pain.' He absentmind-edly touched the place where the scar on his chest was.

'Rafael stabbed you in the back with his sword. It went right through and came out there.' I nodded to where his hand was.

'Did it all really happen?'

'Yes.'

'Reincarnation? Your dimension? All of it?'

I nodded again. 'It's a lot to take in.'

'No kidding.'

He took the beaker from the tray next to the bed and drank a sip. 'I could do with something stronger.' He held up the cup.

'I bet you could,' I replied laughing. 'But you'll have to ask the doc for that.'

'Figured you'd say that.' He drank the liquid.

'You know. Sometimes it feels like a dream. Or a film or something. Like it happened to someone else. Not me. I can't get my head around it all.'

'It would floor anyone, Jonah. Give it time.'

'Time?'

'Yes. You have that now. Take it one step at a time.'

He shrugged. 'I'd love to, but they won't let me out of bed.'

'Physicality is only one side of it,' I added once we'd stopped laughing.

'That part I can deal with.'

He looked at me again. 'It's the mental side that worries me. What if I can't get it all in order?'

'You will. We're here to help you.'

Chapter Twenty-Eight

'You should have told us about the resistance.'

I just couldn't let it go.

Aaliyah and I were in the kitchen. I was preparing a sandwich to tide me over for the rest of the afternoon.

Aaliyah didn't even look up. 'You should have known.'

Touché.

'The two resistance groups are working together?' I couldn't stop myself.

'I told you they were.'

'I know. But it sounds so unbelievable.'

'Why?' She was indulging me, reluctantly.

'Well, we've been at each other's throats for so long.'

'Some of your family and some of mine have. The other people just got caught up in the melee.'

She had a point.

I turned to face her.

There was no reproach in her violet eyes. Curiosity, maybe on how I would deal with all the information I'd heard in the past days.

To be honest, I didn't know how.

The last few days had been a roller coaster. Not just for me, for everyone here. But egotistical as I was, I thought my experiences were the worst.

The impact was just beginning to register, and it was scaring the bejeebees out of me. What could have happened —should have happened—would keep me awake for nights to come. I'd been more than lucky. By all accounts I should have been dead; plastered over the Hashta torture dungeon in hundreds of small parts.

Chills ran up my spine at the memories and gave me goosebumps. My breath caught and I felt the strength seep out of my legs. I leant my butt against the counter and held on with both hands, hoping it was a subtle move.

No chance. Aaliyah had noticed.

Of course she had.

I was shaking.

There was no masking my feelings of dread.

'Just hit you, did it?' she asked without reproach.

I nodded, unable to utter any words. It was enough just attempting to breathe.

Aaliyah stood up and walked the four steps to me. She placed her hand on my arm, The warmth was soothing. Hooking my elbow, she softly pulled me from my perch and guided me to one of the chairs. With a softness I'd never imagined, she pushed me down on the seat and pulled up another chair to sit next to me. All the time allowing physical contact.

'What you went through would floor anyone,' she said softly. 'It's only natural that it will impact you.'

I nodded.

'You almost died, Gabriel. In a very messy and painful

way,' she continued. 'And not only that, it was by your father's orders.'

Her last comment slammed me harder than I cared to acknowledge.

'We hate each other,' I stammered. 'I expected no less from him.'

She huffed softly and smiled. 'Yeah, you keep telling yourself that.'

'I mean it,' I tried lamely.

She cocked her head.

I gave up.

Yes, it did haunt me that my own flesh and blood had not only condemned me to death, but in a manner I would not even wish on my worst enemy. It went beyond hate.

Hate was an emotion. This was completely devoid of any sentiment. Good or bad. And that made it even worse.

I rested my elbows on the table and covered my face with my hands. Waves of emotions washed over me, alternating anger and fear, destitution and emptiness.

Chapter Twenty-Nine

I had unfinished business.

Somehow, someone, had found and tagged me for the ambush last month.

They'd forced us to move out of our conformable penthouse. Not that these digs were bad, we just had a thing with control, and we wanted to be in the previous headquarters. Besides, I was sick of being hunted and continuously looking over my shoulder.

I had no illusions I would be free to walk the streets without looking over my shoulder anytime soon. We were at war. It was part and parcel of the situation we were in. But we'd felt safe there. Now that was gone—again.

I wanted to know how they'd found me. We all did.

Ebony's team had combed the CCTV streams from every camera anywhere near the LA financial district, searching for the cars that ambushed me. There were no sightings after the ambush, they seemed to have disappeared into thin air. So, they went back more than a month before the attack reasoning that the perps wouldn't be hiding then.

The dashcam on my car and the streams Sly had followed me with, delivered details on the cars themselves. Enough to find them after painstaking hours of shifting through the enormous mountain of data. The team used AI to speed up the search and found the old pick-up. It had been abandoned in the rough side of LA and was now nothing more than an empty husk. The wheels had been replaced with bricks and both doors were missing. By the look of the blackened interior, someone had set fire to the cabin.

We wouldn't find any clues there. It wasn't worth the risk of exposure.

On to the other vehicles.

The black F150 was reported stolen, so Sly didn't expect to get any leads there. He turned his attention to the battered van. We had the plates, but they turned out to be stolen too. So then it came down to the specific dents, vague lettering on the sides, and hopefully some residual paint that had resulted from them pushing me off the road. The manoeuvre that pushed and rolled my car must have damaged the van. Sly's team searched for the van in the dealerships and repair shops. No luck. We reasoned it had been written off, like the pick-up.

'Now what?' I asked as we sat before the computer array.

'We keep looking.' Sly was never one to give up. 'Do you remember anything about the guys in the car? Tattoos, scars, anything that would be unique to one person.'

I sat back in the chair and tried to remember the details of the ambush.

'Anything out of the ordinary.'

I shrugged. It was hard to concentrate on the specifics. I hadn't then, preoccupied as I was with staying alive.

I closed my eyes and tried to imagine the ambush as a film I was watching. One I could fast forward and re-wind if need be. I pictured myself in a cinema, outside of the action, viewing it from multiple sides. It was another technique my mother taught me to deal with difficult situations.

The car on the make-believe screen hurtled off the highway ramp, bounced head over heels multiple times and came to rest on the grass. I looked around in the images my sub-conscious gave me. I could see the pickup and the Ford parked in the grass verge. Guys getting out. Their features were fuzzy, so no help there. The white van was nowhere to be seen. Ok. So they hadn't transported me with the van.

I saw one of the two men from the Ford approach the overturned car with something in his right hand. I tried to zoom in. It was a syringe. The other guy, a smaller man with grey-blond hair spoke to concerned bystanders who rushed to help. I couldn't hear the words, but they looked reassured and left the scene to go back to their cars.

The big guy bent down to stick his hand in the window, and I assumed he'd injected me. He then called to his companion and together they manhandled my limp body out of my wrecked car and on to the grass. The smaller guy checked they were alone, then they lifted me up and walked to the Ford, where they shoved my limp form into the back of the cabin.

I watched from my imaginary perch while the Ford left and was quickly joined by the red semi that had been the final side of the box.

The semi. That was it. The truck. We hadn't investigated that yet.

'There was a big red truck behind me.' I informed Sly. 'It boxed me in. It was there when my car rolled over and when they took me away.'

'Are you sure' Sly raised an eyebrow, it hadn't been obvious on the streams or the dashcam.

'Completely.' I answered resolutely.

Sly turned to his team and told them to look for a big red truck that had shared the road.

'Did you see a registration?' He asked me hopefully.

'No.' I disappointed him. 'The first time I noticed the truck, it was too close to see the plate. The only thing I was aware of was the massive bull-bar on the front of the grill and the devilish skull.'

'What skull?'

I sat up straight.

I closed my eyes and pulled the image back up. 'There was a big skull on the top of the grill. It had red lights in the eye sockets. The teeth were pointed, not like human teeth. Monster type.'

'What colour was it?'

I concentrated. 'Grey with streaks of black and a sickly green.'

'How was it attached?'

'It was mounted on a metal stake that looked like it was part of the bull bar.'

'And the semi was red, right?' I heard the sound of fingers hitting the keyboard. He was relaying the information directly to the team.

'Yes. Fire-station red.'

'You didn't see the driver?'

'No. Like I said, it was so close I could only see the bull bar.'

Sly turned to his team and filled them in on the latest news.

My excitement sent shivers up my arms. The skull was

quite unique. I'd never seen one before. And together with the description of the truck we might get lucky.

It took another four hours, but the team finally got a lead. They found a Facebook post of a hood ornament that resembled the skull I'd described and was mounted on the front of a massive, red Mac truck. The proud owner stood next to the grill, his smile a yard wide.

The man was what I'd come to view as a typical biker-come-truck-driver. Okay, I'm generalising, but he fit the picture. About as tall as Jonah, big—but flabby, fat, not muscle—tattoos all over his arms, chest and neck. He was dressed in a Harley Davidson T-shirt with cut-off sleeves, a faded pair of jeans that hung way too low and leather cowboy boots. His grey-streaked beard and unkept hair completed the picture.

The kind of guy I would steer clear of.

'That's it?' Sly asked, pointing to the truck grill and skull.

We have a name and a Facebook site. We'll dig deeper and find an address. Maybe pay this fine upstanding man a visit.'

I smiled for the first time today.

A lead.

Finally.

Chapter Thirty

Sly reported in three hours later.

They'd found the name and address of the truck driver, along with the company he worked for. Neither rang a bell with me. Sly's team dug further and cross referenced the trucker and the owner of the haulage company with names we knew were linked to the Establishment. They even brought up the old list I'd brought back form Taxore just after I met Jonah.

It was there that they found a match.

The truck company owner.

Just as well I hadn't put money on the trucker.

On the surface, and based on his Facebook profile, the owner; Dwayne Patricks, seemed like a wholesome, happily married, civilised businessman. But when I zoomed in on his eyes in the photos, I acknowledged a dark depth that belied the first impression. While the team trolled deeper, Sly and I made plans to visit him.

The address of the trucking company was the same as his home address. On google street view we could see it was an enormous level plot between the hills and mountains to the east of Los Angeles. Out of the suburbs, but within good driving distance to generate the business he needed.

There were three main buildings on the left side of the plot we deduced were for the business. Two massive rectangle boxes, most likely warehouses, and a generous workshop surrounded by parts and tyres.

The front of the right-hand warehouse had a one-story block of offices attached. The parking space in front and to the side of the office was filled with pick-ups and four-wheel drives. Typical of this kind of setting. A sign on top of the office building read "Dwayne Patrick Haulage" in the same bright red as the semi that had boxed me in. Beside the second warehouse we saw a line of trailers waiting, and two trucks, both big red Macs.

On the right-hand side of the plot stood a vast, two-floor, picture-book mansion in cultivated gardens that wouldn't have looked out of place in an episode of Cribs. To the back and side, it bordered dusty fields where horses roamed.

The stark white building with its dark windows and its ostentatious grounds stood out in the dusty valley. This was almost dessert, but here the gardens flourished. The big fountain in front of the house spewed valuable water into the sun-drenched air and sent a thick haze of mist to the two BMWs and the Bentley parked next to the entrance steps.

This was the place.

Dwayne certainly put a lot of value on status. It screamed narcissism to me.

Way too familiar.

The flat open character of the enormous plot and the absence of any kind of vegetation would make it almost impossible to approach the offices unseen. The house had more greenery, but it was all low shrubs and flowers. We also catalogued the many CCTV cameras and decided against a home call. A large doghouse and pen were located to the edge of the driveway, with good views of the house and surrounding grounds, completing the security measures.

This was one seriously paranoid man. He obviously had enemies. Now—with us—he had some more.

Ebony joined us in the computer room around the whiteboards as we tried to figure out how to get our hands on Dwayne.

'There has to be dirt on him,' she remarked after we brought her up to speed. 'With that kind of security, he's got something to hide.'

We pondered the information the team had unearthed.

Dwayne was a forty-something former college quarter-back, married to the then head-cheerleader. They'd been childhood sweethearts. In the last two decades, the family had been expanded with four children and, according to Facebook, a few dogs, horses and an alpaca.

'How long have they been married?' Ebony asked studying the photos of the happy family.

'Twenty-one years,' Sly answered.

'I'll bet the fire has gone out of that marriage. Find a mistress, he's bound to have at least one. Looks the type.'

I couldn't have agreed more.

'On it.' Sly went to instruct the team.

As expected, he did have a mistress.

Actually, he had two. Both half his age, one working at the office and another with no connection to the company. He alternated between the two women, spending as much as three nights a week away from home. There was no way his wife would not be aware of his extra marital activities.

Dwayne had a routine. Not a good idea for a man with enemies. But then again, he was unaware of us, his biggest threat.

It made it a lot easier for us. Sly's team watched him for two long weeks. Way too long for me. Now we thought we knew who was behind my abduction, I wanted revenge, and waiting for weeks was not on my agenda. I sulked and was frankly difficult to be around.

Finally, Sly was comfortable with the latest recon and we prepared for a strike. The second girl—Amanda, the one without connections to the company—lived seventeen miles from the haulage company in a quiet, remote, ranch-style, one-story building. It was surrounded by a tree filled garden and vast fields offering us much better options for a stealthy approach than the company location. The closest neighbour lived almost a mile away.

There was a security system and one of the team found multiple firearms registered to Amanda. That, plus the multitude of guns registered to Dwayne, meant we would have to be careful.

We'd established that Amanda lived alone, without pets, which endorsed our choice. The office mistress had two children, one of which was probably Dwayne's, and we wanted to minimise any collateral damage. So, she was ruled out as an option.

Sly outlined his plan at the big table in the computer room. We were all concentrating on the details when Jonah walked in supported by a cane. As one, we stopped our discussion while he slowly walked towards the table. Sly pushed a chair his way and he sat down next to Ebony.

I was astonished to see him up and walking, bringing

home that it had been almost a week since I'd seen him. I'd been wallowing in my own misery at the delayed revenge and totally ignored the big man. I felt terrible.

I nodded to him when he looked my way, unable to do more in my shame. I couldn't read anything from his face other than full concentration on getting to the chair without falling. I glanced at the others, Ebony was glowing, so happy to see the big man up again. She laid her hand on his shoulder once he was seated, and he covered her small fingers with his. Looked like they were an item again. Good.

Aaliyah, on the other side of the table, was less happy. The new Jonah had not rekindled their romance. Sure, she was happy he was alive and seemingly doing well, but he had little recollection of their trysts and wasn't interested in picking up where they'd left off. I didn't begrudge her a relationship, but I was happy she was no longer a third wheel on the Jonah - Ebony wagon.

'So, what's the plan?' Jonah broke the silence.

'We surround the ranch next time Dwayne stays over and move in just before dawn,' Sly explained. He gestured to the hologram image on the 3D creator. It showed an eerie blue-green three-dimensional representation of the ranch and its surrounding grounds. It enabled us to simulate several attack plans and debate the impact.

'We'll be streaming the mission,' he added. 'You can follow it here with Ebony.'

Jonah nodded, resigned to the fact he couldn't be part of the missions, yet.

'How many in the team?' the big man asked.

'Seven.'

He cocked his head in agreement and studied the hologram.

I smiled. It was good to have the big man around again.

Chapter Thirty-One

Three o'clock in the morning found us flat on our stomachs crawling steadily closer to the ranch.

The enhanced night goggles made everything light up a sickly green. It was momentarily disorienting. I can see reasonably well in the dark, but the blackout here was a whole different story, so even I needed the goggles. The ranch was so far from civilisation that the only light came from the house itself. There was no moon, and thin clouds masked the little glow there was from the stars.

It was pitch black.

The goggles were state-of-the-art to start with. Now—after Ebony and Tajan's improvements—we had almost daylight detail. Light cancellation technology allowed us to move our line of sight through dark and illuminated areas without the usually expected and painful flashes. This partnership between the two scientists was an enormous bonus. They combined the best technology from both dimensions and even improved on that.

The outside of the ranch was exactly as we expected.

The trees and shrubs, coupled with the intense darkness, would shield our advance. There were two sentries patrolling the grounds outside the main building. They walked together, falsely trusting in their security measures and the isolation. Their attention to detail was minimal; limited to randomly flashing their light at the ground and foliage around them.

I counted three vehicles in the parking lot to the side of the building. Two large pick-up trucks, one sporting Dwayne's company logo on the side, and an SUV. None of them came up warm on the goggles, so we deduced they'd been there for a while. This was an all-nighter for whoever was inside. We'd expected the ranch to be quiet with everyone sleeping by this time of the night, but the lights were still on in the living room and the kitchen. We counted four people inside. Three sitting on what we assumed was the sofa and one walking back from the kitchen.

The guards walked past where I lay hidden. Sly let them move from view before he indicated to Aaliyah and Jaime to follow and dispatch them. They would, if possible, be kept alive. But there was no guarantee. Secrecy was the main goal here. The three of us remained flat on the ground. We'd wait until the guards had been taken care of, then proceed to the house.

The last two in our team were positioned high up on the hills surrounding the area, just in case back up was needed.

A click in the earpieces heralded the next step. The patrol had been taken care of.

We raised ourselves up to a crouching position and, under cover of the darkness, made our way to the front of the ranch building. Aaliyah and Jaime would proceed to the back of the building and make their entry that way. It would also shut off any escape routes for the occupants.

I took up position next to the door, to the right of Sly. Tyrone covered the left side, holding the short pump action shotgun.

Another click, Aaliyah and Jaime were inside. Sly counted silently from three backwards with the fingers of his left hand in the air. On one, a well-placed shot-gun blast to the lock threw the door open and off its hinges. Sly rushed in first, with Tyrone hot on his heals, and threw a stun grenade into the centre of the living room. The one-hundred-and-seventy decibel blast echoed in the small room, throwing everyone back into their seats. The flash disoriented them even more.

Our team crashed into the living room at the same time as Aaliyah and Jaime pushed through the kitchen door and covered the scene from that side. I stayed out of sight for the moment, as we'd agreed.

Three of the living room occupants were plastered over the sofa, they held their eyes shut and had their hands over their painful ears. The last person, a woman, lay on the floor up against the wall to the kitchen shaking her head to clear the incessant whine she no doubt was experiencing.

Sly and Tyrone pushed the men to the floor, their hands behind their necks, and frisked them for weapons. Jaime did the same to the woman and threw the small handgun he retrieved on the floor, far away from her. He pulled her up onto her feet.

Tie-wraps were coiled around the men's wrists, and they too were pulled to a standing position. The largest of them, identified as Dwayne, shouted obscenities and attempted to push Tyrone away.

Sly nodded and Tyrone punched Dwayne in the ample gut, effectively shutting him up.

The woman, Amanda, gazed at her so-called lover with

clear contempt. No love lost there then. Good to know. We could use that.

'Now,' Sly broke the silence. 'Shall we get started?'

He stood in front of the four prisoners.

Tyrone pulled Dwayne upright. He looked like death warmed over. The blow to his stomach had clearly floored him.

'Dwayne,' Sly addressed the big man. 'You are going to tell me exactly what I want to know.'

'Like hell.' Dwayne spat out his reply, his face gaining some colour. 'Go fuck yourself, whoever you are.'

Sly signed audibly. 'Now that's not a good way to start our conversation. Believe me Dwayne, you will tell us what we want to know. Sooner or later.'

Dwayne glanced at the team, Tyrone, next to him, the stoic Sly, Jaime, holding Amanda and Aaliyah.

'Who the fuck are you?' he shouted.

'Let's just say we have an interest in the Establishment.'

The recognition was there. Dwayne's eyes flitted from Sly to Amanda and back again.

'What?' he tried. I noticed he didn't ask which establishment.

Sly stayed quiet and stared at the truck company owner.

'I have no idea what the fuck you're talking about.' Dwayne filled the silence. His glances shifting back to Amanda and the other two prisoners. 'You're at the wrong address here. I'm a businessman. I own a trucking company. Unless you want something hauled across the country, there's nothing I can help you with.'

Sly turned to the man standing next to Dwayne. 'What about you?' Again, stolen glances at the others. He lowered his eyes to the floor and shook his head.

The last one was the same. Silent. Evading eye contact.

So, back to Dwayne. 'Shall we try again?' Sly addressed him. 'We know you're involved in the Establishment. We're aware your company trucks have been used in clandestine missions to abduct people and move contraband for them.'

Dwayne's features took on a pale hue. His gaze landed on Amanda again and he swallowed hard.

'I don't know what you're talking about,' he tried again. His words had less conviction than before, the tone less confident. His shoulders sagged slightly as he searched for a way out of the situation. I saw him flex his shoulders in an attempt to find a way out, but the tie-wraps were tight on his wrists and didn't allow for any movement.

He took a deep breath and straightened his spine.

'Arrest me if you want. I have no idea what you're talking about. Whatever police department you're from, this conversation is over. Anything you want to say, you can do to my lawyer.' He stared straight ahead past Sly, determination on his features.

'We're not law enforcement.' Sly surprised him.

'Then who the hell are you?'

'Call us a private organisation. One that opposes the Establishment.'

Again, Dwayne observed the team.

The absence of police identification on the Kevlar vests registered.

Chapter Thirty-Two

'I should never have become involved with you.' Dwayne turned to Amanda.

'Shut up, Dwayne.' Her voice was hard and threatening.

'She tricked me. Then blackmailed me to front this whole mess. It's her. I'm the victim here,' he continued to vomit words.

Amanda stared at him. If looks could kill, he would have been squirming on the floor in agony.

'She seduced me. Filmed the whole thing. Manipulated me to do…. things, and filmed everything. She forced me to go along with her fanatical nonsense. I don't even believe in god. So why would I want to be caught up with this sick group of religious fanatics.'

Yeah, right. He was about as convincing as a bad salesman.

We played the trump card.

I walked into the room in a calculated manner, curious to see how Dwayne reacted to my presence. It would be a clear message his mission had failed. Okay, his part hadn't, he'd delivered me to my people, but as far as he knew, I should be dead. Or at least incarcerated on Taxore. Earth was the last place he would expect me.

I stared at him. My eyes locking on to his.

No reaction.

He barely glanced my way, more interested in Tyrone's shotgun trained at his gut.

I scrunched my brow. How was this possible?

'No reaction,' I said into the microphone link.

'Not from him,' Jonah answered in my ear. 'Look at the woman.'

I turned to face Amanda.

She tried to cover her surprise, but it was clear in her eyes and in the tightness of her lips. She averted her gaze— too late—I'd seen the recognition.

She knew me.

She knew who I was.

What that meant.

I looked back at Dwayne. Big, stupid, front-guy Dwayne. He'd been used. That much was clear.

We'd been looking at the wrong person.

'Find out who she really is,' I sent over the microphone.

'Already on it,' Ebony replied.

I walked over to where Amanda stood between two of Sly's men. She avoided looking at me, stared at the ground between her feet, then at Dwayne who continued to rant about how he'd been played.

He was just another man who'd let his dick do the think- ing. I had no pity for the likes of Dwayne.

'Amanda, right?' I addressed her.

She was a beautiful woman. Her long dark hair perfectly framed the delicate features of her face. Mixed heritage gave her the best of both worlds, a coffee-coloured skin and soft features. Luscious lips needed no fillers and the hint of green in her eyes made them mysterious. Her body was magnificent, full in the right places with a tiny waist and legs that went on forever. She was a beauty. I understood Dwayne's infatuation.

She tried the innocent, scared look. It was convincing, until you looked in her eyes. They were hard. Cold. Full of contempt. This was not a nice woman. More the psycho type. She was quick to notice I wasn't falling for her ruse.

Her lips pulled into a wicked lopsided smile that ruined her features and accentuated the hard lines of her jaw and the shadows of her face. A classical Jekyll and Hyde moment.

The sound of her chuckle was mirthless and sent an involuntary chill up my spine.

'Gabriel,' she stated. 'Right?' Mocking me.

I waited for her to stop laughing.

'Care to tell me your real name?'

She remained silent; her vicious smile fixed to her stare.

'I guess not. Well, no matter.' I moved slowly to stand directly in front of her.

'Surprised to see me?' I asked.

'Not really. They did say you were resourceful.'

I stared at her.

'How was the family reunion?' Her voice turned sickly sweet, with a hint of arsenic.

'All I expected it to be.' I answered, turning away from her.

It was clear to me we wouldn't get any information out of her. Not here, not now. She was enjoying it too much. So, I turned my attention back to the spineless puppet.

'Dwayne,' I started as I walked back to face him. 'We have to talk.'

He nodded, flinching as he looked past me to Amanda who no doubt glared at him.

He pulled himself up straight and, in a semblance of courage, looked me in the eye.

'What do you want to know?' He stated resolutely.

'Your men ambushed and abducted me.'

'That was you? I knew she was after someone. A few of my men and some of her guys did that job.' He nodded his head past me to Amanda.

'What do you know about those people?' I asked. 'I want to know everything you know about what Amanda here is caught up in.'

I turned back to her with a smile on my features. There was nothing in her face. A total blank space. She was definitely a proficient actress.

'She's mixed up with some religious fanatics. They're full of shit. Total wackos. Stories about aliens, Gods. That kind of thing. Wacky.'

'I know about that stuff,' I answered. 'I want to know who they are, and where I can find them.'

He looked confused. 'They talk about aliens, like they're among us.' His gaze jumped from me to Amanda and back again.

'They are, dipshit. You're talking to one,' Amanda butted in, laughing.

Dwayne looked at me closely. His eyes travelled from my head down to my feet and back up again.

'Joke, right?'

I refrained from answering, which confused him even more.

'That's a joke, right?' he tried again, to Amanda's continued mirth.

Dwayne took a deep breath. 'They meet here, at the

ranch. Every week, usually on Friday or Saturday. Weirdos. All of them.'

'Could you identify any?'

'Sure. It would be my pleasure, especially if I can stick it to...'

He never finished his sentence. A round hole appeared in the centre of his forehead just above his brow. Time stood still as I watched a single drop of blood congeal at the edge of the wound and drop over the edge. Slowly, his body toppled over backwards.

'Snipers!' Sly yelled, bringing me out of my reverie.

We ducked for cover as rapid fire erupted through the large windows, breaking the glass and sending shards in all directions. I dove over the large wooden table, upending it as I fell to use it as a shield. From the corner of my eye, I saw Amanda deliver a vicious kick to the crotch of the man on her right. He went down like a brick wall. She swivelled on one leg, and her knee caught the other guy holding her. He joined his companion writhing on the floor. I tried to make my way to her, but a barrage of sniper fire erupted and forced me back behind my temporary fortress.

She smiled at me, turned and ran out of the room.

I crawled over the floor in an attempt to reach the door and pursue Amanda, but was stopped by the incessant rain of bullets, one of which passed through the fleshy part of my left upper arm. Angry, I crept back to the minimal safety of the thick tabletop and fumed.

Sly called in the extra team he had stationed on the ridge as a failsafe. They quickly made their way to the sniper's location, making short work of the two guys shooting at us. We stayed under cover until Sly gave the all-clear.

'Is she among the dead?' Jonah asked over the intercom.

'No. She must have gotten away. We're checking the buildings.'

'Send up the drone.' Sly called to Tyrone from the ranch house. It was equipped with heat seeking functionality and would find anything alive.

I walked outside into the emerging dawn. The sun had just cleared the small hill to the east and lit up the slight haze that covered the ground, turning it almost silver. The bright red of the sunrise heralded rain to come later today. I turned as I searched the horizon. On the hills I saw the silhouettes of Sly's men as they combed the undergrowth for any more enemies. The drone flew overhead in steady grid lines, the sound resembling an irritatingly oversized mosquito. It probed into dense undergrowth and clearly lit up any living creature on the pilot's screen, but other than Sly's men, no humans.

'Anything?' I asked the pilot.

He shook his head. 'Couple of rabbits. Nothing else.'

I moved away to hide my disappointment. Amanda would have been a fountain of information. She knew who I was, that meant she was aware of the existence of Taxore and my family's company. She had to be somewhere high up in the hierarchy of the Establishment to be so knowledgeable. Maybe even in the inner circle, or at the least close to it. We'd had her in our grasp, and now she was gone.

Shit.

I joined Sly at the bodies. Five dead besides Dwayne. The people inside the house, mowed down by their own snipers, the two snipers themselves and a man who'd emerged from the shed when the shooting started. Dwayne had been brought outside too.

Thankfully, small glass cuts were the extent of the injuries on our side. That and the rapidly healing bullet hole in my arm.

Sly nodded to my bloody shirt. I answered by shaking my head. He shrugged. He was used to my speedy recovery.

'Search them,' he ordered his men turning back to the bodies. 'Then take the house apart. We're looking for anything electronic. Phones, Laptops, Tablets. Anything that can store information. Documents too. Bundle everything up in the lead cases and we'll investigate it when we get home.'

There were a few "yes, sirs" and everyone got to work. With seven of us, the task should be handled quickly.

Three hours later we were on the road back to the safe house with a collection of phones from the dead men, three laptops, an iPad and a burner phone we'd found under the floorboards in the bedroom. Those last ones were particularly interesting. Especially as they were accompanied by a printout of what looked like mobile phone numbers.

Ebony's team would be kept very busy in the coming few days.

Sly had also pulled out all the photo albums, magazines, videos and anything that might give us a clue to who Amanda really was and what she'd been doing at the ranch.

With his dying breath, Dwayne pointed to her as the ringleader, though I wasn't so sure he was as squeaky clean as he suggested. It was his name that had been on the list I brought back from Taxore. Not hers. Anyway, Ebony would find out.

Nothing was as it seemed.

As usual.

Chapter Thirty-Three

Back at the headquarters, Sly's men brought the bags and boxes of secured items into the house. All the electronics were in lead-lined boxes to make sure no hidden trackers could be activated. They would be unpacked in the bunker, then dismantled. Whatever was on there would be decoded and presented by Ebony's team. I was cautiously optimistic there would be interesting data on the machines after reading through the paperwork we'd found. It was a treasure trove.

There were invoices and transport documents that showed large movements of good, some of them guns and ammunition. Scrutinising the paperwork, we had to assume most of the loading documents were false, I couldn't imagine Dwayne and Amanda sending bananas halfway around the US, but at least it gave us an indication of the operation's scale and their involvement.

In addition to that, we'd found a ticket-to-heaven in Dwayne's left forearm, which strengthened my impression he wasn't the innocent schmuck he'd made himself out to be. It was too coincidental.

Jonah walked into the room and surveyed the piles of documents.

'Looks like it was a success,' he stated enthusiastically, with just a hint of disappointment that he'd not been an active part of the mission.

'Mixed,' I answered. 'We have a lot of information, there has to be a potential lead there somewhere. But the woman got away. That bums me out.'

'Can't win them all,' he reassured me in a very non-Jonah kind of way.

Was he getting mellow in his old age?

I smiled at the thought.

We were seated around the conference table in the video room. The massive screen at the end of the table showed images of data found on the devices. There were all kinds of information. Maps, documents, voicemails, emails. You name it, it was there. Now came the tedious task of shifting out the good from the rubbish. That would take time.

'We've been able to decode a lot of the data on the laptops and the team is running the phone numbers from the impounded devices. The only ones we haven't cracked yet are the iPad and the burner phone. They're proving to be a challenge.' Ebony had the floor.

'That's where we expect to find most of the quality information,' Sly added.

The room sat all seven of us easily. The comfortable chairs were placed around the oval table facing the screen. The boardroom itself was sound- and sight-proofed, the large windows coated with a substance that distorted the image when seen from outside the ceiling high windows.

Ebony was careful. To a fault. It crossed my mind these

security arrangements were not just to keep the Establishment out, I still had to find out what it was exactly that Ebony did to bring in the kind of money she had. Odds were, it wasn't completely legal, so the security made sense.

Jonah joined us, as he was prone to do now. His health was improving rapidly, and he'd even been spotted in the gym. No heavy weights, just baby steps, but he was back in his element.

I loved having the big man around again. Even if he was constrained to the house, he still helped. And just his presence gave us all a motivational boost.

Aaliyah was absent. She had business to attend to, or so she'd declared this morning. With that, she was gone. I had no idea when she would be back, but that was just the way things were with her. I think, deep down, her heart was breaking. Jonah and Ebony were an item, and there was no room for a third person.

'There are references to the Establishment,' Ebony continued. 'We know we're on the right track here. But what we've been able to decode has no real value as yet. We need to get into the iPad and the burner. The team is working on them. The paperwork was useful to cross reference some of the things we'd already found.'

'We found some streams we've identified as CCTV from the financial district, with you on them,' she nodded to me. 'We think that's how they found you. They've been monitoring the feeds from some of the buildings. We're pinpointing which ones as we speak. Maybe those companies have links to the Establishment. That would be a bonus.'

So, it had been facial recognition. That was a setback. We'd hoped the Establishment wouldn't have the use of that technology yet. But that was naive. They had almost unlimited funds and we knew they'd recruited extensively in technology teams and gamers. Add that they may also have access to Taxorian technology, and we had to assume they were almost as proficient as Ebony's team.

The next day brought good news.

'The team did it,' Ebony said over the phone proud as a peacock. 'They decoded the iPad and the burner phone.'

'You will not believe the information on them.'

Her enthusiasm was contagious. I found myself smiling in anticipation. It was about time we had a breakthrough in our quest.

We gathered around the meeting table and one of Ebony's wizards shared what they'd found, projecting it on the big screen. The first image I saw was a mail referring to some kind of event.

'The Establishment's inner circle, the Ventus Dei, has organised a global assembly. It will take place here in the US, at a remote location in the hills of Colorado somewhere.'

I was stunned.

'They seem to do this at least twice a year, according to the documents we found. The date is five weeks from tomorrow. No doubt the location will be heavily fortified, but this is an opportunity we can't pass up on. We have to act on this.'

'Hell, yeah,' Jonah answered for all of us.

I felt goosebumps all over my body. The Inner Circle. The de-facto leadership of my father's company here on Earth, all together in one place. It seemed frivolous to me that they would congregate like that, but I recognised the arrogance and narcissism which made it very believable.'

'How sure are we of this information?' Sly asked.

'We have no reason to believe it's planted. They didn't know we'd targeted Wayne. So, there's no reason why we should doubt the validity.'

'How about we cross check?' I suggested.

They all looked at me curiously.

'Benedict,' I stated.

Jonah nodded. Yes, if we could get hold of Benedict, we might be able to certify the information. In our last, very brief communication he'd indicated he was on a fast track to the Inner Circle. He would no doubt know if a summit was planned.

'He contacted us yesterday,' Ebony surprised me.

I raised an eyebrow and glanced at Jonah. He already knew.

'Last night,' the big man explained. 'He sent a message through a secure channel asking when we would come to confession again. He said it was time we came to church.'

'Actually, it was addressed to the operative who'd spoken to him in the cathedral last time.' Ebony added.

'Makes sense.' I mused. 'Do we use the same lady? Or someone else?'

'Someone different.' Sly interjected. 'Just in case it's a trap and they're looking for her. We can't be too careful.'

'It has to be someone the Establishment is unaware of; someone they will not have any images of.'

'Everyone here is ruled out.'

I nodded. Our team was too obvious. The way they'd used facial recognition to ambush me proved how unsuitable we were for any kind of undercover mission.'

'Leave it to me,' Sly closed the discussion.

I was curious what Benedict wanted to share with us. He only contacted the team when there was important news.

Maybe it had to do with his ascension to the Ventus Dei. At least it offered us a chance to verify the data we'd found.

'That's not all we found.' Ebony's voice brought me back to the meeting. There was more?

New images flickered across the screen. I settled down to what would definitely be a lengthy session. Finally.

Chapter Thirty-Four

'Gabriel,' Jonah stuck his head around the door to my rooms. 'There's something you should see.'

'Not now,' I answered.

My head was splitting, the headaches more frequent now that I'd stopped sleeping. I didn't want to see anyone or hear about the next problem we'd encountered.

I was sick of it all. Running around in circles. Always one step behind the Establishment.

Sure, the information we'd gathered in the raid was helpful, but not nearly as much as Amanda would have been. If we'd held on to her, then we could... Blah, blah, blah.

I hadn't taken any rest in days, obsessed with finding the next clue and deciphering the data we had, to figure out what my father was up to. There was something. Something terrible. I should know. I had to know.

It was driving me bat crazy.

Two days of binge drinking hadn't helped either. Even with my tolerance, I'd gone way too far.

The big man entered the room and stood in front of me. I tried to covey that I wasn't interested in talking now just by my features, then looked down again at the empty glass I had in my hands.

'Yes, now,' he stated resolutely.

I looked up, anger foremost in my emotions. Who the hell...? Well, he was my friend. That was who.

'You can't lock yourself in here forever, Gabe.' His features were creased in worry.

'I don't want to see anyone,' I answered.

'Well, that's not an option, is it? You're part of the team here. You remember teamwork? People working together. Not sitting in their rooms sulking all day.'

The heat of anger flushed my face and my breath deepened.

'You're not helping. This...' he gestured to the mess around me. 'This isn't helping. Not you, and not us.'

I glanced around at the books and documents strewn over the table, some of which had spilled on to the floor. I'd seen them fall but couldn't be bothered to pick them up. There were empty bottles of liquor all over the place, interspersed with crumpled snack bags, the only sustenance I'd had since my self-imposed isolation.

He pushed papers off a chair, pulled it forward and turned it backwards, he sat facing me with his arms resting on the back.

'What's going on, Gabe?'

'None of your business,' I snapped back.

'Yes, it is. As long as you're part of this team, it is my business.'

'Then maybe I should leave.' It sounded childish and spiteful to me as soon as the words left my mouth.

Jonah's laugh didn't help much.

I sat in stubborn silence.

'Get off your butt and come to the meeting room. Ebony has some important news. Something she said you need to hear.' He pushed himself up, swivelled the chair and moved it back under the table.

When I walked into the room, they were all there except Tajan. Aaliyah had a seat on the left side of the big table, Ebony and Jonah were opposite her. Even Tyrone was present. Sly walked from the kitchen holding a tray of soda cans and sandwiches which he placed in the middle of the conference table. Jonah attacked the sandwiches and Ebony took a can of soda for each of them. Aaliyah pulled the tray towards her and started munching on a BLT.

I would have preferred something a lot stronger than soda, but it was only eleven-thirty in the morning, so I guess that wouldn't be appropriate.

I walked over to the sideboard and leaned my butt against the hard wooden surface in a stupid act of defiance. I wouldn't sit with them, not yet. The fact that they had summoned me, irked me. It felt disrespectful to me at that time. Mind you, everything agitated me. I blew up over the slightest thing, either implied or just the result of my paranoid imagination.

Ebony smiled at me, not impressed by my sulking.

The missing Tajan walked into the room accompanied by one of Ebony's team. They set up a computer and linked it to the big screen.

Ebony stood up and joined them at the head of the table next to the screen. She nodded to Tajan.

'We received some information from Taxore,' the mousy man started the meeting. 'Something worrying.'

All news from Taxore was worrying, so it was nothing new. I continued to sulk.

'A group of Taxorian soldiers have been transported to Earth.'

Now that grabbed my attention.

'When?' Jonah interrupted.

'Three days ago.'

'Why didn't you tell us earlier?' I challenged.

Ebony cocked her head at me and gave me her best patronising look, making me flinch. 'We received the information forty minutes ago. About five minutes after we called this meeting, and Jonah had to go fetch you.'

Touché.

I looked down, my face colouring in shame.

'How many?' Sly picked up the meeting.

'We think three or four.'

'Do we know what their mission is?'

'Us.' Ebony stated clearly. 'Or more precisely; Gabriel.'

All eyes turned to me.

It made sense. Dad would be really pissed off at my escape. That meant a lot of pain for Michael and the rest. My father had lost face. My escape was a direct hit on his power and control, he'd see it as a personal affront. That almost made me smile.

'How do you know?' Jonah's question pulled me out of my reverie.

Tajan and the engineer looked at each other, then to Ebony who nodded.

'You might want to sit down, Gabe,' Ebony suggested.

I scrunched my brow in question. What kind of news was coming? Wasn't this bad enough already?

I pulled a chair back and sat down, apprehension sending goosebumps up my arms. Sly slid a can of coke my way and I caught it before it careened off the table edge.

All attention was focussed on the screen. A news reel

started with the anchor commenting on a mass killing in a small desert town west of Vegas.

A feeling of dread started at the base of my spine and sent tingles up my back. My headache intensified with stabs to the rear of my skull as unwanted thoughts began to form in my mind. I held on to the can and focussed my gaze on the recognisable images that filled the screen.

'Five people were slaughtered in what looks like a targeted attack on a diner outside the small town of Pahrump.'

The picture zoomed in on the diner surrounded by police and first-responder vehicles. The air was filled with smoke coloured by the blue and red flashing lights of the cruisers. Uniformed officers had set up a perimeter around the smoking remains of the diner, while the fire brigade showered what remained of the right side of the building with water hoses.

I could see dark stains of what looked like blood leading to a form on the ground shrouded by a black body bag. My throat constricted and I gripped the can tighter.

'The police are interviewing any potential witnesses and have not commented or released any more information on who is responsible for this atrocity.' The anchor's voice sounded metallic to my ears. Alien.

The shot moved from the diner to a group of people standing desolate to the side of the scene. Some were crying, others hugged each other. The journalist walked over to the group, followed by the camera and tried to inter-view them. A middle-aged man, who lived a few hundred yards from the diner, finally reported he'd heard a lot of what sounded like big motor bikes or terrain vehicles. Loud exhausts. He'd closed the windows and turned up the tv, acutely aware that he didn't want to interfere, whatever was going on. Then later, when it had gone quiet, he'd looked out the window and seen the diner alight.

'A biker gang?' The reporter pushed him.

'I don't know. I didn't look.'

'Did bikers come here more often?'

'Lots of people came here, bikers, off-roads, trucks, all kinds.'

'And there were issues before with these gangs?' The reporter was fishing for statements.

'Nothing like this.' The man shook his head and turned to his neighbour, zoning out the reporter. The camera panned out to cover the smoking remains of the diner.

The screen went black momentarily. Then photos of the inside of the wrecked diner appeared.

'These are from the Vegas police report.' Ebony explained.

Bile rose unwanted and I swallowed hard to force it back to my stomach. I felt the colour drain from my face as more photos appeared on the screen.

These were the uncensored ones. No body bags here, just plain blood, guts and corpses.

There were massive red stains and pools of blood everywhere. Whoever had done this, had gone to town on the people who'd been in the diner. Even with the fire and water damage, the brutality of what had taken place was abundantly clear in the state of the bodies. These people hadn't died well. No gun shots, all wounds were blade related. Deep cuts, hacked body parts. And blood. Lots and lots of blood.

I put the can down on the table, not trusting my shaking hands to keep it upright.

Jonah's features darkened with every new image that appeared on the screen. Even Sly, our stoic military leader had to swallow audibly when yet another bloody photo shook us to our core.

'The Taxorians?' I broke the silence with barely a whisper.

'Yes,' Ebony answered.

'How do we know for certain?' I held on to hope. 'They mentioned bikers.'

Ebony nodded to the engineer and a final photo came into view.

My blood ran cold, my throat constricted, and I couldn't breathe. I couldn't take my eyes from the horror on the screen.

A bloody form hung on the wall over the remnants of the Wurlitzer that lay smashed on the floor. Cook's knives hammered through the hands held the body in place. The copious amount of blood on the woman's chest was clearly the result of a gaping hole in her throat which had been cut from ear to ear.

She had been tortured. Her face was a mask of pain, the eye sockets were empty and bloody. Burns on her arms and body could have been the result of the fire, but I doubted it. Dark bruises on her bare torso told the story of multiple blows sustained while she'd been alive.

This was the waitress.

The kind woman who'd given me the benefit of the doubt and taken care of me when I came back to Earth. She'd trusted me enough to feed me and let me use her phone to call Sly. And now she was dead. Tortured. Slaughtered.

I felt sick.

But it was what was above her still form that really drove it home.

Letters were easily discernible on the previously white

wall between and above her arms. The bright dripping red of the words clearly determined what they had been written in.

I read them.

Then again.

The bile in my throat threatened to spill out. I read it again. And again.

Each word burned itself into my retina, mind and soul. I would never un-see this for as long as I lived.

This was personal.

"You're next, Gabriel." Was written in blood above the tortured form of the innocent waitress.

It was a message to me.

Personally.

And there was only one sadist who would be so outspoken. So in my face. So psychotic.

'Ibrahim,' I broke the silence.

Ebony nodded her head.

'He's back on earth.'

'Yes,' Tajan validated. 'He and two others. We think they're all Hashta.'

Could it get any worse? The Hashta loose on Earth?

'She died because of me.' My voice was barely more than a whisper but sounded deafening in the oppressive silence. 'They all did.'

No one answered. There was nothing to say.

We sat there digesting the implications of the Hashta on Earth. Of Ibrahim hunting me—us. Of the slaughter that had taken place just to send me a message.

'How did they find the diner?' Sly asked.

'Social media, probably,' the engineer answered. 'The waitress posted on Facebook about a bachelor prank where the groom had been left in the desert without money or a phone, dressed in weird clothes.'

My cover story.

'And they put one and one together?'

'Yes. Most likely.'

'My fault,' I repeated.

'Nothing you could have done about it, Gabe,' Ebony interjected. 'You didn't know, you couldn't have.'

I turned to her, finally tearing my eyes from the bloody images. 'And now they're dead.' My words were harsher than necessary, but I couldn't help myself. Once again someone innocent, someone nice, had died because of me.

'If I'd stayed away from the diner, they would be alive now.'

'Yeah,' Aaliyah broke through my self-pity. 'Or if you'd died on Taxore, or a thousand other things that didn't happen and cannot be changed.'

Her words stabbed at my hearts, and I felt my rage threaten to overpower me.

'Cut the pathetic self-pity, will you?' she continued. 'We're at war. Us against your father, my brother and the rest. People die in war. Soldiers and innocents. Isn't that what all this is about? Bringing down our families to protect the people here. To protect our loved ones on Taxore.' Her anger matched mine.

'This is personal. It can't get any more specific. This has happened, Gabe. And yes, it's addressed to you. So, pick yourself up out of that swamp of dramatic self-loathing and do something about it.'

I was flabbergasted. Slammed into my seat. I didn't know what to do.

I wanted to hit her, shut her up.

Anything to stop the flow of words that cut me deeply.

But she was right.

'Ibrahim died before I did, right?' Jonah changed the subject.

'What?' I was confused, what the hell did that have to do with what we'd just seen.

'My body deteriorated. It died on me. So why hasn't his? If he was reincarnated before me.'

His words struck a chord. Why was that? I'd forgotten that Ibrahim was basically a replica. It helped me channel my thoughts. Way to go, big man.

'It depends,' Aaliyah answered. 'Could be that his body is still functional because he didn't come to earth earlier.'

It was a possibility.

'Or,' I interjected. 'They gave him a different quality body.'

'There's a choice of qualities?' Jonah asked bewildered.

'There is,' I explained. 'Your body was what we call a grunt's. It's the vessel made for the slave trade. Biologically designed to have a restricted durability.'

'Why?'

'Basic business sense. You sell a product that lasts forever, or one that needs to be replaced every so many years. Quality forces you out of the market. The business wants to sell new grunts, not immortal ones.'

'Business, huh?' he asked sarcastically.

'Yes.' Aaliyah joined in. 'Grunts are no more than assets to Taxore. A component in the product chain. Necessary, but temporary. To create a version that lasts longer would undermine your profit. It's just business.'

'Unless you're the grunt,' Jonah said with an edge to his voice.

'Yes,' Aaliyah challenged him. 'But Taxorians aren't.

They're the producers. The business. Grunts are no more than a product to them.'

'And what about other vessels.' Sly steered the conversation away from yet another confrontation.

'Pre-growths for Taxorians are basically an improvement on their previous body. The same, but without the defects. In essence an improved version, minus a use-by-date. And then there are the ones in between. The bodies created for the human allies that have the ticket-to-heaven. They are much better quality than the grunts, but not designed for eternity.'

'Bet they don't tell their allies that,' Jonah remarked.

'Probably not. But then, no one's been back to tell on them, have they.'

'And you think Ibrahim has one of those bodies?' Ebony brought the conversation back to its roots.

'It's possible,' Aaliyah answered.

'He's Hashta,' I offered. 'They wouldn't invest all that work in a grunt's body. Cal-Tan obviously saw his potential, so at least a "ticket" quality.'

'Why not the pre-growth?' Jonah asked.

I pondered the idea.

'Cal-Tan wouldn't. Even if he sees Ibrahim as a kindred spirit, and I think he does, he won't trust him. They're too much alike. He will have recognised Ibrahim's ambition and psychopathic tendencies. It's what attracted him to the man to start with. But he needs to have an ace up his sleeve. If he controls the duration of Ibrahim's second life, he will in effect control the man.'

Jonah nodded. 'Sounds logical,' he concluded. 'So how long does that body last? And do they have any weak spots?'

We shrugged in unison.

'We don't know.' Aaliyah answered. 'On Taxore they

live for about two hundred years. But none of them have been sent back, so your guess is as good as mine.'

'Unchartered waters.'

I nodded.

'No way we can know, without finding one of them.'

I looked up in shock. 'Go after Ibrahim?' I couldn't believe what I was hearing.

'Maybe.' Jonah proposed.

Chapter Thirty-Five

'Where's Tajan?' I asked at breakfast next day.

Yes, I was back in the team.

'He's gone back to Taxore,' Ebony answered.

I looked at her incredulously. 'Why?'

'Because I asked him to,' Aaliyah answered. 'He's more use to us in the resistance.'

I stared at her. Just when I thought she was becoming more empathic, she turned one-eighty.

'Was that what he wanted?' I asked sarcastically.

She looked at me, disdain in her eyes. Aaliyah still had no patience for emotions and clearly found mine inappropriate. But I'd become fond of the mousey little man, we all had. He'd made an enormous difference in bringing Jonah back. The real Jonah. Without him, the big man wouldn't have been here. To me, it felt like a blow that he'd been sent back to Taxore.

'Yes,' Aaliyah deigned to answer. 'He did. He wanted to see his family. Make sure they were alright.'

My earlier righteousness deflated like snow in the midday sun.

'Will he be safe?' Jonah asked.

Aaliyah shrugged. 'As safe as anyone can be. Our dimension is a dangerous place.'

'Are you staying in contact?' The big man sounded worried.

'I am.'

'Good.'

Chapter Thirty-Six

Aaliyah returned after two days absence.

With her characteristic flourish, she barged into the dining room and took control.

'I've had a message from Tajan,' she announced.

We all looked at her in anticipation, our mouths full of the delicious home-made Thai meal we were devouring with gusto.

Sly pushed an empty plate and utensils her way, and she sat down, pulling the serving dish towards her.

'Cal-Tan has completely halted the supply of grunts to Taxorian customers,' she stated.

I was confused and shrugged my question. 'Why would he do that?' It was his livelihood. The blood of the company.

'Tajan didn't know. He was as confused as you are. I hoped you might be able to shine a light on the reasoning.' She didn't add "because he's your father" but the words hung in the air, nevertheless.

I pondered the conundrum. It wasn't like Cal-Tan to pass up on revenue like this.

'It's strange,' I thought out loud. 'The pens must be full now with the escalation of violence between fundamental groups here. And he has your family's stock as well.'

'According to Tajan, he now controls all the religions, so the whole supply chain.'

'All of them?' I was astounded at my father's power expansion. My mother had indicated he wanted the monopoly, but I hadn't expected it to happen so quickly.

'Yes,' she answered between mouthfuls.

'There must be hundreds of grunts waiting to be sold,' I mused.

'There are.' Aaliyah validated. 'Tajan said the harvesting has even been increased.'

'Sounds like he's stockpiling,' Jonah suggested.

'Yes. It does,' I agreed. But why?

'Has he ever done anything like that before? Stop trade?' Aaliyah asked.

'Once, I think. Though not to our dimension. He and his father suspended all supply to the Eighth dimension long ago to pressure them into a better deal. Maybe he's putting the screws on the Council in Taxore.' I shrugged.

'Is that plausible?'

'Not really. I mean he already has the monopoly; he can dictate the prices. So why pull the supply?'

'Could they be destined for another dimension?' Ebony suggested.

'Maybe. But what use is there in antagonising Taxorian customers? Cal-Tan's a savvy businessman. I can't see him ruining one market just to push another one. He might decrease the supply slightly, but never bring it to a standstill.'

'Unless he's out for power,' Jonah mused.

I shrugged again. It was as good an explanation as any other. 'Could be. I mean what else is there to strive for now he has full control of the slave trade in the First dimension?'

I racked my brain for another explanation but couldn't find one. My father's mind worked in strange ways. I could never guess what he was thinking. He did it on purpose, to keep us on our toes, and to disorientate us just in case we had power aspirations. He was truly the only person who even remotely knew why he acted as he did.

'Anyway,' Aaliyah added. 'It's strange. Even for Cal-Tan.'

I appreciated that she didn't make it personal by referencing the family ties.

Aaliyah continued her narrative. 'There's more.'

She had our attention.

'Cal-Tan is recruiting soldiers. Not just any candidates, mostly from the bad side of Taxore. He's even visited the prisons to get volunteers. Seems he has the power now to get criminals released ahead of their time.'

'Why doesn't he just recruit the pirates? The other families must have more than enough soldiers.' I contemplated. 'If, like Tajan says, he now controls all the families, he should have an abundance of mercenaries.'

'Everything points to a major offensive,' Jonah chimed in.

I had to agree, but what was the target?

'Could they have identified a new dimension?' I speculated.

'It's possible,' Aaliyah answered. 'Tajan didn't mention that, but he probably wouldn't know. He's not partial to that kind of information.'

'Do they do that often?' Jonah asked. 'Find new dimensions?'

I shrugged. 'Yes and no. There are hundreds of dimensions. About half of them have been mapped by our scientists. We know they're there. But not all are profitable or even inhabited. Cal-Tan has a team investigating the profitability of prospect dimensions. They produce a business case, and he ultimately decides whether any actions will be taken.'

'Then what?'

'If deemed interesting, he'll send a probing party to the dimension to determine what commercial opportunities it has. That is reported back to him, and the final decision is made. The profitable ones will get attention.'

'The kind of attention that merits mercenaries?'

'Possibly. It depends on what the commercial angle will be. The dimension is classified as either a supply or a demand dimension. Demand dimensions are coddled to generate the commercial success. Supply dimensions are plundered. So yes. It is possible that Cal-Tan found a dimension to pillage.'

'How could Tajan find out which it is?'

'He probably couldn't. Cal-Tan will keep the information close to his chest. In time, an increased supply of a product could become apparent, but that will take time to trickle down. Especially if he's selling outside of Taxore. It will be difficult to recognise because we don't know what product they would be harvesting.'

'No way to know, then if this is the reason?'

I shook my head.

I had one last angle. But I kept that one silent for now.

'Okay,' Ebony stated resolutely. 'Let's not dwell on it.'

I agreed, but at the back of my mind that irritating

voice whispered that it could be important. Maybe he'd found a new dimension where he could sell Earth grunts. That would necessitate an increase of his harvests here. I was apprehensive what that would mean for the escalating violence between the religions. An all-out holy war was in the cards. We had to act fast and stop whatever it was he was doing.

'Penny for your thoughts.' Ebony stood beside me and nudged my shoulder.

I smiled. Not successfully. She waited patiently for my answer.

'Everything Cal-Tan does is part of a long-term strategy. I'm wracking my brain to figure out where we fit in all this.'

She raised an eyebrow with an unspoken question.

'I can't shake the feeling it's connected to Earth,' I explained. 'It's too much of a coincidence with the heightening conflict between the religions here we know is the Establishment's doing. We need to be vigilant. Very vigilant.'

'Maybe Benedict has an answer,' Jonah suggested.

'Could be. Or at least an idea.'

'Or it will become clear at the Establishment summit.' Ebony proposed.

I nodded.

The tingles still ran up and down my spine. The old man was up to something. Something we had to find out in a hurry.

Whatever it was, it wouldn't be good.

'Can we ask Tajan to look into more details?' Jonah asked Aaliyah.

She shook her head. 'He doesn't feel safe there anymore. The Hashta have turned on our own people now, led by Bashir. They are interrogating anyone they think is suspect. Most of them don't return home, and those that do speak of terrifying and brutal torture. They're searching for the resistance.'

I could imagine the situation with Ibrahim in control. He would leave no stone unturned. Although he himself was on Earth now.

'Tajan should be back here by tomorrow.'

It was the best way forward, though his intel would be dearly missed.

'Do you have other contacts?' Ebony voiced my question.

Aaliyah shrugged. 'I do, but they're reluctant to step up at this time. We'll need to let things calm down first, then we can try again.'

Chapter Thirty-Seven

The meeting with Benedict was scheduled for two days later.

Once again, we'd found out online when he was taking confession in the basilica and briefed the middle-aged man who would be our intermediate.

He was a mousy, mixed-race, fifty-something, completely unimpressive person. Unmemorable. Exactly what we wanted. He would blend in with the regular congregation in the immense basilica.

We'd agreed to let Benedict take the floor first and tell us what he knew. He'd effectively called the meeting. We would observe the proceedings from Ebony's headquarters with the aid of the mule's custom glasses which sported a built-in camera and microphone. From the control room we would be able to guide the conversation, speaking directly to our operative though his hearing aid.

At seven twenty-three I stood with my back to the wall in the command centre and observed the bank of screens that covered the opposite wall.

The interior of the church filled three screens. Its familiar ostentatious marble columns and stain glass windows seemed oppressive. A big difference to the last time I'd viewed the basilica. It wasn't necessarily the building. It was what it had come to stand for. Too much had happened.

I know, it's not fair. The church itself, like all the religions, wasn't the culprit in this fight. It was my father and all the humans he'd corrupted. They were the bad apples in the basket. But, for me, the stench of their decay and debauchery overpowered any good that may have been there.

This was getting to me.

It always had.

But now, since my abduction, it had taken over my life even more.

I felt sick to my stomach.

I remanded myself and turned my attention to the screens.

This wasn't about me. It was much, much bigger.

I was seriously becoming even more of an egotistical prick than I'd always been. Shame coloured my cheeks and I felt very vulnerable. I glanced around but no one was watching me. Only Ebony. She never missed a beat. I shrugged and pulled my lips into a pretend smile. Her eyes laughed and she made me feel a lot better.

Not for the first time, I was happy Jonah had introduced me to our tech wiz. She was one in a million and I'd come to love her deeply.

The images from the mule's glasses were concentrated on the pews and the confessional. I counted two people in front of our man. That would give him time to clandestinely survey his surroundings while he mumbled prayers kneeling at the pew.

His viewpoint moved slowly from left to right.

Initially, we saw nothing that alarmed us. But closer scrutiny showed members of the congregation who were definitely not concentrating on anything spiritual. Their eyes took in who came in and who left the church. Everyone was scrutinised deeply, and I could see their lips move in for us secret words. I could imagine they were linked to a control centre something like the one we were in.

'You think the security is because Benedict has an important position in the Establishment?' Jonah asked no-one in particular. 'Or because they don't trust him?'

I shrugged. 'Could be either. But I hope the first.'

'Yes.' Ebony chimed in. 'Though, let's base our security on the presumption they have doubts.'

We all nodded. It was the logical thing to do; be careful.

The mule had a need-to-know knowledge of our operation. Just in case he was intercepted by the Establishment, there was little he could tell them. I hoped it wasn't necessary, and if the shit hit the fan, that it was enough to keep him safe.

The sounds of the church were subdued. Muted mumbles from our man, the buzz of the others deep in prayer, the shuffling of new believers taking their place in the pews in line for confession.

Soft light illuminated the view as the door of the confessional opened and an elderly lady made her way from its dark depths to one of the pews. There she settled down to her penance.

The man in the pew in front of our guy stood up and made his way to take his place in this archaic custom. I marvelled again at the strange traditions the church had constitutionalised. For someone looking in from the outside, it was all very peculiar. But that was just my opinion.

The minutes passed by slowly. Very slowly. It was a chore to stay calm.

Ebony, observant as always, handed me a cup of coffee. It gave me something to do. I smiled my thanks.

We waited. There was nothing else we could do.

Finally, after what seemed endless, the man vacated the confessional, so our messenger stood up from his kneeling position and made his way through the door into the dark interior. The tiny overhead light did little to illuminate the small claustrophobic cubicle. Heavy, muted curtains reinforced the dark and stuffy atmosphere.

The messenger sat on the bench and waited for the slide to open between him and the archbishop.

'Forgive me father, for I have sinned.' He started the ritual. 'This is the first time I have been in a confessional.'

'For which sins would you ask the lord for forgiveness?' the voice from the other side of the intricately carved lattice said. I recognised the soft but strong voice of Archbishop Benedict.

'Well, actually,' our man continued. 'I'm not here of my own accord.'

'Please elaborate.'

We could hear the surprise in Benedict's voice.

'I was asked to come.'

'By whom?'

'You, your grace.'

The silence was total. I imagined I could hear the cogs in Benedict's mind grinding.

'You said it was time I came to church,' our man added. Again, silence.

'We have mutual friends?'

'We do, your grace.'

'Do they hear the words of the lord?'

'They are aware.'

Just in case someone was listening in, we'd instructed the messenger to stay cryptic as much as possible.

'The goal has been reached,' Benedict stated, equally as careful. 'There will be a ceremony soon.'

It was the validation we needed. Benedict was going to be initiated into the Establishment's inner circle.

'When?'

'Three weeks.'

'We know.'

The sharp intake of breath signalled Benedict's surprise. I smiled internally; he'd underestimated us again.

'Where?' the messenger asked.

'There has been a location change,' the archbishop answered. 'The original location was no longer appropriate.'

The messenger stayed silent. Benedict didn't have to ask whether we were the ones responsible for the move.

The silence was loaded. The messenger watched as a small rolled-up piece of paper was passed to him through the lattice of the wall separating them.

'For your penance, you must pray five Hail Mary's, three of our lord's prayer and read John 34.36. Have you understood your penance?'

'Understood.'

'Good.'

The messenger opened the door and left the confessional. In line with his persona, he knelt in the pew, put his hands together and pretended to pray.

In fact, he scanned the people seated and kneeling

around him. Five in all. No one warranted suspicion. Then his vision turned slightly to the right. Nothing suspicious, other than the observants that had been there before he spoke to Benedict. Left—the same. He bowed once last time towards the altar and left the church.

Chapter Thirty-Eight

I read the transcript of the podcasts diligently every Friday. Then re-read them again the next day, just in case I'd missed anything.

The information in the podcast was remotely interesting, but there was no hidden message from the resistance, or from my mother.

That concerned me. It had been a while and I'd still not heard from her. I was worried. What if dad had found out? What if she'd been tortured? I wouldn't put it past Cal-Tan, he'd ordered Ibrahim to interrogate me with whatever force was needed. And then kill me. The man had no constraints on anything as fickle as family ties. His vengeance would be bottomless if he found out she'd been undermining him all these years.

But there was nothing I could do. I had to trust her, and Maron, that she would stay invisible to Cal-Tan and be safe. Well, as safe as she could be.

I hated my helplessness. I wanted to protect her. But it was impossible.

With Tajan here, Aaliyah's information line had dried up as well, so there was precious little news from the home front.

It drove me nuts. Aaliyah wasn't much better off. Both of our families were still there, still in dire straits and there was nothing we could do about any of it. Not without endangering their, and our, lives.

I still hadn't told anyone about my mother's involvement. There was something intangible holding me back. I racked my brain to find a reason, especially as I trusted the team with my life, but I couldn't bring myself to share the information. Maybe because it concerned my mother, maybe something else. I couldn't get a handle on my rationale, so I decided to keep everything close to my vest for the time being.

I would just have to wait.

And read the podcast.

A week later, there was finally a message.

Not good news. But I hadn't expected any.

Cal-Tan was indeed amassing a large army of mercenaries. He needed them to keep control of all the grunts in the overfull pens. There had been no slave auctions. None had changed hands for more than two months causing a lot of unrest and shortage on Taxore. There was still no explanation on Cal-Tan's motives which made everything so much more volatile. Mum thought it was linked to the thirty-second dimension that had only recently been discovered. Cal-Tan had visited it twice. An unheard-of personal involvement. So maybe that was it.

Or maybe not.

She was worried, I could tell.

So was I.

What was Cal-Tan looking for in the Thirty-second? A new market, or something more sinister. Whatever it was, there was nothing we could do about it from here. It was just another thing to add to the list of what we would handle once the Establishment was on its knees.

She asked how I was. Tears pricked at the edges of my eyes as I decoded the words.

I answered in the comments cryptically that I was doing well and had recovered fully from my last visit. She wouldn't believe that any more than I did. But I still hoped it gave her a bit of peace.

I hinted we were making progress, which was true. But it was painfully slow. All except for the upcoming Establishment conference. I omitted that in my reply. It wouldn't have helped her.

I pressed send and the coded comment was posted under the rendering of the podcast.

That was it.

There was no more I could do. To be sure, I monitored the podcast daily after the first message.

Three days later there was another message. Cal-Tan had started to experiment on moving grunts to the Thirty-second dimension. Just a small number to start with, while his scientists observed the effects, if any. Mercenaries had also been dispatched there and he himself had made yet another visit. Whatever was unique about the new dimension, it definitely had my father's attention.

'Maybe that's what he needs the grunts for?' Jonah suggested when I reported the info.

I shrugged. 'Looks like it, but it still doesn't make sense

for him to suspend all sales on Taxore. There has to be more to it than that.'

I'd asked as much in my coded reply to the podcast.

Another comment had appeared an hour later suggesting a power struggle on Taxore.

'Cal-Tan is doing a bid for a seat in the Council,' I surprised the team.

'How do you know this?' Ebony asked.

'I have a contact with the resistance,' I reluctantly answered, gazing clandestinely at Aaliyah who raised an eyebrow.

'And you didn't think to inform us you were in contact?' She asked, her words dripping with righteous venom.

It was the same conversation as weeks ago, only now I was the one withholding information.

'It's very fragile,' I tried. 'The fewer people who know, the better.'

'Not even us?' Jonah joined the sentiment.

'Let me guess,' Aaliyah butted in. 'Need to know?'

I felt shame colour my face bright purple. Words eluded me and I just nodded.

'Way to go, Gabe,' she said as she stood up and left the room.

My paranoia had just cost me a lot of the team's trust.

Not my finest hour.

'I'm sorry,' I tried at dinner later that day.

Jonah, Sly and Ebony continued their meal in silence. Aaliyah honed the edge of her knife to the side of the table. She looked up momentarily, then went back to the wet stone.

'I should have told you,' I continued.

Ebony pushed her plate away and looked at me. 'Why didn't you?'

'I don't know. Not really.' I shrugged.

Jonah huffed his reply and continued to attack the lasagne on his plate.

I turned to him. 'I deserve that. But I really don't know.' I tried to bring my thoughts into words. 'I trust you all. Without any reserve. With my life.'

'But not with someone else's,' Aaliyah answered for me.

'Must be someone close to you,' she added.

I nodded, not trusting myself to speak.

'Very close.'

Her tone made me wonder if she already knew about my mother's involvement.

'You're on the wrong path, Gabe,' she surprised me. 'Carry on this way and it will eat you up inside. And make you useless to our cause.'

'You've changed since you came back,' Ebony commented. 'You're isolating yourself. Pushing us away.'

I stared at the plate in front of me, my appetite gone.

'I know it was terrible what you experienced, but we're here to help you get through it.' She placed her hand over mine.

My first reaction was to pull it away, but I stopped myself. Not quickly enough, I registered the disappointment in her eyes.

The silence was loaded and oppressive. I wanted to scream, cuss, throw things. Hit something or someone. My anger was only barely under the surface, and it consumed me, day and night.

Yes, I'd isolated myself. I had to. I didn't trust myself enough not to explode and hurt someone. Someone from this family. My days were an endless battle for restraint and the nights were even worse. I would go for midnight runs, anything to tire my body and shut down the incessant rage that pushed me to take action. On the runs I would push myself past what—even for me—was healthy. I would climb cliffs in the dark, part of me wanting to miss a hold and plummet to the rocks below.

The ferocity of my rage scared me. It was almost an obsession, a hatred for my father with a passion I hadn't known I was capable of. With every mile I ran, I felt less and less in control of my own madness. In all my musings there was one question that consumed me.

Was I becoming my father? Was this rage inevitable, hereditary?

'Tell us, Gabe,' Jonah pushed.

'I can't.' I whispered.

'You're not Cal-Tan,' Aaliyah stated. 'You don't have to follow in his footsteps, not if you don't want to.'

Once again, she'd hit the nail on the head.

'When Bashir killed my father,' she continued, staring at the knife she twirled in her hand. 'I alternated between pain and rage. Like you're doing now.' She nodded at me.

The only thing I could do was continue to stare at the table in front of me.

'I wanted others to feel the same pain. To know what it was like. I wanted to hurt them as much as they had hurt me.'

'My father was a tyrant, I know that. He's done terrible things. But he was never like that to me. He was my rock. My life. Even though I opposed his actions, I still respected and loved him beyond anything. You have people like that in your family, for sure.'

I nodded.

'I was lost,' she continued. 'Like you.'

'How did you find your way back?' I whispered.

'I held on to the one thing that was pure in all of it. The

love my father had for me. I concentrated on that, on what it meant to have been the recipient of so much love. I looked further. Past what he'd done, past Bashir, to the rest of my family. To the people around me.'

She raised her head, and a thin smile adorned her lips.

'Even to you lot,' she continued as she looked at all of us. 'The most dysfunctional group of misfits I have ever seen together in one space.'

There was a light chuckle of agreement.

'This—whatever it is—shouldn't work. It defies all logic. Humans, Taxorians. Your family, mine. Sworn enemies. Yet here we are. Kicking butt.'

I raised my chin a little and watched her as she spun the knife between her fingers.

'We can't live in the past, Gabriel. It will consume us. We didn't choose where we came from. Who our families are. We're not responsible for that, or for what they do. I'll never forgive Bashir, or my father for many of the things he did in his lifetime. But it's not me. They are not me.'

'Oh sure, I have a temper. One that has saved my life more than once. It's part of me. Like yours is part of you. You can let it take control, or you can control it. Your life is not determined by Cal-Tan. Not if you don't want it to be.'

She laid the knife down on the table in front of her and looked me dead in the eye. Aaliyah cocked her head, silently demanding an answer.

I nodded.

She smiled, placed the knife back in the sheath around her calf, stood up and left the room.

'Not much more to say,' Jonah summed it up, then turned to Sly.

'What's for dessert?'

Chapter Thirty-Nine

'We have to do something about the Hashta,' I declared after dinner next day. 'As long as they're in the picture, there will be unacceptable risks for our mission.'

'They are a big unknown,' Jonah chimed in. 'It would be best to get them out of the equation before we attack the Establishment. We don't need them interfering.'

Sly sat to the side observing the discussion without comment. Like me, he'd noticed the intense fear the mere mention of the Taxorian assassins had on Tajan. The small man pushed himself as deep into the chair as possible in an attempt to become invisible. That was the extent of the terror the Hashta generated.

I felt for him. He'd come to Earth to be safe. And now he knew there was no escaping the Taxorian reach. He was as much on their death list as Aaliyah and I were.

'We have to take them out,' I stated resolutely.

'Any idea how?' Sly chimed in, his normal practical self. 'Without endangering everyone here,' he added dashing most of my ideas to smithereens.

The silence said it all.

We all studied the empty plates or our glasses of whatever beverage we had. There was pitiful little inspiration.

'They're here to find us,' Aaliyah broke the quiet. 'We need to pull them into an ambush.'

'From what I've heard about the Hashta, that will be immensely dangerous, at least for one of you,' Sly pointed out.

'It's a risk we must take. They're dedicated to their mission.' I joined in. 'We have no idea what the extent of the Establishment's investigative powers are. You can be sure they'll exhaust any and all opportunities to find us. It's become an honour thing. Cal-Tan's status depends on their success, at least that will be his point of view. He's given them a mission. They will never give up. Not until they have our heads.' I gestured towards Aaliyah and myself.

The loaded silence continued.

'Undoing my treason, and the effect it has on the resistance, will be Cal-Tan's primary goal. He can't handle the betrayal by his own blood. From his point of view, I've undermined his power.'

'You have,' Aaliyah concurred. 'The resistance is making the most of your escape. Unrest is increasing and the Council is being pushed to intervene.'

'Can they do that?' Ebony asked.

Aaliyah shook her head. 'Not really. They are too dependent on Cal-Tan for their own status and the economy of the whole dimension. He has them by the balls.'

'He sees my continued existence as a personal affront,' I continued. 'I defied him.'

'That obsessiveness could make them vulnerable.' Sly

mused. 'If they are certain of their success, maybe we could use that against them and reverse the situation.'

'Is there no way we could avoid tackling them?' Ebony asked, worry lines creasing at the edge of her eyes. She held on to Jonah's hand with a vengeance. I understood, she just had him back, confronting the Hashta had definite risks and she didn't want to chance any new deaths.

'We have to,' I explained. 'They are relentless. You have to remember they're basically immortal here on Earth. They can go on forever. Not that Cal-Tan has the patience, but you know what I mean.'

The pressure was immense. I definitely wasn't looking forward to a reunion with Hashta, and three to boot. But it had to be done. Their presence could thwart all our efforts. If we wanted to have a chance at success, I would need to face my demons. All of them. Believe me, my body shuddered just with the concept of standing in the same room as Ibrahim again.

'We can't make it too obvious,' Jonah was already looking forward. 'They're not stupid. If it's too easy, they won't go for it.'

'You're right. It has to look as though they found me. They need to be comfortable in their prowess. Then we can ambush them.'

'You need to understand the Hashta are experts at investigation.' Aaliyah added. 'They are renowned for their paranoid nature. It will not be easy to pull the wool over their eyes, especially as there are three of them.'

'Do we know what they look like?' Sly asked.

Ebony shrugged. 'Other than Ibrahim—we have a composition drawing of him and some CCTV from the mosque—no. We haven't identified the others.'

'You can be assured they have a specific presence. These

are not timid or easily impressed individuals,' Aaliyah explained. 'They will seem aloof and comfortable in their perceived superiority. It's inbred, I don't think they can act otherwise.'

'Like most macho men in Los Angeles. About half what you encounter in the streets.' Ebony sighed.

There were some smiles and short laughter at that, lightening the mood slightly. But it didn't make our quest much easier.

'In Taxore, they stand out through their presence and their clothing,' Aaliyah optioned. 'I don't think they'll wear the customary black and gold cloaks here. It would be too obvious. But they will probably still prefer black.'

'Narrows it down slightly.'

'And they will be my skin colour, with at least shoulder length black hair and most likely beards. And they have specific markings.'

'What kind of markings?'

'Ritual scaring. Like your tattoos, but not exactly.'

Sly sat forward, suddenly even more interested.

'Where do they have these markings?'

'Usually on their torso and, if they achieved a high status, on their faces. It's a sign of superiority.'

'A medal of sorts?'

'Something like that. They scar themselves for every successful mission.'

'Won't it be difficult to see any markings?' Ebony countered. 'They'll be clothed.'

'Yes, but that in itself could be a tip-off,' Aaliyah continued. 'Dark men dressed head to toe in this temperature would stand out.'

We nodded. They would be obvious, under the right circumstances.

'We will have to be extremely vigilant. The team here will be on surveillance twenty-four seven,' Ebony offered.

'How are we going to lure them into a trap?' Jonah asked to no one in particular.

The sixty-four-thousand-dollar question.

'What about the attack on the diner,' I asked Ebony. 'Do we have any surveillance videos or anything that could give us a glimpse of the Hashta?'

'We've been scouring the images rescued from the fire. It's not much. Hailey has been sweeping through all CCTV from the neighbourhood and has identified that they headed northwest, through the Death Valley National Park. She's been following three bikers that exited Pahrump just after the call came in to the police. We can expand the search and start from there.'

'Maybe we can then at least get a better look at them. Who knows, we might get lucky that they're on a surveillance camera somewhere and we can catalogue their faces.'

'It's worth a try.'

The next day found Jonah and me working out in the gym again. The big man was back into his pre-death regime and his physique was once again impressive.

'There was a message in the podcast,' I surprised Jonah. 'Seems Ibrahim has been pulled back to Taxore for something.' I couldn't keep the relief out of my voice.

He put down the dumbbell, looked at me intently and raised an eyebrow. 'What exactly did it say?'

'The butcher is back home,' I repeated the message.

'And the others?'

'No mention of them.'

He looked disappointed.

'It's good,' I said. 'We can ambush the other two before the Establishment's meeting. No doubt Cal-Tan will send Ibrahim back for revenge after we've exposed him.' I much preferred to take on the Hashta in smaller numbers. Ideally one-by-one, but I'd take the situation we had now. Ibrahim still installed more terror in me than the rest. Maybe because of the up-close-and-personal time we'd shared. I couldn't shake the idea that luck wouldn't stay on my side. He'd been about to kill me twice, and both times I'd escaped with the help of others. I sincerely hoped I could make that a hat trick if I confronted him again. But the memories ate away at the little confidence I had.

Jonah seemed less impressed. Actually, not at all. I swear he was looking forward to it. Some kind of competition maybe, or just plain and simple revenge. Always a strong incentive for the big man. I hoped some of his confidence would rub off on me.

'So, there's only two of them,' he mused.

"Only" wasn't really the way I would describe it, but ok.

'We'd better inform Ebony and Sly.' Standing up, he looped the towel around his neck and dried the sweat off his face with the end.

'That makes sense,' Tajan commented. 'We've been following only two of them for the past days.'

'You found them?' I asked, surprised.

'We did,' Ebony came to Tajan's rescue. 'But wanted to find the last one before we informed anyone.'

Still not willing to jinx things, I thought to myself.

'Where are they?' Jonah asked.

'L.A.'

'On their own?'

She shook her head, 'regrettably not. Seems they've joined up with a small group of bikers.'

'What group?' Sly asked, his face a mask of anger.

Made me wonder what the history was there. It was a question for another time.

'A splinter group of the Outlaws called the Outcast,' Ebony answered, closely observing her security manager. Whatever it was he was bothered about, she knew the cause.

A flash of rage coloured his face even darker. He recovered quickly, but we'd noticed. He was aware of the biker group, and there was hatred there, that much was clear. We didn't need to ask for more detail, not at this moment.

'How many bikers?' I asked, trying to get the meeting going again.

'Ten max,' Ebony answered. 'It's a small group.'

'But they're affiliated with a larger one?'

'Yes, we need to be careful. Ideally, we wouldn't involve them at all.' Again, she glanced at Sly.

'Do we know if this group has any connection to the Establishment?' Aaliyah queried.

'I haven't heard of them before,' I said. 'That's no guarantee, but bikers haven't been a staple in the recruitment as far as I know.'

'Makes sense,' Sly joined in. 'They like to stay independent of anything outside the biker community.'

'Maybe it's just the motor bikes that brought them together temporarily.'

'Yes, and the attitude,' Aaliyah added. 'I can see the attraction. Birds of a feather and all.'

'Do we know where they are now?'

'In the clubhouse, just outside of Compton,' Tajan responded.

'What about photos? Do we have clear images of them.'

'We're hacking into the local FBI office. They monitor the gangs, including the Outcast. We expect they have surveillance on the club house,' Ebony interjected.

'And any CCTV in the neighbourhood,' Tajan added.

'We should have something more concrete by the end of the day.'

That would be a definite bonus.

I'd have to ask Sly what his connection was with the Outcast, but the look on his face indicated today wasn't the right day.

The images came in early the next day.

They showed two very impressive dark-faced men. Both at least six foot four or five, athletic build, black hair down to their shoulders and immensely intense eyes. The violet irises stood out immediately. Their arrogance at not even disguising their atypical colour was astounding, even to me. The older of the two sported scars on his face, some intentional, some from what I expected were fighting wounds. The two stark honour lines from the outer edge of each eye down to his chin were the most prominent.

This was a Hashta, there was no doubt. Even without the customary clothing, there was no mistaking the arrogance, the narcissism, and the utter lack of empathy this man exhumed. My mind went back to San Francisco and the Hashta we'd encountered there. This was a carbon copy, only with both eyes intact.

Shivers ran up and down my spine unwanted. The Hashta were the embodiment of the boogy man. Worse than any sociopathic serial killer Hollywood could dream up. This wasn't fiction. They were real, and they were here.

The second man was just as intimidating, but younger. In most of the streams he was a step behind his elder, the hierarchy apparent. Not a junior, no way, but not as experienced and revered as his companion.

My father had sent the best, that was obvious. It spoke to how serious he was in finding me, his wayward son. It wasn't desperation, that was an emotion Cal-Tan was unfamiliar with. He never doubted himself, or his actions. He was the quintessential narcissist. It was part of his strength.

My hearts beat loudly in my ears. Thump, thump. I was certain it was audible to the others. My limbs were shaking despite my resolve. I'd talked myself into a semblance of courage yesterday evening, assuring my frayed nerves that I was up for this. That I was not alone this time. I had the team behind me. They had my back. This time I would triumph; I would not let my fear rein. I would stand up to them and persevere with my dignity intact.

Yeah. Right.

Chapter Forty

'I owe you all an explanation,' Sly announced after dinner.

'You don't owe us anything,' Jonah answered, echoing all our sentiments, while shoving yet another spoonful of curry into his mouth.

'Yet here it comes. Whether you like it or not.' Sly's lips curled up in an infrequent smile.

He glanced at Ebony, who nodded.

'You saw someone in the streams who probably looked familiar. One of the Outcasts.'

'None of our business,' Jonah tried.

'Yes, it is. Because they may be our best bet to neutralise the Hashta.'

We were silent.

'I grew up in Compton,' Sly continued his narrative. 'The bad side of L.A, for those not familiar with the city. I never knew my father; mum brought me and my brother up on her own as a single parent. She did a great job, but the odds were stacked against her. My older brother died in a gang war, protecting a gangster who couldn't care less about his soldiers. Mum sent me to the army after that. I joined at sixteen. Army first, but finally found my new family in the marines. I did numerous tours in places I don't want to think—let alone talk—about. They made Compton look like a ride in the park.'

'When I revolved back to civilian life, I came back to LA. It was worse than I remembered, but it was my home. I made a life there, married my best friend, my childhood sweetheart, and started a family.'

He stopped for a moment, the emotion in his features showing his struggle. 'Latitia was my everything.'

Was?

I stopped myself from asking.

'We had four sons.' His smile returned as the images became clear in his mind. 'Four strapping men now.'

He glanced to the right at Ebony who'd taken up position beside him. He took her hand in a rare show of affection.

'Latitia came home one day with a small homeless child of about ten. The little girl had tried to pick her pocket but got more than she bargained for.'

He chuckled at the memory. Ebony blushed bright red.

She smiled and squeezed his hand.

'Latitia grabbed my hand before I could take her purse. Then pulled me in front of her, looked me deep in the eye and let me go. I was confused. She offered me her purse, just held it in front of me and said I could have it if that was what I really wanted. I just stared at her, not sure what was happening.'

'She brought Ebony home.' He looked at her lovingly. 'The daughter we'd never had.'

'They took me in. Made me part of the family. Gave me

something I'd never had before: a home. Even put me through college, then MIT,' Ebony added.

'You're family.'

Sly sighed deeply, another memory taking its turn.

'Latitia was diagnosed with terminal cancer five years ago,' he almost whispered. Then he looked back at Ebony, the love clear in his face and eyes. He took her hand in both of his.

'Ebony took care of us. Made Latitia's last year the best it could be. She paid for the treatment, our life, everything. Then when my wife died, she took care of the family.'

'Our family,' Ebony added.

'Our family.'

'The man in the CCTV stream?' Jonah asked what we all were thinking. 'He's your son?'

Sly nodded. 'Yes. My eldest; Caleb. He took it very badly when his mother died. Went off track and joined a biker group. Not for the status or anything like that, for a new family.'

We stayed silent.

'I've contacted him.'

Sly was all professional again.

'He's aware of the threat the Hashta pose. For him, for his new friends and for his family. He has a wife and two small children. My grandchildren. There's nothing I wouldn't do to keep them safe.'

I'd completely mis-interpreted the recognition I'd seen in Sly and his resulting anger, when we watched the CCTV. I thought it was aimed at the bikers, it wasn't, it was focussed on the Hashta who now threatened his family's safety.

'We'll be coordinating with him and at the same time we'll evacuate his family,' Ebony explained.

'Very carefully,' Sly added. 'It can't throw any suspicion on Caleb.'

'They've been under constant surveillance since we knew of the Hashta's presence.' Ebony said.

'And Caleb will help ambush the Hashta?' Jonah asked carefully.

Sly nodded.

'Is he aware of the immense risk?'

'He is.'

'What's his background?' I asked. 'Did he follow your example? Does he have military training?'

Sly shook his head. 'He's a black belt in multiple martial arts, does cage fighting. So very disciplined, but no formal military background.'

'Any chance we could bring someone in undercover?' I asked.

'I wouldn't,' Aaliyah chimed in. 'It would be too convenient. Too much of a coincident. The Hashta don't believe in those. They would immediately be alarmed. We need to keep the situation as close to normal as possible. Even evacuating the family is a risk.'

'It has to be done,' Sly stated resolutely.

'It will be,' she conceded. 'But be aware of the risks.'

We nodded.

No one here would underestimate them.

The Hashta were too dangerous for that.

And there was too much at stake.

Even more than we'd thought.

Chapter Forty-One

We decided we couldn't count on manipulating the Hashta to a place where we felt comfortable. Their natural paranoia would send off all kinds of signals with the first suggestion of an ambush.

We'd have to let them lead the mission.

Strange as it was, it was the only option we had.

The waiting game was killing us. There were only a few weeks left before the Establishment's meeting and we wanted to get at least these two threats out of the way before then.

Finally, after what seemed like an endless wait, Caleb contacted us with a possible opening.

The Hashta were restless, they wanted action. They'd received information from somewhere—we concluded Taxore—about a possible contact of mine. Someone they could use as leverage. A woman who I'd been with.

My heart sank.

Kate. The woman who'd comforted me in my hour of need after Raphael killed Jonah.

Ebony place a hand on my arm in support. 'She's okay, Gabe. We have her under surveillance.'

I looked at her and cocked my head in a silent question.

'Ever since you met her,' she answered me with a smile.

'You knew?' Stupid question. Of course she knew. I smiled.

'There's a team at the diner,' Sly added.

I looked at him incredulously.

'The chef,' he added. 'And the handy man.'

The extent of Ebony's reach never failed to surprise me.

'If anything happens, we'll take her underground,' Sly assured me.

My shoulders relaxed and I felt an enormous sense of relief. Kate had been such a breath of fresh air for me, she'd put me back on my feet and given me the will to go on. Even if she didn't know anything about me or my quest. She'd taken me for what I was and loved me for a day. A day that had made an impression. A day that could not— definitely not— result in her death. I would make sure of that.

'They have the address of the diner and plan to kidnap Kate Friday or Saturday night, on her way back to her home or at the house. Caleb has been drafted to help them.'

'Won't that put him in the firing line?' I commented.

'He's aware,' Sly answered, effectively ending that discussion.

'We need you to go to the house and stay there. Kate isn't aware of our presence,' Ebony explained.

'She trusts you. It might get hairy, and she'll need a friendly face.'

'I don't feel right, putting her in harm's way,' I countered.

'You didn't,' she answered. 'At least not this time. She

came into the crosshairs as soon as you two had a thing. It's not something you can change now. The only thing we can do now is make sure she stays safe, and we get those bastards.'

'What's the plan?' Jonah asked. 'Do we need them alive?'

'No,' Aaliyah and I said in unison. 'Too dangerous and no added benefit.'

'What about information?' Sly suggested.

'Not feasible,' Aaliyah spoke up. 'They're Hashta, they'll never give up anything. They've been trained not only in delivering pain, but also in receiving it. Nothing you could do would make them talk.'

'So they're dead,' Jonah summed up in his typical style.

We nodded.

'Perfect,' the big man announced.

I guess he was joining us on the mission.

Caleb came through.

The Hashta planned to kidnap Kate two days later, after her evening shift. They'd planned to ambush her while she walked the quiet lane from the bus stop to her house. It was a sleepy neighbourhood with little traffic after eleven o'clock at night. There would be four in their team: the two Hashta, Caleb and another Outcast. The latter would stay with the car. For this occasion—and to transport Kate—they'd take an electric SUV instead of the noisy Harley Davidsons.

Surveillance indicated Kate would typically arrive at the bus stop at eleven-twenty-five. The short walk would take approximately twelve minutes, the first five of which were still in a well-lit area. Once she turned the corner onto her street there were less streetlamps, the lights restricted now to subdued mostly decorative garden lamps. Some of the houses had movement detectors connected to floodlights near the garages, but they could easily be avoided. The mostly elderly neighbours were expected to already have retired at that time of night and no one would be out.

We would intercept the Hashta as they got to the house, but before they got to Kate. At least that was the plan.

Ebony assured me she would make sure they could only attack close to the front door. We wanted to minimise the impact on Kate as much as possible. Stealth was also needed because we planned to be in and out without leaving a trace. Sly had organised a "clean-up crew" as backup, just in case.

There would be five of us in the street and house: Jonah, Sly, Aaliyah, Termain and me. Ebony hinted there were others close if needed and that they would assist in the set-up. She didn't elaborate and I didn't ask. Another small team would be a few streets away with our own vehicles parked in the lot of a small company Termain had contacts with.

Equipped with Ebony's night vision technology, we would be in place way before the Hashta, so we could follow their every move.

Chapter Forty-Two

The small sliver of moon disappeared behind the sketchy clouds, elongating the shadows of trees lining the road and enveloping the houses in an eerie atmosphere. Few lights were on at this hour, most of the inhabitants already in deep sleep.

The mist muted the sounds of occasional night owls, a car in the next street and Kate's footfalls.

She pulled her coat closer over the flimsy waitress uniform. It was great in the humid heat of the diner, but on these occasional cold nights it was more than inadequate.

Kate shivered. The cold, but also from a strange premonition that sent tingles up and down her spine. The butterflies in her stomach enhanced the feeling of dread. She tried to console herself with the knowledge that she'd walked this street hundreds of times at this hour. Nothing had happened then, nothing would tonight. This was a nice neighbourhood. Crime, especially violent crime, was reserved for the town centre, not here. She would be okay. It was just a few hundred metres to her house. Nothing to be worried about.

So why did she feel eyes on her? Why did the apprehension try to push her to move faster? Preferably to run.

Kate's right hand slipped into the handbag she wore over her shoulder and her fingers curled around the small tear gas canister her father insisted she carry at all times. She'd vowed never to use it, never to need it, but now she was glad of his over-protectiveness. Her tight grip on the canister tempered the anxiety a bit. But she still stole glances into the shadows and moved sideways to walk in the middle of the road. There was no traffic here at this time. And it felt safer. Further away from the shadows that had never bothered her before.

A light was still on at the house two before hers and she heard music through the closed door. A party. The multitude of cars and occasional bikes in the driveway spilled out on to the street and she had to skirt one big pick-up that took up almost half the road.

The happy sounds made her feel better. That, and the idea there were others nearby.

The door opened and three people came out, one staggering off the two steps and landing flat on his face in the grass. All three laughed at their clumsy friend and one helped him to his feet. She recognised her neighbour, a lovely man who'd come to live here a few months ago.

'Hi Kate,' he called, trying unsuccessfully to hide his intoxication. He needed his friend's support to keep upright.

Kate laughed along with them. Their happiness infectious. Happy sounds spilled from the open door and made her feel much better.

'Want to join us?' the neighbour called out. 'Night cap before you go to sleep?'

Kate laughed. 'Thanks Bert, but not tonight.' She smiled and felt a lot better for their short interaction. 'Next time.'

'You're on.'

Kate walked on to her house, her step much lighter for the contagious laughter of her neighbours. She reached the front door and pulled out her keys before the unsettling feeling of a stalker returned. Before she put the key in the lock, Kate looked behind her and to the side. Nothing.

She turned back to the door, admonishing herself for her paranoia. A trait she wasn't familiar with.

She chuckled softly at her silliness, put the key in the lock and pulled the door slightly to let the lock turn.

Goosebumps suddenly assailed her and the dread she'd felt before returned with a vengeance. She shivered with terror as she turned the key, then turned suddenly to look behind her again.

This time, there was someone there. A dark tall man, dressed in black, imposing and terrifying. The automatic light turned on again and the threatening scars on his menacing features made her scream.

He grabbed her, his hand over her mouth stifling the sound and pushed her against the now unlocked door. It gave and they fell back into the hallway, out of sight of the street.

Kate kicked and scratched at her attacker. Her attempts at escape drawing blood from the man's face. In the dim light it looked strange. Not right. But she continued her desperate defiance.

The Hashta turned her around, his hand moved from her mouth to her neck where he squeezed on her throat until she couldn't breathe. His other hand was around her waist as he pulled her backwards into the dark living room, intent on subduing his victim. The second Hashta, closely followed by Caleb, quickly slipped into the house behind his mentor and closed the door, his eyes on the party next door. He made his way to the living room where a strange sight awaited him. The older Hashta lay on the ground, a big pool of purple blood quickly expanding from the massive wounds that had slit his throat.

The woman was nowhere to be seen.

He hesitated for all of a second, then grabbed for the sword on his back. One second. One too many. My short swords pierced his back through his hearts to burst out of his chest. I turned the blades violently to the side, effectively shredding his organs and stopping his life. His hesitation had killed him.

The body slipped off my swords into a heap on the floor. I quickly jumped over the corpse to the kitchen where Sly stood with a still shaking Kate.

From the corner of my eye, I saw Jonah check the second Hashta was truly dead, and he and Aaliyah grabbed the amulets, smashing them into thousands of small pieces. To be absolutely sure, Jonah would also crush the Hashta's forearms, just in case they had an implant.

I moved quickly to Kate and took her softly by the arms. My touch shocked her, and she pulled back, the pupils of her eyes wide and black in shock.

'Kate,' my voice was soft. 'It's me. Gabriel.'

She looked at me, or more accurately, through me. Her flight mode still prevalent. Then slowly I started to see recognition.

'Gabe?' she whispered.

I smiled and stroked her upper arms in reassurance.

'It's me,' I answered.

'Gabe?'

'Gabe!' She pushed herself into my arms, her face buried in my chest. I held her close, with her arms tight around my waist. My hand moved up to stroke her hair and neck, as I softly made soothing sounds.

I held Kate close for minutes, no sound around us. Just us. Then her body started to shake slightly, sobbing sounds emitted from her mouth, which was still buried in my chest, as Kate slowly let go of the numbing tension she'd experienced. I held her even tighter and rocked slightly from side to side, kissing the top of her head.

What seemed like a long time later, her form relaxed, and she stopped crying. Kate lifted her head and look me in the eye.

'Gabe?'

I nodded.

'What…. How… what's going on? Who were they? What are you doing here?'

I smiled and carefully lead her backwards to a waiting chair. Kate let herself be guided and sat down, still clinging on to me. I knelt in front of her, holding on to her hands and keeping close.

'I'm so sorry, Kate, I whispered.

'What for?' She looked perfectly surprised.

'For bringing this to you. For subjecting you to this violence.'

'These men.' She looked past me through to the living room where the forms of the Hashta were still visible on the rug. 'Who are they? Why are they here?'

'They're here for me,' I explained. 'They wanted to use you to get to me.' I felt shame colour my face as silent tears congealed at the side of my eyes.

She looked at me and cocked her head in amazement.

Slowly she let go of my hands and brought hers up to cup my face. Her features full of warmth.

'It's okay,' she said. 'I'm okay. Thanks to you.'

'You wouldn't be in this mess if it weren't for me,' I answered.

'It's okay. You're here.'

I pushed my body up and took her in my arms again. So thankful for this wonderful woman.

We held each other.

Then she softly pushed me back, her hands holding on to mine again. 'Who are they?' she repeated.

'They're assassins.'

She raised an eyebrow.

'From your home?'

'Yes.'

'They were looking for you?'

I nodded.

'To kill you?'

'Yes. I'm so sorry you've been caught up in this,' I repeated. 'We'd hoped to get them before they entered the house, but with the party next door, we couldn't risk taking them down earlier.'

She nodded her agreement.

Kate pushed herself up off the chair. 'I want to see them,' she announced.

'I don't think that's a good idea,' I tried. But she was adamant.

We got to our feet, and I held her close as we walked into the living room.

Jonah lit the small lights beside the TV, concerned not to alert the neighbours. Up to now there had been little sound and no struggles because the surprise had been complete. The Hashta had been dispatched quickly. It had been almost too easy.

Kate held on to my waist as she surveyed the room and its grisly contents.

'Their blood,' she noticed. 'It's purple.'

'Yes.' I dreaded explaining it to her. But she had a right to know. 'They're not from this dimension.'

'Then neither are you,' she concluded correctly, looking up at me.

'I'm not,' I answered, a knot in my throat, apprehensive on how she would react.

Everyone was silent as she observed me closely. She cocked her head and moved one hand up to my face, then back to my chest as my hearts thumped.

Kate nodded. Then placed her head back against my chest and held my waist tightly.

I let out my pent-up breath.

Jonah's smile said it all. It was okay. We'd succeeded, and Kate was all right.

A familiar face popped around the door. 'You okay, Kate?' Bert asked, surprisingly sober.

Kate registered his sobriety and how he didn't even flinch at the bodies lying in the living room. She nodded.

'Good.' Bert nodded at Sly and Caleb and moved back out of the house. I realised he'd been the extra Ebony mentioned. The "party" had been set up to push the Hashta into a small area where we could keep an eye on them.

'We have to get out of here,' Caleb brought us back to the current situation. 'Clean up this mess and leave.'

'You have to come with us,' I told Kate. 'It's not safe for you here anymore.'

She nodded. 'With you?'

'Yes. We'll go to our safe house.'

Again, she nodded.

'Let's get some of your things. Just the important ones and a few clothes. We'll get you anything else you need.'

Kate moved to the bedroom, still holding my hand, and we gathered some essentials together. Clothes, papers, her passport, a few pieces of jewellery and a photo album.

'I'm not coming back, am I?' She asked.

I shook my head.

She pulled open a cupboard and added a few personal keepsakes to the bag on the bed.

'What about them?' She gestured to the room as she zipped the bag.

'Sly's men will take them away, clean up here, and make sure there are no traces left.'

I picked up the bag, slung it over my shoulder and guided Kate out the back door. We walked a short distance to a dark SUV parked in the next street.

Just before we turned the corner, Kate looked back one last time, shrugged and then turned back to me. I saw a tear in her eye, but she smiled, squeezed my hand and followed me to the car and our ticket out of her neighbourhood.

I was acutely aware, as she was, that this would probably be the last time she would see her home.

Chapter Forty-Three

Late that night we were still talking.

She lay beside me in the bed, her arm over my waist and mine holding her tightly to my side.

'Quite the day,' she joked.

'I'm sorry,' I answered, guilt still one of my most prevalent emotions.

'Don't be. You didn't do this.'

'It was because of me. If I'd never opened the door to the diner, it wouldn't have happened.'

She squeezed me tightly and kissed me. 'Well, I'm still glad you did.'

The silence felt comfortable, and I secretly echoed her sentiment. My emotions surprised me. I hadn't consciously thought of her in the past months, but as soon as she came into view goosebumps appeared up and down my arm.

She raised her upper body onto her arms and looked at me with a gleam in her eye. 'So, you're an alien?'

I nodded, my smile wide. 'Fraid so.'

'Wow, So I'm really sleeping with an alien.'

'We haven't actually slept yet,' I pointed out.

She laughed, the sound so melodious and warm it instantly made me smile again.

'How do I know you're not bullshitting me?' she asked semi-seriously.

'Last time someone asked that I ended up with a fork in my hand,' I answered, thinking back to when Jonah introduced me to Ebony.

Kate cocked her head. I explained and she laughed along with me.

'Kind of drastic,' she joked.

'Typical Jonah.'

'Are there more restrained ways?'

'Lay your head on my chest,' I suggested. The warmth of her body back against me felt so familiar, as though we'd been made for each other.

I waited for a moment. 'Now what do you hear?'

I felt her press her ear closer to my chest. She stayed still for more than three minutes, concentrating intensely.

'I hear your heart,' she commented. 'Strong, regular, but with an echo.' She lifted herself up again so that she could observe me. I smiled. Her curious features warmed me.

'I have two hearts,' I announced. 'We all do.' I made it sound so normal. Yeah, who am I kidding?

'And purple blood?'

'Yes.'

'Anything else?'

'We heal extremely well here on Earth. Not so much on Taxore. And because of the way our hearts and blood work we have an exaggerated oxygen supply to our muscles. Which makes us very strong here.'

'Handy.'

'Definitely.'

'Taxore. That's home?'

'It was.' The thought sent a stab to my hearts.

'But not anymore?' Her voice was soft and filled with emotion.

I shook my head.

'Tell me,' she urged me.

So, I did.

I unburdened all the pain and anger of the past year. Kate listened and held me tightly when the pain was too much.

Once I finished my monologue, I felt empty, but content for the first time in forever. My muscles relaxed from a tension I'd carried around me for centuries. Relief flood into my system, and even though my body felt exhausted, my mind and essence were rejuvenated.

I'd hoped to console Kate, and—once again—here she was, making me whole again.

Pangs of guilt crossed my mind. For my egoistical unburdening, and her loss. Something I should have prevented but couldn't.

'You can't go back home,' I suggested carefully, softly stroking the side of her beautiful face.

'I gathered that.' Kate smiled observing me completely without blame or anger, but I felt the disappointment in her form.

'There will be more of them, and you're on their radar now.'

She was quiet for a while after that. I felt the tension in her small body and pulled her even closer to me, hoping I could console her.

She relaxed. 'Okay. Well then, I'll live somewhere else.' Kate squeezed me and settled down happily with her head on my chest.

I kissed the top of her head. She was so resilient; I wasn't sure I would have reacted so pragmatically if my life had been upended in the same way so suddenly. Again, I thanked whoever had brought this exceptional woman into my life.

Chapter Forty-Four

All eyes were on the upcoming Establishment meeting.

We'd found the coordinates in the cryptic reference to the bible Benedict had passed on. He'd referred to the juncture of two highways, then given a hint on the name of the building.

It would be a challenge. That much was abundantly clear.

The coordinates led to a resort called the Lord of the Mountain, high up in the Colorado Rocky Mountains. The website described it as the ultimate combination of luxury and back-to-nature, though the emphasis was on luxury. The massive manor housed a hotel, a conference centre and, during the winter, a ski resort.

The manor house was situated in the midst of a two-hundred-acre estate surrounded by forests, high mountains with sheer cliffs and a wide fast flowing river to the east side.

Don't ask how, but Ebony managed to obtain blueprints to the buildings, seven in total.

There was the main house-come-conference centre,

sporting extended extra wings housing an abundance of guest rooms, a spa, a gym and a cinema. Barns and garages were located to the south, adjacent to a generator powered by wind and water which stood next to the river.

The place was self-sufficient. It was off grid. No electricity lines. They even had their own water cleansing facility and an underground river. No dependency on outside utilities at all. The resort had a private communication network with a fifty-foot-tall antenna allowing for links with Internet and telephone services.

The perimeter of the estate was protected by a high electric fence in most areas to--according to the website-- keep out bears and mountain lions, and steep unforgiving cliffs in the rest. It was designed to be impenetrable.

A good choice for a clandestine gathering.

The manor house was as enormous as it was misplaced in the scenery. It was a three-story Georgian style mansion with extensive side wings. The tall windows either side of the marble columns framing the massive wooden door, were impressive and hinted at high ceilinged rooms inside. The entrance was dead centre of the manor and the symmetry was perfect.

A wide driveway led from the large ornate steel gates, along a tree bordered road, past immaculate lawns and flower borders up to the marble steps of the entrance. It was a classic, magnificent building. Impeccable in its maintenance, it looked as though it had stepped right out of the Bridgerton tv series.

From the blueprints and an online brochure, we deduced there were a multitude of large living rooms, a ballroom, studies and kitchens in the main part of the house. We concluded the conference would most likely be held in the grand ballroom that sported an antique oval table easily seating twenty-four. The open fire on the short side of the room and the banks of bookshelves and panelling finished the old English gentry look.

They certainly did value their pretentiousness at the Establishment. It was all focussed on status, perceived superiority and entitlement.

It looked like Cal-Tan's home in Taxore.

We laboured over the blueprints, brochure, online photos and satellite images for a long time, searching for a way in. It would be difficult. The place was a bastion.

Jonah was once again a permanent fixture of the strategy sessions. He was doing better than anyone had expected. His health had come back in leaps and bounds after the first week of recuperation, and he was close to his old self. Both in musculature, attitude and impatience.

He insisted he was more than capable of pulling his weight again, literally, in any mission we set up, and made it abundantly clear that no one—absolutely no one—would stop him from joining this mission. He was in. With a vengeance. He'd proved his worth at Kate's house.

I almost felt sorry for the enemy. Almost.

His strength had returned, and every day saw more sparring partners limping out of the dojo or visiting Doctor Patil for stitches.

The big man was back.

Jonah stood at the head of the table scrutinising the blueprints. I could see he was becoming irritated by the lack of opportunities on offer. But he kept himself in check, a new characteristic I greatly appreciated.

He looked up at Sly.

'What do you think? What's our best line of action?'

'A full-on attack would only cause the people in the mansion to bunker down, and there would be no way we could get in. It's a solid building, with its own utilities, and self-sufficient in all the important aspects. There's no way we could mount a siege if the surprise element of an attack failed. They could keep us at a distance indefinitely.'

'And a siege like that would attract too much attention. Police are about forty-five to sixty minutes from the hotel. We don't need that interference,' Sly remarked dryly.

Jonah nodded. I mirrored the action. It made sense.

'What about sabotaging the generator?' the big man asked.

Sly huffed and shrugged. 'Maybe. But it leaves too much to chance, we don't know whether they have a backup inside, and it still doesn't answer how we could get the team in.'

'And the roof?' I asked.

'We could, but that would mean abseiling form a helicopter and that would alert the Establishment.'

'Parachute in?' Jonah was not beaten. 'Or hang gliders. Landing on the roof.'

Sly shrugged.

'Could be an option, but how do we get off the roof quickly enough to control the situation?' Jonah asked.

'We couldn't,' Sly agreed. 'We expect the conference to be on the ground floor, in the grand ballroom. The roof is two levels up and the only real entry option is at the end of one of the wings. It would take too long to secure the area.'

'Is there any way we could use underground utilities like sewage to get inside?'

'No,' Ebony answered resolutely. 'The pipes aren't wide enough to hold a person.'

'What about air conditioning. Or climate control?'

Again, another idea was rejected.

Conclusion: we were not going to be able to force our way in using traditional methods.

We were running out of options.

'So we can't get in from above, or below?' Jonah concluded.

'Exactly. And the doors or windows are not really an option either, because of the security we expect.'

'We need someone on the inside. Someone who can literally open a door.'

'How?'

'Any chance of getting in with catering or the staff?'

Sly shook his head. 'They'll be vetted too within an inch of their life, and time is too short to get an undercover in.'

'Then we're screwed,' Jonah concluded.

'Only thing left is to ambush some of them on the way in or out of the grounds. But the impact of that will be much less than if we can surprise them mid-meeting. Or better yet; if we could stream part of their conference real time,' Ebony mused.

'There might one way,' Aaliyah joined in the conversation for the first time. We all looked at her with deep interest.

'Gabriel and I could transport into the mansion and open up a doorway for your team.'

'That would let us have access from the inside,' I acknowledged. Her idea had merit. It gave us an option. A very slim one, but one none-the-less.

'Could others transport?' Sly asked.

'That's debatable,' I answered. 'Humans don't handle transportation well. It wreaks havoc on your bodies and metabolism. There's no use having a team transported in, just to puke all over the place.'

Ebony turned to our new resident Taxorian expert. 'Is there anything we could do about that?'

His brow creased and he stared at the blueprints. 'There may be,' Tajan answered carefully.

I cocked my head in question. He avoided my eyes.

'Your father—sorry, Cal-Tan,' he continued. 'He tasked my colleague Ser-nay to find a way to transport humans from this dimension directly to another one. Not Taxore, we know that's very detrimental to their health.'

'To where?'

'I'm not sure. I think the new dimension they found.'

'The thirty-second?' That dimension had a habit of popping up.

'Yes. It has an atmosphere that greatly resembles the one here.'

'And he wants to transport humans there.'

Tajan nodded.

'What for?' Ebony asked.

'Direct sales.' I said, realisation sinking in. 'Cut out the reincarnation.'

Everyone was silent. The implications were clear. If reincarnation wasn't necessary anymore it would open the door to a more direct harvest. My father wouldn't have to wait for a subject to die, with or without his involvement.

'And did she succeed?' Aaliyah broke the silence.

'She was still working on it when I left.' Tajan turned to her. 'But she was making good progress.'

'Do you know the details of what she worked on?' I asked.

Tajan nodded. 'We worked closely together, always bounced ideas off each other. And we tested each other's work.'

'Could you replicate what she invented?'

'Maybe.' He was hesitant to commit. 'There were still questions open when I left.'

'It doesn't have to be a long-distance transport,' Ebony interjected. 'We could try to get as close as possible, then transport inside.'

'The distance might not be the determining factor,' Tajan answered. 'The principle is still the same. The body has to be broken down and moved in time and space, then recompiled at the destination.'

'What would be the extent of the damage to a human system?' Sly asked.

'That depends on the health of the individual. It could be anything from major indigestion to heart failure or a stroke.'

'Do you know what aspects of health are most determining for success?'

'A strong heart. Good arteries, healthy respiratory system. That kind of thing.'

'Is it something we could try?' Sly asked.

'Maybe. But it's very risky and we'd have to be careful to stay off the Establishment's radar. I know they are monitoring movement, but I'm not sure what they can identify.'

'It would be an answer to our challenges,' Ebony encouraged.

'If it's possible.'

Chapter Forty-Five

Sly found volunteers in his team to attempt transportation. They knew the risks, or what had been explained about them. Nothing was concrete. No one really knew what to expect.

I recalled that my father had initially tried to transport humans to Taxore with devastating results. Hardly any survived and those that did were irreparably damaged. That was why my family ultimately decided to reincarnate the life essence into host bodies that resembled ours more than humans.

Reincarnation avoided the issue with transportation and created grunts with more stamina, strength and duration. A better product.

As far as I knew, Jonah and Ibrahim were the only reincarnated human essences whose host body had ever transported to Earth. And Jonah's had not been a success. No human bodies had transported.

The risks were massive. Yet still Ebony's loyal team supplied volunteers. It was testament to the devotion these people had for our friend. Other than Sly, I still didn't know why they were so dedicated to her. I could find no other hold she might have on them than love, and family.

The three volunteers: Tyrone, Paul and Nasheed were subjected to a full regime of health tests, including full body MRIs, blood and DNA tests and vigorous stamina and strength appraisals.

Paul was ruled out as a potential for transportation, due to a previously hidden vascular weakness in his DNA. Tyrone and Nasheed passed with flying colours. Doctor Patil still wasn't satisfied. He pulled in a mental health expert and screened their mental health. Again, they passed.

Tajan and Ebony in the meantime, worked on adapting new transport amulets to the human physiology. A lot of it was science, but there was still an element of guess work. Educated guesses, but nothing definite. No guarantees.

The first transportation attempt was a nerve-racking experience.

To avoid any needless complications like walls and solid objects, the first tests took place outside. We didn't want to make it any more difficult than absolutely necessary.

I watched from a distance.

Nasheed had been thoroughly prepared, not just by Doctor Patil, but also by Aaliyah and me. We discussed the feelings he would encounter. The stress and pains that were inevitably linked with the procedure. Jonah joined us with his experience transporting back to Earth.

Tajan and Ebony had agreed to transport Nasheed a distance of ten metres. He would stay in the same field.

Baby steps.

It was about the procedure. And sustaining his health.

The questions remained. Would he come back? And if he did, would he be in one piece?

Nasheed stood silently in the middle of the clearing. He held the transporter in his left hand, the fingers of his other hand on the dial, waiting for the nod from Ebony.

Time stood still. Beside the soft calls of birds in the trees bordering the clearing, it was completely quiet. Eerily so. We were so far away from the inhabited world that not even traffic sounds disturbed our silent vigil. No planes flew overhead, we were completely isolated.

Ebony glanced at Tajan. I saw the tension in her body and in the way she wrung her fingers through the material of her sweater. She was acutely aware of the responsibility she carried. This was one of her team. He trusted her to bring him back. To make it all work.

No pressure, right.

Jonah stepped up to her and laid his hand on her shoulder in support. Her hand moved up to his and she leaned into him ever so slightly.

With a last deep breath, she nodded.

Nasheed turned the dial and the air around him shimmered. In what seemed like slow motion, his form blurred and disappeared.

Time had no meaning as we concentrated on a spot to the right of where he'd disappeared. I held my breath, not daring to upset the continuum.

The air moved. The image of the trees behind it blurred and was replaced by a human form. The outline came first, then blurred again, and came back. It solidified and became identifiable as Nasheed.

He stood in the exact same stance as when he'd left, only ten metres further to the right. His form was the same.

His clothes the same, no blood, none of the terrible effects I'd imagined might happen.

We were rooted to the spot. No one breathed. No one moved.

Then Nasheed's form slowly slid down to the soft grass as his legs gave way.

We ran to him. All of us.

His hand raised, and he waved us away.

As one, we stopped.

I could see him struggle to breath. His chest was heaving, pulling in the fresh mountain air. His skin was pale, almost sickly. When he raised his head, the eyes were bloodshot and crunched in obvious pain and agony. But still he motioned us away.

Nasheed placed his right hand on the grass and pushed himself up off the ground. He staggered, almost falling again, but managed to righten himself. Slowly, he straightened his back, took deep breaths and looked us in the eye.

'I'm okay,' his words, hardly more than a whisper, resounded in the silence. Freeing us from the constraints of worry and apprehension.

We moved closer.

Nasheed did his best to disguise the slight tremor in his body. It was only just noticeable, but we were looking for any side effects, so hiding them would defeat the purpose. Doctor Patil waved to Tyrone who brought the pick-up closer. Nasheed would go to the infirmary and be subjected to a barrage of tests to determine whether he'd suffered any permanent damage. Jonah helped Nasheed take the three steps to the open passenger door. Initially his movement was careful, controlled, and slow. The second step was already better.

We stayed back as Tyrone drove off to the house. There

was little we could do here, so we dispersed and made our way back.

Jonah joined me in my car.

'What do you think?' he asked. 'Will it work?'

I shrugged. 'I really don't know. He had quite a reaction. Better than I expected, but he was nowhere near action ready when he hit the ground. That's a big risk. We don't have the luxury to let anyone recover from transportation.'

'What about me?'

Oh no.

Not that again.

'We've been through this, Jonah,' I answered exasperated. 'Your body is not suited to it in its current state.'

'There's nothing wrong with my body,' he countered, angrily slapping his chest. 'I'm just as strong as before.'

'Yes.' I chose my words carefully. The big man's temper was also back up to his old volatile self. 'You've recovered fantastically. In all aspects, you're back to your old self.'

He nodded.

'But.'

His face clouded over.

'You died,' I continued. 'Twice.' His eyes shot daggers, but I pushed on. We had to get this out of the way.

'Your body has been damaged. It's too soon to know if that is permanent or not.'

Jonah bit his lower lip.

'We can't risk it, big man. Not now, not when we need you and your axe. You're leading the outer group into the mansion. That will already put you in the line of fire. We can't chance any complications before that.'

He was quiet.

Jonah stared out of the window to the safe house. We'd

arrived and the car was stationary again. I turned towards him but stayed silent. The hunched stance and deep furrows in his crunched brow showed his inner conflict. He knew I was right. Not just for him. For the mission. We couldn't risk a blotched entry. It was a one-time thing. One chance.

Slowly he tilted his head to the side and looked at me. 'I still think you're all being overly dramatic about it all. I'm fine. I'm strong.'

'Yes,' I smiled. 'And we want to keep you that way.'

We were two weeks away from the conference, so there was a clear and pressing deadline to solidify our plan.

We had three scenarios. The first, only Aaliyah and I transported in and somehow opened a door. In the second we were joined by Nasheed and Tyrone. The third was a no-transport option that wasn't really viable.

The outcome of Nasheed and Tyrone's test transports was the determining factor in finalising which of the first two scenarios we would effectuate.

Doctor Patil reported on Nasheed's health as Ebony and Tajan tweaked the settings of the transporter. There had been no permanent damage and Nasheed recovered within three hours, the only remaining symptom his bloodshot eyes. It was expected to pass.

After doctor Patil gave the-all clear, Tyrone repeated the transport and came through with much better results. Except for throwing up, he had no real side effects.

'Happens to me all the time,' I chimed in. 'Transportation plays havoc on your intestines.'

'What did you do to minimise the effects?'

'Breathing exercises. Before and after the transportation. The more relaxed you are, the better the results.'

'Mindfulness?'

'Something like that.'

Bolstered by the positive results, we repeated the tests another two times after which Tajan tweaked the transporter again. After every attempt Nasheed, Tyrone and two more volunteers were subjected to the same thorough stream of tests with surprising results. Their bodies were actually adapting to transportation. Each time they showed less negatives, even the nausea became tolerable with the mindfulness training. It was looking good.

There would be six of us in the initial probe team. I started to feel more confident.

One thing we didn't know was what kind of reception we could expect once we were in the building.

There would no doubt be resistance.

There would be security; probably a lot, with all the high-ranking people expected to be present.

Ebony and her team organised a meeting.

Chapter Forty-Six

Preparation was key in this mission.

It would be a singular occurrence. No re-runs. We had to nail it first time.

I was still astounded by the arrogance of the Establishment in organising a conclave of this proportion. It screamed the pretentious narcissism of my kind. They thought they were invincible.

Sure, we'd attacked some of their strongholds, messed up the delivery of souls and been a definite irritation. But we were frankly no more than a flea in their coat. At least that was what they thought.

Their perceived superiority wouldn't let them consider any real threat to their authority. They were so sure of their safety they couldn't imagine we would know about the meeting, let alone target anything as big as this.

At least, that was what we were counting on.

My father is no fool.

Neither—and I admit to that reluctantly—is my brother Michael. Despite their egos, they would definitely have demanded state-of-the art security in and around the conference. As much to impress the so-called partners as against any threat from outside.

I didn't expect my family there. It was a Terran thing. Cal-Tan would stay far above anything as trivial as a meeting of lowly minions. And with all the happenings on the Thirty-second dimension, Michael would be kept busy in other places. Maybe, just maybe, there would be a delegate from Taxore, but I wasn't betting on it, they tended to just let the humans do what they had to and direct from a safe distance. I was good with that, in no hurry for another family reunion. I was still reeling from the last one.

Besides, it was the high placed humans we were after.

But it wasn't enough to catch them, we had to expose the conspiracy. That would mean showing the world what these people were doing and what they had planned for their fellow man. The proof had to be irrefutable. What we were going to tell them was beyond human comprehension. There could be no doubt.

'We want to stream the conference real time on all major networks,' Ebony surprised us.

I'd thought big, but not that big.

'Worldwide,' she added for extra shock effect.

Okay. That was mind blowing. Worldwide. Could she do that? Of course she could, otherwise she wouldn't have brought us here or suggested it.

'The team has hacked into CNN, Al Jazerra, BBC, Al Arabiya, Fox News, Euro news, all major news channels, and social media, X, Facebook, Insta. My guys are standing-by to stream whatever you can film in the mansion.'

'So it's up to us to give them something to show,' I added. There were nervous nods all around.

It was risky.

Not only were we going to invade the mansion, but we also had to do it in a covert manner and film whatever we could of the proceedings before we made our presence known. That would require some finesse.

Like I said; risky.

The rest of the afternoon was taken up with finetuning the details of the attack. Things like where we would gain entry and how we would move unseen to the ballroom.

And… what we would do after that?

There was some contention. Jonah wanted to go to town on everyone there, take out as many as possible. Aaliyah agreed. Ebony and I were more restrained.

Streams were one thing. They would expose the Establishment. But that was only part of it. We needed to do more to successfully bring my father and all his cohorts down. We were in it for the long haul and that meant showing some constraint.

The icing on the cake would be to bring the conspirators to justice and obtain their confessions. I argued why filming the proceedings would not be enough. The streams could be labelled as fake, as staged. If we captured high-profile people and they spilled the beans it would eventually help our ultimate goal: to definitively bring down the Establishment and unequivocally stop the violence they'd instigated.

I understood Jonah's and Aaliyah's need for revenge. I felt it too. But I refused to let it overwhelm me and determine my actions. Not this time. Not with these stakes.

There was another major challenge for this operation.

How would we know where to transport into? We couldn't look into the mansion and as none of us had ever been there, I assumed we had to place our trust fully on the blueprints. They showed where the walls were, doors, windows and so on. But not where the security converged. How many stood guard and where? What obstructions would be in our way?

'We'll use drones,' Sly announced.

I raised an eyebrow. 'Drones? Wouldn't they be too obvious?'

'Not if they're up high enough.'

'I'm no expert, but won't that cloud the details?' I tried.

'If there was only one, yes,' Ebony chimed in. 'We're going to launch three infra-red drones that will cover the exact same area. The images they gather will be laid over each other and form a detailed picture.'

'That will work?'

She nodded, a smile on her face. 'It will. We've been testing it for a while now. The last adaptations have been made and it's good to go.'

'What will it show us?' Jonah asked.

'Heat signatures, where people are,' Sly explained. 'And we'll create a more detailed blueprint of where obstacles are by following people's movements in the mansion for multiple days. We've already started. The patterns show where they walk, what they avoid and so on. We're building a floorplan which will help us avoid furniture and other impediments.

Chapter Forty-Seven

Jonah and I watched as the images streamed in from the drones.

Initially three distinct, blurred, renditions of the area appeared side-by-side. Ebony super-imposed them on each other revealing every leaf on the trees almost three miles down.

The drones had undergone rigorous testing, ascending ever higher to determine the limits of their camera's reach.

'No higher than four miles,' Ebony declared. 'That will keep them clear of international and commercial flight lanes while still providing the detail we're looking for.'

The drones flew in perfect unison, their cameras seamlessly linked to avoid image distortion. Ebony guided them over a small town, hovering the drones over the town hall. The cameras focussed and zoomed in on an office where five people were easily distinguishable: three seated, one standing to the side, and the last walking around what we perceived as a table, keeping his or her body angled towards the group. It was a presentation of some kind.

With a shift of the joystick, the scene changed to another room. This one with multiple groups of people around what I deduced were tables. Three figures stood in a line at the far right while a procession of people filed past them suggesting a cafeteria. The images were remarkably clear, allowing us to distinguish between individuals figures with ease. It exceeded my expectations.

'Let's see what the difference is if we bring it down to half the hight,' Ebony suggested.

The images clarified and we could make out the figures' extremities. Whether this would significantly aid our investigation remained debatable, except perhaps to identify if they were carrying anything, such as a weapon.

I realised what a massive benefit this technology would be for our mission. We weren't going in blind anymore. Maybe somewhat visually impaired, but definitely better than before.

'Moving back up,' Ebony narrated her actions. 'We can go into smaller details on the day. Now we need to plot the general layout.

She manoeuvred the controls, and the drones flew up and away from the town, over the forests until they arrived at the mansion.

Ebony combined the new images with ones the team had already gathered in previous flights.

The floorplan started to take form. I could see forms appear, tables, staircases, what looked like other furniture. There were clear walkways, and overlaying the images in a time frame, we ascertained distinct patterns that translated as security routes.

The images continued outside, and we mapped the coming and going of the security teams. There were two dog teams, one walked clockwise, the other in the opposite direction. They encountered each other twice in their rounds and proceeded on to cover the grounds. The presence of dogs worried me. Not so much for myself—I was going to transport inside the building—but for the main body of the team we had to let in.

The breach had to be meticulously timed. Both in and out, to avoid chance of discovery before we were ready.

Technology was a massive benefit, but ultimately, it was still a people's action, and the risks were great.

'Leave it to us,' Ebony dismissed the big man and me. 'You can go make yourself useful somewhere else.'

We took the not-so-gentle hint and left the computer room.

'You looking forward to this?' Jonah asked as we made our way to the kitchen.

I shrugged. 'Yes, and no.'

'How so?'

He moved to the American style fridge and pulled open both doors to peer inside. I heard him rummage around to find something to still his ever-present hunger. His appetite had been fully restored with his physique and it was bottomless. There was no feeding this man. Luckily Sly kept the kitchen fully stocked, and repleted it again after the big man had been on his customary rampage.

Jonah placed a plate of pulled turkey, a large segment of Cheddar cheese, some greens—for show I would imagine— a hunk of roast beef and a pot of pickles, placed them on the table and closed the fridge. He wasn't done though, the big man turned to break a big piece of rye bread off a new loaf that was cooling on the countertop. A plate, some utensils and a big glass of water later, he finally sat down behind his banquet.

He looked up at my smiling face.

'What?' he shrugged.

'Just good to see you back.'

He raised an eyebrow as his teeth sank into the bread.

I shook my head and laughed.

'You hungry?' He indicated the food on the table.

'I'll pass,' I answered. 'I ate two hours ago.'

Again, the shrug. We'd all eaten a hearty meal together. But there was no satiating this guy. I guess the reincarnation had enhanced his appetite even more.

I retrieved a soda from the smaller drinks fridge and sat down opposite Jonah. He ate in silence as I sipped the drink.

Finally, he put down his fork and pushed the empty plate away. I observed the damage. Half the turkey was gone, the cheese was reduced to mere crumbs and the beef was also substantially less than ten minutes ago.

He patted his now full belly and settled back to drink his water.

'And?' He started the conversation. 'Why are you in two minds about the mission?'

'I'm not exactly debating it,' I answered. 'It's more that I have conflicting emotions.' I stared at the soda can, slowly turning it in my hands. 'On the one side, we're finally getting closer to our goal. We have a real chance to expose the Establishment and everything it stands for. We can end this controversy.'

'Isn't that what you wanted?'

I looked up. 'Yes. Of course it is. And it will be a relief to finally put an end to all this.'

He smiled.

'There's just a nagging feeling at the back of my mind that questions whether it will be the end.'

'What do you mean?'

'Cal-Tan. I can't imagine he'll just shrug it off and accept defeat.'

'We're sending the drones to the area again tomorrow,' Ebony announced. 'They should arrive in the middle of the night. Then we can start to scope the area around the building and the mansion itself during the next night.'

'No daytime flights?'

'No, just to make sure no one identifies them. It's also much quieter in the airspace at night. The place is off the beaten track, but still borders on one of the major continental flight paths. We don't want anyone looking out a plane's window and seeing the drone.'

Chapter Forty-Eight

The day had arrived, or should I say the days. It would take more than two days in all once we got to the mansion.

We had to assume the guards were observing all incoming and outgoing traffic in the area for at least a day in advance of the meeting. We would. So, we expected the same from them.

We avoided the main roads, preferring to take back roads or even rough tracks. Our four-wheel drive vehicles were all terrain enabled, so not a problem.

From our perch deep in the forests we observed the mansion with a combination of the drones, telescopes and heavily camouflaged team members crawling through the dense vegetation. All relayed images back to our position and the headquarters manned by Ebony, her team and of course Tajan.

We camped during the wet, cold night under camouflage nets in small basic tents, and abstained from lighting fires. We weren't there for comfort.

The weather expectations were more of the same for the coming days. Rain and sleet were expected during the nights, with possible cloud breaks in the afternoon. The sun would be absent, as was the moon. The conference coincided with the waning of the moon and cast the landscape in deep shadows.

Rain dripped off the trees onto my shoulder to join the steady flow moving down my coat. Even though the material was watertight, I felt cold and clammy. Twenty plus hours of either drizzle or pelting rain was taking its toll. A freezing drop of water found its way in between my hat and coat. It felt like a needle as it touched my skin and descended under my sweater. I shivered involuntarily. I hated this kind of weather, but in this case, it would be a benefit, it would camouflage our presence.

At the mansion, there were few people outside in this terrible weather. Only the guards with the dogs, and even they would be handicapped by the incessant rain. Everyone else had chosen to stay inside, in the dry warmth that shone through the big windows. From where we were, it looked cosy.

It wasn't all good news. We would have to lose our wet clothes as soon as we transported inside. A trail of wet footsteps would be a dead giveaway. We'd agreed to swap coats to dry ones as close to the transportations as possible and we hoped for a short respite, maybe just a light drizzle. We were also wearing over-boots; these would be discarded just before we transported.

We'd have to wait though.

The visitors were only just arriving. Most of them would stay the night in the luxurious hotel rooms so they could join the intended speeches and the celebrations which would no doubt follow the official aspects. The valets had their hands full keeping the VIPs dry under massive black umbrellas as they made their way from the luxurious cars to the steps leading to the mansions inviting entrance. They hurried inside as quickly as possible, all anxious to get out of the pelting rain we were destined to undergo.

The streams showed a steady flow of people arriving at the mansion. Some we recognised immediately; others were more anonymous. We identified Benedict as he arrived in a chauffeured SUV. He looked up at the mansion, ignoring the valet with the umbrella as he surveyed the surroundings. Benedict turned slowly on his axis and took in all he could of the area. Finally, to the valet's relief, he walked up the seven stairs into the mansion.

His presence at the meeting gave me mixed emotions. On the one hand, he was potentially an asset. Someone on the inside. Not that I had an idea how we could benefit from his presence. But at this point in the mission, I was glad for any positive addition.

On the other hand, we were once again putting someone in danger. Make no mistake. His life was definitely hanging by a thin thread. If the Establishment found out he was a traitor to their cause, he would undeniably be dispatched in a very painful and educational manner. If he wasn't exposed, he would potentially be caught in the cross-fire once we made our presence clear. Jonah indicated Bene-dict was no stranger to danger, but this could possibly be one step too far. I was also concerned about Jonah's emotional connection to the archbishop. I hoped his friend-ship would not take off his edge. Not distract him.

I had no illusion that this would be an easy mission, or that we would exit the event without any damage. It was war. In war there were casualties. I just hoped they would be on the Establishment's side. The team knew the danger. They walked into whatever was waiting for us with open eyes. But that was the theory. My experience was that emotions would be very different if anyone from our team was badly wounded, or even killed. And that was a very plausible potential outcome.

The pressure on our shoulders—not just mine—was enormous. It almost buckled me. Everything we'd done in the past two years had been gearing up to this moment. This was our one, single, chance to completely expose what my dimension was afflicting on humanity.

The future of mankind was resting on our success.

No pressure. Right?

We'd planned our transportation for early evening, after dinner when the Ventus-Dei was expected to convene in the ball room. Benedict's information had been sketchy at best, but combined with what we saw in the preparations, and just general common sense, this was what we would use as our guideline. Ebony's team would continuously measure our progress and every movement inside the mansion, through the drones. There was still room for conjecture, nothing was certain. But they definitely offered us an educated guess.

I was grateful for that.

Finally, it was time to move.

The incessant rain had diminished slightly, offering us a short window in which to transport into the mansion. Ebony's team monitored all movements inside the vast building, and we awaited their green light. They would tell us when to activate our amulets.

We waited impatiently, but silently, just outside the

perimeter of the gardens on the eastern side of the building, as close as possible to the library where we would materialise.

Minutes dragged by slowly.

Involuntarily, I counted the seconds. It didn't help. But it gave me something to do.

A soft click in my earpiece signalled the moment had finally arrived.

I discarded the over boots and, standing on my rain jacket, I turned the dial on the amulet around my neck, glancing at the rest of our six-man team.

The familiar queasy feeling assailed my gut as I felt myself pulled harshly to the side, as the technology dispersed the atoms of my form to reassemble them thirty metres further on, inside the library.

That was the plan.

What seemed like forever was just a fraction of a second. The wet trees that had surrounded us were replaced with a dark, somewhat dusty room with ceiling high bookcases and old leather chairs. A bureau at the far end of the room held the only light form in the room, which shone an eerie glow over the leather-bound books.

I glance around at my fellow transporters.

Aaliyah was to my right. Naturally, she had gone through the experience without any noticeable effect, she was used to the procedure.

Tyrone, Nasheed and Clyde had weathered the experience reasonably well and looked ready for combat. Steve stood retching beside a deep leather chair. His face was pale, and he strained to stand. Tyrone moved towards him, but he waved him off, taking deep breaths. A minute later he'd recovered enough to proceed with our mission.

'One person is in the hallway,' Ebony's voice informed us. We waited at the door.

'Now!'

Tyrone opened the door a crack and slid a camera snake out into the corridor. There was no one around so we hastily made our way out of the second-floor room and into the labyrinth of corridors beyond.

We hugged the shadows, blending in with our dark clothes and camouflaged features, as we made our way forward to the designated areas. The team split at a servant's staircase and Aaliyah, Clyde and I slowly descended to the ground floor while the rest of the team went to the utility room that bordered a flat roof. There they would let the rest of the team into the mansion.

Part of the team would stay on the second floor and take up position on the mezzanine that bordered one side of the vast ball room. They would secure that area and have a vantage point overseeing the events below. Aaliyah, Clyde and I would slip into the ballroom, hopefully undetected, and stay in the shadows below the balcony.

Communication would be minimal during the mission. Clicks and the images from the head cameras the only way the on-site team could convey any information. Ebony's team kept up a brief commentary on the area around us as we slipped deeper into the building.

Secrecy was our ally. Without it we'd be unable to film the proceedings.

Disrupting the Ventus-Dei was not enough. They had to be exposed.

That would be the most difficult part of our mission: staying our impulse to attack until Ebony had sufficient material to univocally expose the real villains in this building.

She was in charge.

Ebony was the one who would ultimately steer our movements, our patience. Unless exposed, we would wait with our interference until she gave us the sign.

It would be tense. Difficult.

Chapter Forty-Nine

We reached the ballroom without issues.

Thank you, team.

The floor plan had been spot-on, preparing us perfectly for a stealthy passage from the entry point to the main event.

The team was complete. Twelve of us in total inside the building. Aaliyah, Jonah, Sly and his team, and me. The rest was in the grounds, waiting for our signal.

The ballroom was enormous and entering would be a challenge. There were constantly people moving in and out of the gigantic open double doors. No matter how stealthy we were, gaining entrance was an obstacle that would require precise timing and speed. The planters either side of the doors offered us some shadows, but it was debatable whether we could enter without identifying ourselves. We had to concede that the continuous traffic, and the open character of the situation made it almost unusable for us. There had to be another way in.

A consternation in the meeting offered us a break.

Two of the speakers were engrossed in a heated argument, with others standing up from their chairs to either support them or attempt to calm the tempers. All eyes turned towards the altercation, with staff even stopping to watch the proceedings. The bickering escalated to a fight when the original speaker pushed his opponent to the floor and was in turn attacked by his victim's supporters. The ensuing brawl was a way for Aaliyah and me to move into the room unseen using the dark shadows.

The grand ballroom was aptly named. It stretched out over at least ten-thousand square feet. Three-story high floor-to-ceiling windows adorned the length of the vast chamber on the right side. On the left, the wall height was only broken by four doors and the mezzanine's ornate balcony that ran the length of the room. It originated above the grand entrance and tapered down to a curved staircase at the far ends. Sly, two of his team and Jonah sneaked on to the mezzanine from the first floor, this would provide a great vantage point for us. The soft clicks in my earpiece indicated they were in place. I answered with my own signal.

The expanse of the chamber was divided into several areas with the use of furniture, plants, and more modern room dividers.

The lighting had been dimmed to offer the meeting an almost medieval character. All lights focussed on the centre of the room where the action was, now very appropriate with the fight. Security rushed from the side to pull the two men apart and deposit them back in their chairs.

Aaliyah and I had made our way behind the vast array of plants and containers to a vantage point opposite the centre of the ring of chairs. The shadows of the tropical plants and the balcony hid us from view while it still gave us a great overview of the scene in front of us.

I counted eight guards interspersed over the lit area near the centre of the room. They were all armed with semi-automatic guns slung from their shoulders. Most of them sported a large hunting knife in a leather scabbard on their hip. To me, it was all show. The guns would be impractical in the busy room, and the knives were Rambo style, more for effect than actual usability.

The open expanse in front of us was ringed with twenty-four high backed chairs in a semi-circle, though the label "chair" would not really do them justice. They resembled thrones, what you would expect in a bad Camelot film. There was no table, effectively opening up the central area in front of the chairs for presentations.

All but one of the thrones were taken. This was the Ventus Dei. The inner circle.

Nineteen men and three women flanked the person in the centre throne.

My breath hitched as I observed the familiar form.

Michael looked completely at ease on his throne; his back stiff against the high-back and both hands flat on the ornate lion-head arm rests. My brother's face was the epiphany of a tyrant's stern visage, with his hooded eyes, thin unsmiling lips and creased brow. He was enjoying it.

'That Michael?' I heard Ebony in my ear. I slowly nodded my head up and down. We'd agreed to no verbal contact from our side. If they had a question we would answer with clicks or movement. The images from our head camera would show our reply.

'You expect him?'

My head moved from side to side. Hell no, I hadn't expected him. Not in person. This conference must be even more important than we'd thought, to merit the heir making an entrance.

We watched the proceedings from our vantage points as the cameras and microphones on the headsets recorded everything and streamed it back to Ebony. Her team patched it into the major networks worldwide where millions of people could view the abomination that was taking place in this ballroom.

Peace had returned to the circle. A tall man stood in the centre of the space turning slowly to address all the people seated. Every few minutes he consulted the tablet in his hands as he relayed the statistics like a regular CFO.

The past year had been a good one for the Establishment with an increase in souls, both in volume and quality.

'The emergence of the religious hostilities has provided us with the intended benefit. The two sides, Christian:' he nodded to one of the bishops seated to the far right. 'And Islam.' Another nod to an imam next to the bishop. Seemed the hostility between the two religions hadn't reached this room.

'Both sides have done fantastically in harvesting souls. The total is far beyond our expectations with an increase of more than one-hundred and fifty-six percent.' He paused for effect. There were approving nods all around.

The speaker continued his well-rehearsed dialogue. 'The holy war has proven itself, not for the first time.'

'We will continue to expand the hostility,' the bishop stated directly to Michael, who nodded his agreement.

The speaker picked up his narrative. 'The terrorist attacks need to be amped up to force a full-blown holy war. That will net us more male casualties. Now, we have too many women and children. As you know,' he indicated towards the others. 'They have no value for us. Collateral damage. It's the males we want. A bloody war will get us exactly that.'

'What's the time frame?' Michael asked, no longer interested in the numbers.

The imam took up the narrative. 'We will increase the violence in synchronised increments, pulling in more countries, especially those around the Mediterranean, Middle East and Northern Africa. Our calculations show the hostility will reach boiling point after the new year.'

'What fail-safes do we have in place?' Michael asked.

'There are back up plans to give the extra push if needed,' the bishop interjected. 'Ones that will not fail to ignite a worldwide spark.'

My brother nodded his approval, the sentiment prevalent amongst the attendees. I slowly moved my head from side to side to include as many of the conspirators as I could. Ebony would home in on their faces and name them in the streams if possible. We wanted to show how immense the Establishment's reach was.

The "CFO" finished his presentation and retired from the circle.

An aide walked into the circle and addressed Michael directly.

'My lord. We have a new high potential to fill the empty seat.' He indicated the one unoccupied throne. 'Naturally, we require your approval.'

Michael nodded, his body tilted slightly sideways as he stroked his chin in thought, his elbow on the throne's arm rest.

The aide bowed and walked backwards three steps, then turned sideways and nodded towards the left main doors.

All attention was pulled to a procession of men who entered the room.

Two men dressed in floor length blue robes proceeded Benedict, four more made up the rear behind him. They were milking this to the maximum. It was a ritual the likes of which you would see in a particularity bad movie.

Benedict was not impressed.

He slowly rotated his head to take in the people seated in the circle. His brow creased and the thin lips pulled even thinner in barely veiled disdain. His erect form and strong aura projected his feelings even more.

The procession stopped as Benedict reached the exact centre of the circle of thrones and he slowly turned to face Michael, his face no longer in my line of sight. But his body language was enough to deduce his contempt.

We'd hoped he would go along with the whole ritual, but it looked as though his natural honesty and abhorrence was winning the battle.

I could see Michael's reaction. His eyes shot daggers from under the hooded brows. The smirk on his lips deepened as Benedict stared directly at him.

'My lord?' the aide didn't sound as confident as earlier.

The temperature of the room decreased a few degrees with the open hostility between the two men facing each other in the centre of what now was an arena.

'This is the archbishop?' Michael asked.

'This is Archbishop Benedict, my lord,' the aide stammered, glancing round at the others for support. None was forthcoming.

Michael made a point of looking Benedict up and down, stroking his chin all the time.'

'I must say,' he began, his voice dripping the venom I recognised so well. 'I had expected more.'

Benedict didn't react.

'They told me you were a man of stature.' Michael shook his head. He pointed to Benedict, his hand travelling from the floor to the top of his head. 'I'm disappointed.'

'As you are not of this world, you may have misunderstood our language,' Benedict answered in a particularly patronising tone. 'Stature is not the same as size.'

Smoke almost came out of Michael's ears, and I couldn't stop a silent laugh.

'And size does not equal status.' Benedict drove the insult home.

Michael's features coloured bright red with the effort to contain himself. He was rapidly losing the battle. I was enjoying myself. It was very refreshing to see my bully brother brought down a few pegs in front of his minions. His standing was slipping fast, and he knew it.

He sat back against the throne, took a deep breath and started again, only a slight edge to his voice.

'I assume you know who you're speaking to.' Michael continued.

Benedict refrained from answering, he simply held Michael's stare. His body language was a mix of stoic control and readiness for action.

'My name is Michael,' My brother continued, unfazed by the lack of reply. 'I am here on behalf of my father.' There was a loaded silence as I wondered whether my brother would actually call Cal-Tan "god". He didn't.

'He is the initiator and the leader of the Establishment and all it entails. My father is the driving force behind the harvesting of human souls.' He kept emphasising the family relationship, probably hoping it would give him more credibility.

'You may be unaware of the reach and importance of the Establishment, so I will give you a short introduction.'

The silence said it all. No one dared interject.

Michael was showing off. This was even better than we'd hoped.

He seemed desperate to impress Benedict for some reason, maybe to recover his injured ego. This was new for me. I'd never seen him so insecure. I wondered what was behind all that. Something was going on back home to make him feel so out of sorts. The big bully image was waning.

'You have been brought before us to decide whether you are worthy of elevation to the Ventus Dei,' Michael declared.

Benedict stayed silent, there was no reaction at all, from what I could see. But that was enough to anger my brother again. I saw the crease in his brow intensify and his eyes harden.

'This is not to be taken lightly. The Ventus Dei is the governing body of the Establishment here on earth. Membership of this prestigious executive board is by invitation only. To gain access you must embrace our goals and missions. Your contribution to our cause must be exceptional, and complete fidelity to my family is mandatory.'

Michael paused for effect and prepared to continue his monologue.

'And what exactly is that cause?' Benedict interrupted Michael's line of thought. He cocked his head to the right as an emphasis.

Michael's brow creased even more, and he glanced to the bishop seated to his right, but he looked as confused as my brother. Michael's hard visage moved to the aide, who visibly wilted under the scrutiny.

'Surely you have informed this candidate on what we do?' Michael asked incredulously.

'They have,' Benedict interposed once again. 'But I want to hear it from you.'

The silence had teeth.

I felt my hearts skip a beat at the audacity of the archbishop. He was pushing all the right buttons in the knowledge that we were present.

Michael sat back in his throne and observed this recalcitrant candidate. I saw admiration barely veiled by the contempt he tried to portray. No one stood up to him, this was a new experience. Especially from a human.

'My family has been harvesting slaves from this dimension for centuries and shipping them off to our home world where they are sold to hard labour,' he began. 'This practise has made us exceptionally rich and powerful. The Establishment was created by my father to improve and expedite the acquisition and reincarnation process and assist in the demand for new slaves.'

'And you only want young, strong men?' Benedict asked.

'The environment where they end up is not for the feint hearted. Also, the reincarnation process is invasive and requires strength of body, mind and soul.'

'You reincarnate them in your dimension?'

'We do. Into bodies more suited to our world.'

'You're an alien.'

'That depends on your point of view. But yes, I come from another dimension, another world.'

'If your family is so successful, what do you need these humans for?' He swiped his hand from left to right to encompass the Ventus Dei members to emphasise his question.

'As I said, the reincarnation process is a difficult process.

It requires a strong will to live. A will to be reincarnated.' Michael's voice sported a dangerous tone, he was tiring of this game.

'And they know that?'

'No. They do not know where they are going to.'

Benedict huffed.

Michael continued, barely holding his temper.

'They have a strong belief that they will go to another place after death,'

'To heaven.'

'Something like that. So they are determined to find what is on the other side of death. This ensures they make it through the process.'

'And then they wake up as slaves?'

Michael stayed silent. The question needed no answer.

'The Establishment has assisted our efforts for centuries.'

'How?' Benedict was relentless. I was surprised at the effect he had on my brother, how easily he manipulated him to expose the slave trade and the atrocities they were committing.

'By recruiting souls, life essence if you will. They recruit young men to believe they will be reincarnated in heaven after death.'

'And?'

'And the Ventus Dei makes that death happen.'

'You murder them?'

Michael gazed at the men and women around him, his anger mainly on the bishop to his side. His patience with Benedict was gone and he was looking for who he would blame after this confrontation had finished. The look on his face said it all, he'd been taken for a fool by the bishop and all the others who had nominated Benedict, a totally unsuitable candidate. Someone would pay for this. For wasting his time.

He turned back to the real object of his anger.

'No. Not directly.' Michael answered, his tone cold. 'We organise conflict where casualties are common. The recruits are tagged and when they die, they are picked up by our technology.'

'Conflict. Like the violence between the Christian and Muslim fundamentalists.'

'Exactly.'

Benedict looked around at the men and women seated in the thrones. There were people from all religions. So-called enemies, all seated here together for a common cause. One that had nothing to do with any deity or dogma. Their only driving force their own status, wealth and comfort, in this life and the next.

This wasn't religion, this was pure and simple greed.

Some wilted under his gaze, others stared back defiantly.

I moved my head in unison with Benedict, filming them, staying still long enough at each face to imprint the features on the streams.

Benedict was playing a dangerous game here. But it was working. Michael was spilling the proverbial beans. All the secrets the Establishment had been so desperate to keep obscure were now being streamed real-time out into the world. And they had no idea. This was better than we could ever have imagined.

'What's in it for me?' Benedict pulled Michael back to the conversation. It was by no means finished for him. 'And all these people here, your allies.'

My brother cocked his head and creased his brow in confusion.

'Surely you were told how we reward loyal humans?'

'If you mean that crap about a new life in your dimension after my death, then yes.'

'That crap?' Michael's voice bordered on shouting. He leaned forward in his throne, his face again bright purple-red with rage.

Benedict stayed silent while my brother almost blew up.

'What is that supposed to mean?'

Still the archbishop stayed silent, with no outward reaction. I wish I could have seen his face, but I had to make do with Michael's.

'You promise us eternal life in your dimension. We would live as kings?' Benedict asked after a painfully long minute.

'You would.'

'Almost heavenly?'

Michael's irritation prevented him from recognising the big red flags.

He nodded vigorously; his patience evaporated. 'Exactly.'

A silence descended over the attendees. No one dared point out the grave mistake my brother had just made.

'Like you and your minions promise the believers?' Benedict drove it home.

'You doubt our promise?'

'Wouldn't you?' Benedict answered with his own question. 'You just explained how you've scammed believers for centuries by offering them a heavenly afterlife, while--in reality--they encounter a fate worse than hell. And now you promise me the same and expect me to believe you?'

The penny dropped.

…With a massive bang.

'And,' Benedict added to the insult. 'No one has come back to prove what you say.'

The oppressive silence that followed Benedict's challenge was broken by a sound I'd hoped never to hear again.

'I have,' A dark and dangerous voice declared from the shadows behind Michael.

My hearts sank as the familiar black-clad figure emerged from the shadows behind my brother's throne.

Ibrahim strode into the circle directly towards Benedict. He towered over the archbishop, and I have to give Benedict credit for his poise and lack of reaction. He was still not impressed. I, on the other hand, was trembling uncontrollably.

'Are you okay, Gabe?' Ebony's voice felt like the warm hug I desperately needed to calm my frantic nerves. She must have noticed my trepidation in the movement of the camera image.

I nodded slowly, trying to steady my unwanted movements.

'Is that Ibrahim?'

Again, a nod.

'Be strong, Gabe. You're not alone this time.'

I swallowed the bile that rose unwanted to my throat, straightened my spine, forced my hearts to calm down and concentrated on the scene unfolding in front of me.

This mission had just become even more dangerous.

Ibrahim slowly walked around Benedict who remained standing, his attention focussed on Michael. The archbishop refused to be intimidated by Ibrahim's tactics.

The Hashta continued. 'I died and was reincarnated on Taxore. I can contest that all my wishes have been fulfilled.'

He came back to face Benedict, obscuring Michael from his view.

'There, and here, I can do what brings me the most pleasure.' He paused for effect. 'I love to cause immeasurable pain. Taxore has given me unheard of new torture options and the opportunity to practice them to my heart's content.'

The vicious smile and cold laughter that followed his words cut through most of those present, I saw several tremble and try to push themselves further into their thrones. They all recognised the psychopath in the Hashta.

Benedict just stood there. Still and poised. Unflappable.

'So they have bullies there too,' he commented. 'Not my definition of heaven.'

Ibrahim laughed—a deep, haunting sound—turned and walked back to Michael. He took up station beside the throne, now clearly visible for everyone as he scanned the Ventus Dei members. They faltered under his penetrating stare.

The silence could be cut with a knife. No one dared react to the situation. They were at an impasse. Benedict stood patiently while Michael fumed in his seat. The deep furrows on his brow and the depth of his hooded eyes showed his inner struggle. He was adamant not to make another mistake.

It occurred to me that Ibrahim was potentially as much a threat to my brother as he was to me. Cal-Tan had no doubt tasked the Hashta with observing Michael, and after the earlier blunder with Benedict, I wouldn't like to be in his shoes. He kept stealing glances to the side where Ibrahim stood still as a statue, a vicious smirk on his face.

'My lord?' The aide finally asked carefully. 'Should we vote?'

Michael glanced again to his left and Ibrahim nodded almost imperceptibly. Michael's insecurity became even more apparent to me with every minute that passed. My brother—the ultimate bully—had been outclassed. His fear of the Hashta was even greater than his hatred for the man.

Interesting.

The aide looked around, first at Benedict, then Michael. He was flustered.

'Leave him,' Michael read his body language. 'If we vote against him, then Ibrahim can take care of him right here.'

Michael wanted to make an example of the archbishop. He was also declaring his intent. No way would my brother let the insults pass. He would vote against Benedict and expected the Ventus Dei to do the same.

The barely veiled threat was clear to all present.

Benedict's life was hanging by a thread.

We had to intervene. I saw a slight movement in the mezzanine reflected in the big windows, Jonah had come to the same conclusion.'

'We have enough,' I heard in my earpiece, prompting me to raise the muzzle of my silenced semi-automatic.

I stopped my intended advance when a clearly flustered guard approached Ibrahim and handed him a tablet. The man gestured wildly towards the image on the iPad, and I could see Ibrahim's brow crease in anger.

The Hashta spoke a few words to the guard and dismissed him, then stepped towards Michael. He whispered in my brother's ear and showed him the tablet.

Michael's eyes opened in shock, and he looked up from the tablet directly at the spot where I stood.

They'd seen the streams.

They knew.

We attacked.

Chapter Fifty

All hell broke loose.

What moments before had been utter silence, was shattered by piercing screams after Jonah and his team fired from the mezzanine. They took the guards completely by surprise. The stream didn't have an elevation and Ibrahim expected to find the intruders directly opposite him. He was right in that aspect, but he hadn't counted on multiple teams.

As soon as the shots rang out, Aaliyah and I moved from our positions. She flanked to the right; I took the left. Just as well, bullets made short work of the plant pots in the area we'd just vacated. The streams had identified where the filming had taken place. Ibrahim pulled a semi-automatic from the arms of one of his security men and sprayed the dark area under the mezzanine without a thought for the Ventus-Dei or staff caught in the crossfire.

Ceramic shards from the pots and black soil pelted my back as I raced for cover under a table. The rain of bullets was relentless and getting closer to my hiding place.

A wild cry from above the mezzanine heralded the entrance of the big man and that team into the melee. They jumped from the balcony, Jonah's trusty axe swinging as soon as he touched the ground. The blade made short work of two guards and Jonah advanced on the Hashta.

Ibrahim threw his now empty gun to the side and struggled to free his curved sword from its scabbard to ward off the madman attacking him.

Jonah's first wild blow was stopped by the sword, the second—with the big man's full weight behind it—shattered the blade into a million pieces. He stepped back and swung the massive weapon again, only narrowly missing Ibrahim's head as the Hashta dove to the floor.

Ibrahim swung his legs mid fall and mowed into Jonah's calves, breaking his balance so much he had to lower the axe to avoid falling to the ground.

I expected Ibrahim to use this to his advantage, but instead he cartwheeled backwards towards the thrones, regained his feet and grabbed the cowering Michael by his robes. He pulled sharply, throwing Michael into the direct path of Aaliyah who'd come up from the right.

My brother's shock was total. Ibrahim had thrown him to the wolves. Instead of protecting him, he was the reason Michael was in such dire straits.

Ibrahim disappeared from view as his guards surrounded Jonah, hiding him from Michael's view. I pushed forward through the melee to help. Not that he really needed it, Jonah's axe swept through the men like a knife through warm butter and Aaliyah had already dispatched two enemies.

From the corner of my eye, I saw Benedict advance on the bishop with a strong dedicated step. He cracked his knuckles and shook his arms as he rolled his shoulders in anticipation of a confrontation. I remembered Jonah's earlier introduction of the clergy man; he was no stranger to violence. I almost felt sorry for the bishop.

Almost.

The bishop saw Benedict approach and took a step back. His eyes flitted from side to side looking for an escape route, to no avail. Benedict continued his determined advance, his steps strong and menacing.

The bishop stepped back, then again, lost his balance over an upturned chair and fell backwards to the floor, his hands up in front of him in defence. He mumbled something about a brother of the church, but Benedict was relentless. The last thing I saw was that he grabbed the fallen man by the robes, pulled him to his feet and hit him squarely on the chin with a roundhouse punch.

Good for you, Benedict.

The Ventus-Dei members scattered at the sound of the first shots, their own survival clearly the only thing on their mind. Most raced for the perceived safety of the shadows under the balcony, others rushed to leave the scene, falling over each other in their haste. Their progress was halted by an unexpected barrage of shots.

Two of Syl's men still held the mezzanine, the entrance from the first floor firmly barricaded to keep them safe. They peppered the doors on either side of the ballroom, preventing anyone from coming in or, almost as important, going out. We wanted the Ventus-Dei to answer for their crimes. They had to be interrogated—online—about the atrocities they'd perpetrated. Either we would, or the police who were already under way.

'E.t.a forty to fifty minutes,' Ebony's voice had announced over the earpieces.

The remote location gave us some time. We wanted to

be gone before the officials came and we still had time to subdue them, then truss them up for the authorities.

A loud whirring sound came through the windows announcing Ebony's helicopter team had landed on the vast lawn in front of the mansion. They would take care of the guards outside first, then come into the building and support our effort. The large helicopter—an Aerospataile Super Frelon—was also our ticket out of the area. Once we'd secured the building, neutralised the guards and trussed up the Ventus-Dei, we'd make our escape. We didn't need the hassle of explaining ourselves. Our presence would generate too many questions. The police frowned on private armies.

Benedict had declared his intent to stay and relay the full extent of the conspiracy to the police. He counted on his reputation and function to gain their assistance.

The close proximity of the Ventus-Dei members and the staff meant the remaining guards couldn't shoot from a distance and were forced to engage in more hand-to-hand combat. Our teams, all ex-military or at least trained by Sly, were clearly at an advantage. The guard's Rambo knives came out of their scabbards, and they held them threateningly. But the way they moved the blades from side to side and the angle at which they held the weapons showed how unfamiliar they were with a knife fight. Sly and his team quickly disarmed two of the remaining guards and pinned them to the ground, hog-tying the men's hands and then their feet with tie-wrap restraints.

There were only a few left. The originals and five who had managed to enter the room despite the barrage from the mezzanine. Six guards in total still fighting.

The team and Jonah would take care of them.

I changed direction and pushed on to where my brother

stood on trembling legs. My big bully of a brother didn't look so impressive anymore. I saw doubt in the way his eyes flitted from one fighter to another and in his erratic movements.

There were too many guards between us for me to get to him straight away. I ended up in hand-to-hand combat with one of them, and saw Michael grab his sword from behind the throne he'd just vacated so spectacularly.

His self-confidence regained with his favourite weapon in hand, he jumped into the melee and slashed at as many of our team as he could. Anger once again overpowering the self-doubt.

Our team had been briefed on the use of swords and other large cutting weapons by people from my dimension but were quite unequipped to counter the slashes with their firearms. They moved out of reach and trained their guns on the sword wielders. A few warning shots at Michael's feet made him hesitate.

I walked over to where he was at an impasse with two of our team.

He lowered his sword when he saw me and observed my approach. His eyes shot daggers at me, the hatred cutting through any moral high-ground I found myself on. He despised me. That was apparent. Though my emotion might not be quite as strong, I found myself revelling in his somewhat hopeless situation. The boot was now on the other foot. I was the brother with the advantage. He, the one with the shorter straw. Quite a novelty.

He followed my every move as I lined up opposite him, my own sword now parallel with my right leg. Even with the fire power at our disposal, Taxorian traditional swords were our weapons of choice, and this was between him and me. Neither of us would degrade ourselves to the use of anything other than up-close-and-personal weapons.

It had finally come to this.

Our centuries of competition for our father's elusive approval. The rivalry. The hatred Cal-Tan had installed in us. It had been inevitable. Everything led to this fight to the death. Both of us knew that without a doubt. It was the only way we could finally settle all those countless years of sibling rivalry and animosity.

I stared directly in his eyes, he in mine. Contempt was the first and foremost emotion I read in his hard face, his upturned upper lip, the tightness in his clenched jaws. But there was something else; fear.

Michael knew I was the better sword fighter. I'd won more sparring sessions than lost. He was fighting for his life. His very eternal existence. He took a deep breath, his nostrils flaring, clenched his muscles and blinked. That one small action alerted me to his attack and as he propelled his bulk towards me, his arm backwards in a slashing motion, I'd already moved to the other direction and easily parried his first onslaught.

I swivelled on the heels of my feet, slashed downwards releasing my blade and nicked his leg. Michael stepped backwards in a reflex to the sudden pain. Purple blood coloured his leg from just above the knee downwards. He glanced down, his ego wounded more than his leg. With a scream of anger, he rushed me. Again, I parried his attack easily and nicked him again, now on the upper arm.

Michael's weak point was his anger. The apparent ease with which I was able to ward off his attacks fed his temper and clouded his judgement. His ego pushed him to intensify his mindless onslaught.

Again, I cut him. This time on his back. And again, only

that time he turned unexpectedly and drew blood from my side. I'd have to reign in my own ego. Even with his temper, Michael was a contender. He wasn't someone to play with.

We slashed and thrust, parried and bled, for what seemed like a lifetime. All sounds of the continuing battle around us faded into the background. I didn't see, didn't hear, other than my brother. My nemesis. Nothing else existed for us.

Fatigue was setting in, our movements slowed slightly, especially Michael's. None of the wounds I'd inflicted on him were life threatening, but together they amounted to a considerable loss of blood. I could see the effect in Michael's erratic movements. His anger kept him going, but even that wouldn't be enough soon.

It had to end.

...I had to end it.

I stood opposite Michael, my feet shoulder width, knees slightly bent, the sword lowered, its blade pointing to the floor. My head was bent down, my view from under my eyebrows concentrated only on my opponent.

His face was flushed and sweat dripped off his brow. Michael grabbed the hilt of his weapon with both hands in an attempt to quell his shoulder's distinct tremor that transcended to the arm holding his sword. His chest rose in short hard breaths, weariness and loss of blood taking its toll. The resentment in his eyes shot daggers at me in a futile bid to impress me.

Michael took a big breath and attacked me with all the force left in him. He swung his sword from the left shoulder downwards slashing for my gut. I jumped back a step, then turned sideways as his momentum pushed him forward past where I'd just been. He stumbled, slashed his sword back again where it clashed full force against mine, shattering Michael's blade into a thousand shards.

I turned, slashed sideways, opened a deep wound in the back of his thigh, cutting the hamstrings and he ploughed to the floor, unable to stand anymore.

I turned to where he sat on his knees staring at the pathetic remnants off his treasured weapon. I stepped forward and raised my sword two-handed up over my head.

One downward slash was all it would take.

Just one.

Time stood still.

And so, did I.

Chapter Fifty-One

'Go on, do it!' Michael screamed.

I stopped the sword ten inches from his exposed neck, my arms shaking with the effort. Every muscle in my body screamed at me to do it, to kill him. The voice in the back of my head shouted that Michael would do the same to me, he would slaughter me without a moment's hesitation. Like my father. They had proven that many times.

But I wasn't them.

I was me.

I looked down at my brother on his knees in front of me. His eyes closed tightly shut, beads of sweat dripping from his brow down his face. Despite his bravura, he trembled uncontrollably.

Time had no meaning. The moment frozen in time.

I stared at Michael, the bane of my existence as a child and as an adult. Images of the torment he'd put me through all my life flashed before my eyes. How he'd beaten me, belittled me, made me suffer. The voice screamed again that I should kill him. I should end the suffering and self-doubt he'd put me through my whole life. The muscles in my arms tensed with the anger I felt in the core of every cell in my body. He was the reason I had hurt so much, why I was no longer able to see my family. He was the reason I was alone.

He....

In my mind's eye, I looked past my brother to what had formed him into the bully he had become.

I saw my father.

I saw him laugh at my failure to stand up to my brother. His amusement when I was pushed to the ground and pummelled by Michael's fists. His disgust when I lost the fights, even though Michael was much bigger than me, much stronger. He was relentless in my persecution. I saw the praise he gave Michael after yet another punishment.

The realisation slowly hit me that Michael was as much a victim of our father's manipulation and sadistic degradation as I was. Sure, he'd complied, whereas I'd rebelled. But in the end, his life—like mine—was formed by one man. One vindictive, narcissistic, sadistic bastard; Cal-Tan. Our father.

The tension in my arms abated and I slowly lowered the sword.

The silence between us could be cut with a knife. It was loaded. Full of emotion and anger. Not just on my side.

The fighting had abated somewhat, our team clearly in control.

Slowly, Michael opened his eyes. His brow was creased with the confusion he obviously felt. He looked at me and slowly shook his head. What was happening?

I took a deep breath and answered his unspoken question.

'I won't kill you, Michael. There's been enough violence in our family, enough bloodshed.' I said. 'No more.'

There was a hint of relief in his eyes, even gratitude maybe, though that might be wishful thinking on my part.

It was short lived.

'I will.' Jonah came out of the fray and strode resolutely towards my kneeling brother.

Michael did a double take. He fell backwards from what he perceived was a ghost. His face was ashen, his eyes questioning what he saw.

'That's impossible,' he stammered. 'You're dead.' He looked at me, then back to the apparition that had invaded his mind.

Jonah continued his advance on my brother.

'Nah. Boring,' he said, his lips curled up in a vicious smile. 'So, I came back.'

Terror caused Michael to scuttle backwards like a crab. To no avail, Jonah kept up his intended approach.

'No! No! That's not possible' Michael screamed. 'You can't be alive. The body died. Its hearts stopped.'

He stared at Jonah, noticed the tattoos, the scars. His eyes opened to their max as the realisation struck him.

'You're in your old body?'

'Yep. The original thing. Much better than the crap your lot gave me.' Jonah's voice was laced with dangerous sarcasm.

Michael looked at me, shocked. He couldn't comprehend what had happened.

'That's not possible. Humans don't have the technology.'

'They do now,' I answered coldly.

He was speechless.

Understandably.

'No. No. No!' He kept repeating himself, as though that would change the situation. 'It can't be.'

Jonah just smiled. A deep, scary, wild smile that froze even my blood and made my hearts skip a beat. He was going to do it. He was going to kill my brother.

I couldn't let that happen.

'Please don't, Jonah,' I found myself saying. 'It's time to stop the killing.'

'I've only just started.' The smile had turned into a grimace.

'I'm not going to ask for him, but as a friend,' I implored him. 'I'm asking you not to kill him. He's a pawn. No more and no less. Cal-Tan is your enemy, not his misguided minions.'

Jonah looked at me incredulously. 'I can't get at your father—yet—so I'll take him in the meantime.'

He pointed his axe at Michael. 'He put me through a lot of hurt, time to return the favour.'

We were back to my father instead of Cal-tan. Jonah was making it personal again.

'It won't help the pain. I know. I've tried. We dealt Cal-Tan a massive blow today. The Establishment has been exposed. Its days are numbered. We've done what we set out to do. More bloodshed isn't necessary.'

'It is for me.'

'No.' I stepped forward to emphasise my words. 'This is your own personal vendetta. It has nothing to do with our cause. Michael is not a threat.'

'He'll go home and report to your father,'

'Good luck with that. Cal-Tan will tear him apart.'

I refused to call him my father. I also had to diffuse this situation as quickly as possible, before it cost my brother his life. But that didn't mean I had to be nice. The truth would be my friend here.

'He's failed him. Failed him big time. Michael will lose

any position he had and be relegated to a nobody. He's not a threat. Not anymore. Killing him will only focus Cal-Tan's anger on us even more.'

I glanced at my brother. The understanding of his predicament had sunk in. His face revealed his understanding. He was screwed, whatever happened. Here he could die —permanently. Back home he would face Cal-Tan's wrath. I'm not sure which option was better.

Michael's nostrils flared as he drew in a big breath. His body trembled with the terror he must have felt.

Slowly he came to his feet, pushing his body up with his right hand. The slashed hamstring gave him a lopsided stance.

'Stay where you are,' Jonah ordered him.

'Or what?' Michael shouted defiantly. 'You'll kill me? Last thing I heard you were going to do that anyway.'

'I still am.' Jonah's voice was dangerously calm. He placed both hands on the hilt of the axe and brought it up to his shoulder.

'Then do it.' Michael had made his choice. Death was better than facing Cal-Tan. I couldn't blame him. But I didn't want him to die.

'No!' I intervened. 'No more.'

'Not up to you,' Jonah threw back at me.

'Don't do it Jonah. Don't let him rile you.'

'Not necessary. I'll gladly end his pathetic life.'

I stepped forward placing myself partially in front of my brother. 'Please, Jonah. Don't.' I tried one last time.

He looked me in the eye, his gaze so intense it was difficult not to falter. The big man was a formidable opponent, and I didn't want to cross him. But in this case, I felt I had to. I saw it register. Jonah was debating it. I couldn't ask for more in the circumstances.

I almost had him.

Then Michael screwed it up again.

'Are you seriously going to let Gabriel talk you out of it?' Michael taunted the big man. 'I thought you were more than that. But no, just another minion to a god's son.'

Jonah's face darkened, his upper lips trembled as he fought to stay where he was, but Michael's words were as toxic as I remembered so well from my childhood.

'Let me live and I will kill you again like the insect you are,' my brother added, pushing the insults deeper.

Jonah snorted, then pulled his lips into a frightening grimace as he gnashed his teeth. 'Nah. Been there, done that—twice. Not a fan. You on the other hand need a lesson.'

I placed my hand on his chest to try and stop what was inevitable. It was useless.

Jonah pushed me out of the way hard, and I stumbled backwards, a shout on my lips as I fell to the ground.

The big axe was raised to the side and swung in an arc annihilating everything in its path. My brother didn't even try to avoid the weapon. He knew what was coming. It was what he'd chosen.

Death by Jonah.

Purple blood sprayed on me from the decapitated body as it fell to the ground. The head tumbled to the other side, the eyes closed, almost in peace.

'No!' I completed the cry that was stuck in my throat.

Jonah stood over Michael's body, watching the blood seep out in a big pool of dark purple. All I could do was stare at the scene.

Another sibling dead.

I thought about my mother. Her pain. And felt a stab deep into my chest.

No one moved. Me least of all.

I felt deflated. Empty. All energy seeped out of me with the blood from my brother's body.

Aaliyah was the first to stir. She approached the body and reached out her hand to pluck Michael's amulet from his still form. I knew what she wanted to do. Without the amulet, Michael wouldn't be reincarnated. There were only a few seconds left to intervene.

'Let him go.' Jonah surprised us all.

'What do you mean? he'll be reincarnated.' Aaliyah was fuming.

'Exactly. Let him experience how it feels. But keep his body here. I want him reincarnated in a grunt's body.'

The big man wasn't finished with his vengeance spree.

'Won't happen,' I answered flatly. 'They'll force grow a body based on his DNA, if he doesn't already have one on ice, which I expect. He'll get a better one than the grunts.'

Jonah shrugged. 'Still want him to go through the process.' Jonah wiped his axe on the cloth of my brother's jacket.

'Your dad will go ballistic,' he stated with a smile. 'What will he do?'

'Probably keep him in limbo for a while before he's reincarnated and punish him again once he is.'

'He'll wish he was dead.' The big man laughed.

I realised he'd achieved both punishments, he'd killed Michael and served up his re-incarnated life to Cal-Tan.

No answer was needed.

Aaliyah stepped back, reluctantly. She glanced my way, but I avoided her eyes.

'Good,' Jonah declared, turned and walked away.

I sat there on my knees. My brother's blood almost

touching me as it drained out of his body. I stared at what was left of him.

My tormenter; my brother. Dead.

I felt drained, empty, pain had replaced any relief I could have that I would no longer be the object of his persecution.

This was what it had come to. The vicious circle was complete, once again.

All my actions ended the same. More pain. For me, for my family.

'We need to go after the stragglers,' Jonah was clearly leading the team. 'Get the streams up and keep repeating them. I want everyone to know about the Establishment. Sly, film the ones we captured, and what's left of Michael. Get confessions on tape. Ebs, break into CNN, any news channel, anything that will spread the news. We've got about another twenty minutes before the cops arrive.'

He was taking the initiative, instead of only killing, he was actually doing what needed to be done. It was progress, of a kind.

He glanced at me. Did he want validation? I stayed silent, back from the rest. Not wanting to join in the briefing.

'Gabriel, you head the group after the documents, while we go after the ones that got away.' Jonah tried to pull me into the action.

'No.' My voice was calm and soft. It silenced everyone. They stopped what they were doing and stared at me.

Jonah raised his eyebrow and observed me quizzically.

I looked at him, then transferred my gaze to Sly and the others. My brothers in arms. People who had jumped onto our quest. They'd had my back, more often than not. Some even saved my life. These were my people. My new family. My cause. My quest. Or more accurately, they had been.

'I'm done.' I stated clearly, standing up.

'You're what?'

I locked eyes with the big man. 'I'm finished. I don't have the stomach for it anymore. I've had enough.'

A weight lifted off my shoulders by just saying the words. I couldn't do this anymore, fight against my family, my kind. Everything I'd ever known for hundreds of years. Yes, they were wrong. They had done terrible things. No. WE had done terrible things, me included. But they were still part of me. Michael had been my big brother. A terrible bully, a tormented soul. Now he was dead. His body lying in a pool of purple blood. Blood that was the same as mine. Not like these people here. Not human. Mine.

Jonah reached out and laid his hand on my arm. I looked up at him. His face a combination of anger and concern.

'You can't leave now,' he said softly, emotion in his features and tone.

But I was adamant.

I knew what I had to do. I smiled an apology but stayed resolutely with my decision.

'Watch me.'

I turned and walked away.

Chapter Fifty-Two

We couldn't go back to Kate's house. It was still on the Establishment's radar and according to our undercover man Brain, they were still observing the house. A new older couple had moved in, the homeowner quick to rent out after Kate disappeared.

Ebony offered us the apartment in Las Vegas, but we were not in the mood for huge crowds. The alternative turned out to be a camper. Not your regular run of the mill, back to nature experience, but a more Ebony-style camper bus with all the luxury of home, on wheels.

We embraced the idea of travelling the eastern states, avoiding highways and large towns, only setting up camp in the vast forests or small villages we encountered.

It was peaceful.

An escape.

Exactly what I needed.

The satellite connection in the camper kept us up to date on what was happening in the world, but we felt quite removed from it all. It was happening around us, not to us.

We came closer to each other with every mile we travelled, and every starlit night beside an open fire, listening to the nocturnal sounds.

I held her close and pulled the blanket closer, revelling in our contact and the peace the forests gave me. I had a lot to process. Not just the exposure of the Establishment and Michael's death, but everything else. Jonah's death, his reincarnation, my harrowing return to Taxore. All of it. Not forgetting the revelation my mother sprung on me.

It had been too much. I needed to get out. I had to get some kind of order in my head.

Chapter Fifty-Three

Chaos reigned.

It was too much to comprehend for the fragile human perception. Too many challenges to their psychic. They couldn't handle it. Not that much, not all at once.

Their beliefs, the understanding that they would transition to a better life, had been shattered. The very foundation of life as many knew it had been pulled out from under their feet. They didn't know where to turn to, so used to having their faith to fall back on in times of need. And now it was that same faith that was causing the chaos, or so it seemed.

As we'd feared, most people identified their religion with the atrocity they'd seen on the streams. They were unable to make a distinction between their real faith and the rotten apples within the churches. En masse, the people abandoned their faith, their places of worship. But they had nowhere else to go and the sense of loss was immense.

The idea that aliens had invaded Earth, had been there for centuries, only compounded the sense of insecurity.

Conspiracy theories were abundant.

It was the US attempting to undermine the status quo in the world. It was a plot to undermine the strength of the churches. It was the Russians' attempt to overthrow the Western alliance by creating adversity. It was the end of the world.

Internet blasted one after the other imaginary plot over the ether. Nothing was sacred anymore now the dogmas had been exposed as a scam.

Or had they? Was it just a few bad apples? Was the whole idea of heaven and God a farce? Or was it maybe, very, very, maybe, real?

Disbelief quickly turned to rage.

The streams had aired on all important news sites worldwide. Where possible, Ebony repeated them, but the big companies came down hard on their security and hacking became more difficult, even for her genius team.

We'd expected the chaos, the doubt and the anger. Ebony had warned us this would be a difficult message to bring. The natural human response would be to shut down. To find excuses. Reasons, why it would not be true.

The remaining information had to be spoon fed. More would risk a total collapse of human society.

The information the team had gathered was leaked to the news stations at a steady pace to keep the story malleable and newsworthy. Despite all the resistance from the government and the Establishment, it stayed as the number one topic for weeks.

Still, the fall-out had been enormous.

After the initial exposure the major religions reacted with complete silence. In truth, they had no idea how to proceed, who to trust. The shock was too profound. No one dared to take the first step in case it wasn't the right one.

There were no contingency plans for a situation like this. Not in the dogmas, and not with the leaders.

Churches, temples and places of worship opened their doors twenty-four seven, but no one came. The believers deserted their priests, rabbi's and imams. They stayed home, unsure what to believe, but shocked to the bone. The radio silence from their former shepherds enhanced the feeling of loss and abandonment.

Two weeks in, the reality dawned on them and the world leaders.

A witch hunt finally started within all the major religions and governments to root out the bad apples. Arrests in many countries showed how serious the authorities took the information we'd given them, they'd discovered or authenticated themselves.

The UN launched a major investigation, aided by the Vatican, the Islamic leaders and representatives of Hindi, Buddhism and Judaism, that went even further and held the magnifying glass to all leadership worldwide.

The churches were adamant to weed out the bad elements before they completely lost their congregation's support. Raids were on the news on a daily basis, no one was spared, all were subject to scrutiny by governmental and spiritual leaders.

Benedict was foremost in the cleansing of the Christian church. His arrest at the mansion had been quickly overturned and he was portrayed justly as a hero. A man who'd risked his life in an undercover operation to expose the conspiracy that was rotting religion out from the inside. Benedict's friendly but stern visage featured on streams and the television daily, consoling people, giving them hope. Slowly he was able to reassure his flock that the poison hadn't corrupted all those in the churches. That there were still many good men and women in all religions. Not every-thing had been a scam and there was still room to believe.

He also brought the religious leaders together in a before then unseen union. They had a common enemy. One that had undermined all their credibility.

Maybe something good had come of this mess after all.

But it wasn't plain sailing.

The Establishment didn't give up that easily. They fought back, their propaganda machine working overtime. They denounced us as a terrorist group intent on black-listing honest pious men and women while they professed to be the true believers. The Establishment explained it had been them that were bringing the dogmas together to bring an end to the religious animosity and finally achieve world peace.

They proclaimed there was indeed a conspiracy, to undermine the churches and the beliefs of the common man, but it was us perpetuating it, not them. The immense wealth behind the Establishment was geared towards creating even more confusion. More disorientation. And it was working, no one knew what to believe.

And then there was the issue of the aliens.

The world reeled from the realisation that there were aliens among them. For decennia, they'd looked to the sky for extra-terrestrial life, and we'd been there all that time, according to what they were told to believe now.

Science was astounded. How was it possible they'd never encountered alternative dimensions? Aliens? Why hadn't anyone noticed anything? Questions were posed that no one had answers for.

The first reaction was disbelief. It was impossible. Scien-tists and military were joined in their denouncement of the impossible.

But they couldn't explain the purple blood.

Or the bodies of two Taxorians found at the scene.

Two major networks had arrived minutes before the police, curtsy of an anonymous tip, and streamed real-time what they saw. They were quickly ushered out of the mansion—the crime scene as the police called it—and their cameras and film confiscated, but the damage was done. They'd filmed and aired the dead aliens, the blood, the strange weapons. The images had been picked up by Reuters and other news services making it impossible to conceal the truth anymore.

The US military, FBI and another service that officially didn't exist, arrived minutes behind the police and quickly took control of the scene, locking it hermetically. No one came in, and no one left until they were fully vetted, interrogated and sworn to secrecy. All phones and technical equipment were seized, never to be seen again.

Ventus-Dei members, the aide and the few remaining guards, were quickly removed from the mansion in military helicopters to an undisclosed location where they would be interrogated. The bodies of the dead guards and the two Taxorians disappeared. Where to? No one knew. Speculation was rampant and the consensus quickly formed that they had been taken to Area 51.

The US senate asked questions, the President asked questions. Everyone did.

No one had answers.

Except us.

Ebony let a steady stream of information seep into the media. She stayed out of sight, her team leaking from different places, in a multitude of languages and locations at the same time, making it impossible to trace.

It was a dangerous tactic. In a world where no one

understood what was happening, someone with information was a potential threat. The authorities were at a loss as to where the intelligence came from. The US government denounced it as a ruse, but the scientific community picked it up and flew with it, drowning out the doubt.

Hers was the only logical explanation, and it quickly picked up support.

We saw NATO mobilise. Images of military power on the news every night.

But they had no idea where to focus their attention. This was an invisible enemy. One that looked so much like themselves that no one could tell the difference. Who were the humans, and who the Taxorians? Confusion reigned.

A general feeling of insecurity was prevalent throughout the world. Paranoia caused people to doubt their friends and neighbours. Were they aliens too?

The foundation of human existence was rocked by the revelation that not only had they already been invaded, but there had been extra-terrestrials deeply embedded within their societies for centuries.

Unbridled speculation questioned every major event in history. From the ridiculous to the outrageous.

Were the aliens behind the sinking of the Titanic?

Was Elvis an alien?

Had he gone home?

Chapter Fifty-Four

The podcasts revealed shards of what had happened on Taxore after the Establishment's exposure.

I slowly pieced the story together from three separate sessions and the picture was disturbing to say the least.

Ibrahim had returned to Taxore with tales that enraged Cal-Tan to the extreme. No one dared go anywhere near him for two days, no one but Ibrahim. Like me, my mother was worried about the Hashta's influence on Cal-Tan, who'd become even more blood thirsty and bent on revenge.

News of Michael's death had also reached her, and I felt the intense pain in the words she'd written. Tears gathered at the edge of my eyes unwanted, as I contemplated the sorrow she must be going through. She loved her children equally, whether they were aligned with her or with Cal-Tan.

She knew who the real culprit was.

As I'd expected, Cal-Tan decided to keep Michael's essence in limbo for a while. Of course he had a pre-growth, but it had not been prepared for reincarnation yet. It was still in deep sleep. I hated being right. I knew Cal-Tan would really let him suffer. Jonah had royally screwed my brother.

Mother was heartbroken. I hoped my reassurance that it had not been me who had killed her eldest would at least lighten the blow slightly, but the reality was he was dead and still out of reach until our sadistic father decided he'd suffered enough.

She also cautioned us that Cal-Tan was plannings something. What? She didn't know.

How we were to prepare for that was beyond me. His potential reaction to what we had done was so broad, taking preventive measures was all but impossible. We assumed he would send more Hashta to hunt us down. Especially as he was now aware of Johan's resurrection. So Ebony monitored as much as she could, searching for new transportations—curtsy of her and Tajan's new inventions—and the team used AI to scan the multitude of CCTV and other streaming devices within a radius of seventy miles from the current headquarters.

Though she never indicated it, I was sure Ebony's surveillance also reached to Kate and myself. More than once she suggested new locations where there was beautiful nature, somewhere we should go visit. They were soft pushes to move. To not stay in one place long enough for the Establishment to find us.

I relayed everything I heard back to Ebony. Every time I spoke to her it tugged at my hearts.

But I needed this time for me, and for Kate. I needed to breathe again after all the planning and the violence. We'd lived our quest day and night for so long I felt empty and deflated once I left the rat race.

Initially, I descended into a deep depression. Something I hadn't expected. I thought once I distanced myself, I would feel better, but the opposite was true. I was without a goal, a reason to live. It was debilitating and I spent days either staring at the scene from my bed or walking through wild and often dangerous nature reserves. I finally found a renewed distraction in climbing. No nets, no safety lines. Just sheer cliffs and me.

In hindsight, not a very good idea, maybe even a bit suicidal. I think guilt was my drive. For surviving, when Michael hadn't. For starting all this—even if that hadn't been me. I blamed myself for everything. My life. My family's woes. All religious conflict on Earth.

Again, not realistic. But that wasn't my main concern at the time.

After a period of black depression and self-doubt, not to mention a pathetic bout of victim syndrome, I finally climbed out of the deep pit I'd dug for myself. Literally climbed. The physical exhaustion I experienced on the cliff faces worked like a balm. A cleansing penitence, if you want.

Whatever, it worked.

But it wasn't all me. Kate stood by me all the time. Bringing me food and drink when I was too pathetic to leave the bed, to bandaging my wounds when a climb didn't go so well. Listening to me whine, rant and question life itself.

Her calm presence soothed me. She was a rock I could always return to. I'd never experienced a romantic relationship like this. One based on empathy, understanding and blind dedication. Whatever I did, she brought me back. I am forever in her debt. Though she sees it differently.

Slowly, I started to feel alive again.

Every night we talked.

Kate encouraged me to voice my emotions. Once I started, the tsunami of words just exploded from my mouth.

I told her about my youth, how much I'd missed a big brother, someone to look up to. The explanation of my family's dynamics brought me to tears and made me angry at the same time.

We laughed, I cried, and all the time she held me, giving me the strength to deal with every challenge I'd experienced during my lifetime.

For the first time in my whole existence, I felt at ease. Relaxed. At peace.

It was a strange feeling, but one I relished.

We enjoyed each other's company, the scenery, travelling and our extended holiday. I could live like this for centuries, experiencing new things every day. I'd never felt like this before, never felt so strongly for any one woman.

The world seemed just a bit more beautiful. Sounds were crystal clear, and colours were bright.

Life was good.

…Until we turned on the news.

Chapter Fifty-Five

It had been seven weeks since I walked out on the team.

What now?

Good question.

I knew Cal-Tan wouldn't let this lie. He couldn't. We'd beaten him. Exposed his business here on earth and brought it to a halt.

During the past three days a sense of foreboding slowly crept into my mind and body. Goosebumps sprang up unasked on my arms, and I felt nauseous and light-headed. Something was wrong. Something was going to happen.

I don't know where it came from, other than the conviction that my father would not let this pass.

We'd effectively ruined his business here on earth. He might be able to salvage part of it, but the cat was out of the bag. The success they'd had in the past would not be reproduced.

My father had a bone to pick with us. Or, more accurately, a whole skeleton. Cal-Tan was vengeful, and we'd made him look bad. One of his sons fought against him, and another had the audacity to die on the battlefield. Not good publicity.

We hadn't heard the last from him, or from Taxore. Of that I was certain.

I racked my brains to imagine his reaction. What would he do? What could we do to counter him? How could we prepare? But I came up empty every time.

It was deathly silent, no news from Taxore after the initial podcasts. Too quiet. I could only imagine the pressure the resistance was under. If Cal-Tan couldn't punish us, he was bound to take his anger out on anyone close to him.

I worried for my mother's safety.

A thought occurred to me, something we'd discussed weeks ago. Cal-Tan had frozen the slave trade to businesses in Taxore. He was recruiting mercenaries. Why? We'd deduced he had a new dimension to trade with and was focussing all his attention and resources on that. A dimension with great commercial possibilities. It made sense. So maybe he wasn't so bothered about Earth right now.

But that explanation didn't sit right with me. It wasn't logical. Not even for Cal-Tan. Especially after our actions.

He had a plan, one that already gave me shivers and sleepless nights.

We'd kept in touch.

The gang and I.

Ebony missed me, us, she said it every time we spoke. And I'm sure Jonah felt the same. It was mutual. Kate and I missed them. I'd greatly underestimated how important this new family was to me. Leaving them behind had felt like an even greater loss than when I left Taxore for the last time. It affected my body and soul.

There was no real dilemma. We would go back. I

needed them to stay sane. Just as how I'd needed this break. It had been temporary, but necessary.

Besides, we had to prepare for whatever Cal-Tan would throw at us, and we would be safer together.

The new normal was something humans had great difficulty adapting to. It ate at the very foundation of their beliefs. Not just spiritually, also in their faith in science. And in their confidence. They had been so sure of their ability to identify threats, either human or not. This revelation hurt them in the depths of their implied superiority.

All scenarios had been centred around humans as the superior species. And now they realised they had been played for centuries. It ate at their perception of self-worth, and with that came anger. Anger, helplessness and fear.

Under those threatening circumstances, humans revert to a perceived security by arming themselves. Gun sales skyrocketed. Former competitors joined forces. All to regain their sense of control.

It wouldn't help.

They couldn't turn back time.

The government came down hard on everyone they labelled an accomplice of the aliens. Paranoia reigned like never before. Or maybe like in the Middle Ages, with the witch hunts and the inquisition.

I'd stayed out of sight. Decided against revealing my true self. My purple blood and alien origin would put me squarely in the enemy corner. So I remained under the radar, as did Aaliyah and Tajan.

The initial gratitude for revealing the scam had been short lived. Jonah was back on the fugitive list, and I knew there were many organisations—not just the Establishment —searching for us. We'd opened pandora's box. Someone had to pay the bill for that.

Ebony had remained blissfully undetected. I had no idea how she did that. But she achieved the impossible. She stayed out of the limelight. No one knew of her existence, let alone her involvement. Good for you Ebs. She was our ace in the hole.

Something told me we would need her more than ever soon.

A clever man would stay hidden.

But it was time to go back home.

The only home I'd really known.

Chapter Fifty-Six

'Are you seeing this?'

Ebony's voice wavered. That in itself was enough to send shivers up my spine. She never, never, wavered.

Jonah and I dropped what we were doing and joined her in front of the super-sized TV.

The images were terrifying.

Utter chaos reigned in the centre of Los Angeles. Terrified people ran in all directions from the centre of the image on the screen. They pushed each other out of the way violently in their hysteria to escape the purple light waves imploding all around them.

Haphazardly abandoned, crashed and burned cars littered the road and made it more difficult for the screaming people to escape. They wove through the obstacles, falling often, but their terror pushed them forward.

My gaze immediately focussed on the dust cloud in the middle of the screen, the origin of the light flashes. Thick dust camouflaged what I instinctively knew was there.

Dread clawed at me with ice cold fingers around my hearts. I knew what this was. I was sure.

This was vengeance.

'The police have no idea what is going on,' the reporter shouted into his microphone. 'But I'm seeing devastation and what looks like dead bodies all around. This has to be a terrorist attack. The dust prevents us from seeing exactly what's going on but by studying the blast we know the attack took place in the vicinity of the Los Angeles Center Studios.'

We were glued to the screen.

'People are being shot with what looks like laser beams. Purple bursts of light that stops them in their tracks.' His voice bordered on hysteria. 'The authorities are clueless as to the kind of weapons these are. No one has seen anything like this before.'

We had.

Aaliyah look at me, my dread mirrored in her creased forehead, tight lips and balled fists.

'What are they?' Jonah asked. He'd seen our exchange of glances.

'Lunaris,' Aaliyah answered. 'Experimental weapons.'

'From Taxore?' Jonah asked.

We nodded simultaneously.

The implications were clear. This was not a human terrorist attack. It was inter-dimensional.

My father had taken our war to this world.

'We're sending up a drone,' the voice on the screen shouted over the consternation. 'To see what's going on in the dust.'

The camera angle changed as it switched to the drone. It rose slowly from ground level until it was above the trees and the three-story buildings. The lens swivelled from the initial ground view to the foreboding black-grey cloud of dust. The drone moved forward carefully, following the road. The pilot manoeuvred it skilfully past the purple bursts that spilt the sky closer to the centre of the attack.

The images showed devastation. Burning cars, bodies strewn over the sidewalk, broken glass from the shop windows. Still, people tried to flee the scene. Some wounded, others simply terrified.

The drone neared the foreboding cloud and hovered forty feet above street level. The camera swivelled from side to side, attempting to pierce the dust and smoke.

We made out figures.

Big humanoid postures sporting the weapons that shot the purple lasers. They were dressed in predominantly white combat gear with dark splotches of grey and muddy-green camouflage. Crossed on their backs were the characteristic swords of my people.

One figure walked out of the smoke and looked up at the drone. His violet eyes were clearly visible as was the rigid grimace on his features. He snarled, lifted the laser and blasted the drone into a million small pieces. The image on the tv screen went blank and the last picture of the soldier burned in my mind. The psychopathic grin on his face chilled my blood.

We watched in silence, stunned at the level of violence. The soldiers gunned down anyone in their way, men, women and children. No distinction was made.

The camera crew were way too close to the fighting.

They moved back slowly, too slowly. A figure appeared in the right side of the image. The cameraman turned, and with him the view. We saw the weapon discharge, then the picture swept up to the sky.

The camera crew were gone.

A new image appeared on the screen. A scene in Moscow, a replica of the situation in LA. Then Washington, London, Beijing, Sydney. All over the world, the massacre repeated itself. Groups of white clad soldiers mowed down any human they could find.

We were stunned.

There was nothing we could say.

This was terror. Intended to break any resistance that might be residual in the enemy. I'd seen it before in other dimensions. Make the first impression count. Scare them into submission.

I glanced at Ebony. She had her hand up to her mouth in shock. Her face was ashen, and tears started to form at the edge of her eyes. Jonah pulled her close into his safe embrace. His brow was creased in worry. He looked me in the eye. I could see he was mulling over the same questions as I was.

'Did we cause this?' he asked, his voice almost a whisper.

'Is this our fault?'

I was numb. The terrible images burned into my brain.

Then my blood went cold as the realisation hit me like a brick wall.

I staggered back. Jonah glanced at me, his face full of concern.

We hadn't thwarted Cal-Tan.

We'd played right into his cards. We'd given him that one last push to do what he'd always intended.

Cal-Tan hadn't amassed an army for another dimension.

It was for Earth.

This was an invasion.

Chapter Fifty-Seven

We're underground now.

We have to be.

Thank goodness for Ebony and her team. We wouldn't have had a chance without them.

Cal-Tan won.

His blitzkrieg had the intended result. No one dared oppose him or the Establishment. Not after the carnage the initial probe caused.

Thousands were dead, maybe even hundreds of thousands.

Thousands more would follow. Cal-Tan didn't take prisoners. He had no use for the wounded. Never one to waste potential, young men were injected with nanos and dispatched to be reincarnated. The rest were executed on the spot.

It would only get worse.

Thousands of people were herded into former stadiums and concert halls, where they were sorted. Those of use were taken to camps. Others were subjected to tests to see if they could serve on Earth in any way. If not... Well, I don't need to spell it out.

There is a world-wide witch hunt on for Jonah and me. Nowhere is safe for us. We are public enemy number one.

The past ten days have been a haze. A terrifying blur.

The invasion threw the world upside down. Resistance was quashed within the first day, curtsy of the Establishment. They still had people in higher places than we'd ever imagined. People in government.

Steve Nolan, the US Vice president took control of America and immediately placed the country under martial law. Only this time the governing troops had two hearts and purple blood.

The same power change happened in many countries, either because of the Establishment's existing influence or just the overwhelming power the invaders possessed with their high-tech weapons.

They've won.

The Establishment is the de-facto ruling power on Earth.

...And they're all after us.

Next in the The Dominion Series

vinci-books.com/insurrection

Hope hides in the shadows.

In just five days, the Cal-Tan crushed Earth with ruthless force. Humanity surrendered—almost. We're the last resistance, hiding in a secret mountain base brimming with weapons… and painful secrets.

Turn the page for a free preview…

Insurrection: Chapter One

Five days.

It only took them five days to conquer Earth.

Humans tried to resist. Armies joined forces with previously internal and external enemies and attacked the invaders. Nothing like a common enemy to break down boundaries.

But the invader's overwhelming fire power and complete disregard for life—their own and that of the humans—quickly overwhelmed the Earthen forces. They targeted government cities in all major nations, devastating the seat of power and killing or capturing the heads of state, then made a streamed spectacle of their long and painful deaths. The message was clear. Anyone who dared to oppose them would be terminated in pain-filled agony.

Casualties were rampant and estimated to be just shy of a million. That number was lower than expected only because the stats were still coming in. The prognosis was at least double.

Cal-Tan was making a hell of a point.

'Is this our fault?' I whispered for the umpteenth time.

'He would have done it anyway,' Aaliyah answered. 'It was just a matter of time.'

I couldn't shrug off our involvement in this as easily as she could. It was my family that was responsible for this genocide, not hers. And I wasn't so sure he would have actually done it if we hadn't pushed his hand.

Who was I kidding? Of course he would have. He'd been planning this for a long time. Something like a mass invasion takes preparation and time.

'We could have warned them,' I continued my useless self-pity rampage. 'Told them the invasion was imminent.'

Jonah looked at me incredulously. 'How?'

I stammered. There had to have been been something we could have done.

'They wouldn't believe us. Didn't even buy into the whole Establishment thing until Ebony sent the last data. And even then, I don't think they actually understood what they were facing. And, not to forget, we didn't know.' He shrugged.

'We could have tried.' I sounded like a broken record and was just about as useful.

'Stop kicking yourself, Gabriel,' Aaliyah sighed. 'We've been over this countless times. There was nothing we could have done. Besides, it's moot. What's important is what we do now. How we combat this.'

'Can we even do that?' Jonah asked.

'We can sure as hell try.'

That summed it up quite eloquently.

'I question whether we should jump in straight away or wait,' Jonah stated uncharacteristically.

Aaliyah and I both looked at him in surprise.

'Don't get me wrong, I want to kill as many invaders as possible. But…'

Never thought I'd hear a "but" in this context from the big man.

'But we don't really know what we're facing. How many there are. And how many of us—any form of resistance—are left. We should plan our response.'

He was right. Though I'd never expected restraint from him. Even Aaliyah had to reluctantly agree.

'What do we do in the meantime?' A small voice asked from the corner.

I'd forgotten Tajan was here, but he was as much a fugitive as we were. More maybe, his stay on Earth was still relatively fresh and he wasn't used to the dimension yet.

After the initial invasion, we'd quickly determined that —besides complete world domination—our team would be Cal-Tan's main focus. He wanted us dead or at least stopped. This blitzkrieg was designed to quell any resistance or rebellion in record time, and he couldn't use our stubborn obstruction or the hope we might perpetuate. He aimed for total command as soon as possible and our continued existence was a threat to him.

Delay was bad for business.

His strategy worked.

We had to go underground.

Most of us, that is.

Ebony and some of her crew stayed put. Their cover stories, whatever they were this time, were still intact and they monitored the situation from there. We reasoned Aaliyah, Jonah, Tajan, Kate and I were probably top of Cal-tan's most wanted list as well as some of Ebony's people who were too interesting for my father to pass up on. He wanted slaves, either dead—to be reincarnated—or alive. It wasn't safe up top anymore for the likes of Tyrone, Caleb and Nasheed. So they joined us, literally underground.

Thank goodness Cal-Tan had never unearthed the connection we had with Ebony. I hoped she would stay safe and out of harm's way. With the Thirty-eighth dimension now also accepting female slaves, she could be in the crosshairs. But I trusted her to stay out of trouble and there was always Sly to contend with, though he alternated between our group and Ebony.

Tajan was lost without her. Aaliyah tried to console him, to no avail. He'd found new reason and meaning for life working with our computer wizard on the inventions they'd created together, and now that was gone. He was effectively a lot worse off than he had been in Taxore. There he hadn't been actively hunted. And his family was on Taxore, he was terrified what would happen to them. I felt sorry for him. My choice had at least been my own. He was more or less pulled into the fray by Aaliyah and the rest of us.

Talking about my other reluctant Taxorian friend. Initially she'd wanted to go off on her own. A one-woman suicide mission to kill as many invaders as possible before they annihilated her. Jonah managed to talk sense into her and convince her anything would be a lot better than what was waiting if she went alone. Cal-Tan would love to get his hands on her, almost as much as he wanted to catch me. Reluctantly, she conceded.

Around us, homes were raided, people executed in the streets and others taken away. There wasn't a family left that hadn't been impacted in some painful and terrifying manner. Daily streams showcasing the invader's intentions dissolved human's resistance to the new order. They became numb to the blood and gore on the TV stations and all around them.

Cal-Tan effectively quashed the resistance by killing human spirit.

They had lost too much and capitulated.

Insurrection: Chapter Two

Underground was a parking garage in the centre of Los Angeles, right in the middle of the affluent financial sector.

After the first invasion wave, we'd moved out of town, but the need to help in whichever way we could, forced us to go back. This was where the invaders were harvesting their prisoners, the men and few women who would be sent off-world.

'Have you heard from your contacts on Taxore?' Aaliyah asked yesterday evening after yet another cold dinner, we didn't dare to start a fire, not even this deep underground.

I shook my head. 'The last communication dated from before the invasion. The coded message was short, only stating Cal-Tan's personal trip to the Thirty-eighth dimension. That alone is food for thought. He's always restricted his own transportation to the absolute minimum, reluctant to put his life in the hands of others.'

Understandable, that's how he himself ascended to power. His father had been reduced to a gooey mush of blasted cells in a blotched transport. I doubt it was an accident, no one believed that where I came from. It was just too convenient and coincided with the development of the Twelfth dimension—Earth—as a supply route for slaves, something his father had countered. Cal-Tan had a hand in it, I'm sure of that. Besides, it's no more than the enactment of a generations old tradition in our family. The son murders the father.

Aaliyah nodded; she'd heard about Cal-Tan's patricide as well.

I shuddered to think what that meant for me but recognised the same pattern happening between us. He tried to kill me, and I wouldn't hesitate to return the favour. After our last confrontation, it seemed like the only option. The brutal tradition would be perpetuated.

Cal-Tan's interest in the Thirty-eighth was starting to get to me. My mother had no idea why he was so engrossed with the new world; he'd never shown so much enthusiasm for anything before, let alone another dimension. She'd reported that vast amounts of grunts, materials and supplies were being transported there but nothing had come back. What could the business model be for that? My father never did anything if there wasn't a solid profit to be gained. He was single-minded in his pursuit of power though wealth, and this would be another important step in his masterplan. I just wish we knew why that dimension was so important.

'This Thirty-eighth,' Jonah asked. 'Can humans live there?'

I nodded. 'It makes sense for the prisoners here to be transported there. The atmosphere is conducive to human life as well as Taxorian. Probably quite like Earth's. And I can't imagine anywhere else, not with the last information. But the big question remains what his goal is. I feel it's important, because it could potentially help our efforts to thwart him.'

I missed my mother's communications. It was the one last link to my past that I wanted to perpetuate, but it had stopped right after the first invader set foot on Earth. Not only was it way too dangerous for all parties involved, but the method we used—coded public messages—hadn't been available due to the disruption of all media outlets. The invaders had shut them all down and now controlled the information sent out into the world. Personal ads and podcasts were not seen as essential. We were running blind because of that.

Our team undertook small forays into the city to hassle the invaders and to stock up on supplies.

Generally, the most difficult thing to acquire at the moment was gasoline. But that was another benefit of hiding in the parking garage. Many of the neighbouring building's permanent residents had left their vehicles in the garage in the lower, private levels, and we helped ourselves to the gasoline still in them. Yes, I felt bad, if anyone managed to leave, they would end up without fuel, but I reasoned our resistance efforts trumped the remorse I might feel, besides, we never emptied them completely.

There was little comfort underground, but staying alive was the priority. That and irritating the enemy. We stole out in the night and raided their depots, setting fire to anything we couldn't use ourselves, attacked outposts where we killed the grunts manning them, and did our best to disrupt the harvesting.

The kidnapped humans were initially held in large buildings in the city centre, but our frequent attacks pushed the containment facilities further out, first to the suburbs, then the industry segments. The large warehouses made it easier for the Taxorians to defend themselves and their precious cargo. Our efforts dwindled after one monumental attack when the risks became too high for both our team and the prisoners.

Seven of us besieged a warehouse on the outskirts of town next to a residential area. In earlier days it had been a distribution centre for vegetables trucked into the neighbourhood.

I saw three loading docks that offered entrance to the vast open, inner area of the building. There were no windows, just a few small ventilation points high up the wall covered in wire meshing and the three offices at the left side of the loading docks. The fenced area around the warehouse was flat with truck bays lining the space between the warehouse and the road and neighbours about twenty metres away on both sides. At the back, high mesh fencing was almost up against the warehouse walls. The proximity to other buildings made that our best entry point.

It went well, up to the point where we threw a smoke bomb into one of the open loading docks. Then, all hell broke loose. Blue laser beams peppered the outside area and pinned us to the walls of the warehouse, after which the invaders started shooting through the panelling itself, leaving massive holes where the material had been literally melted away.

We dove for the ground and scrambled away from the docks; our only real entry point which had just become a death trap. Retreat was our only option. I crept along the building edge and had almost reached the fence at the back just as the invaders swung their attention to the prisoners.

The screams of terror and pain from inside the building made me turn on my heels. I couldn't leave them. Jonah and Nasheed had already entered the building by the time I reached the dock and dispatched two of the invaders. A further two continued to train their weapons on the prisoners with absolutely no regard for their own or the human's lives. Jonah mowed one down. The other was taken out by fire from Tyrone and me. But not before they'd achieved their goal.

More than sixty young men lay at our feet, all of them dead or dying. The invader's firepower had been so extensive some of them had been literally dismembered in the onslaught. There was nothing we could do for them. Nasheed found one man alive, but he died moments later in terrible pain.

The only sound was the drip of a broken water pipe.

The silence was oppressive and pushed heavily on my hearts. This should have been a freedom mission, now it was a slaughter.

'Why did they do that?' Tyrone asked, his voice resonating in the empty hall.

'To safeguard the investment,' I answered, the words cold but true.

'How's that?'

'They will be reincarnated on Taxore,' I explained. 'The guards killed them so that they could be harvested.'

'Sick.'

I nodded.

Prisoners were valuable to my father, dead or alive.

Insurrection: Chapter Three

The hiding place had been compromised.

We had to move again. Preferably out of the city this time, there were no safe places there anymore.

'Load everything in the trucks.' Sly took control of the evacuation. He was back with the group and approached everything in his normal military manner. Exactly what we needed to evacuate.

The seven pickups from the underground parking garage we'd chosen for our hide-a-way stood ready, their tanks full. With its eight levels—five of which were under-ground—it was a warren of spaces to hide in.

The thick concrete and excessive use of steel in the construction protected us from heat sensitive locators as long as we were in the lowest levels. There were three stair-ways in addition to the five unused lifts. We couldn't rely on continuous electricity anymore and standing in a small metal elevator while under attack didn't seem like a good idea anyway.

The parking garage had three separate entrances for

vehicles. Two routes for customers and one for the employees and maintenance teams. The last one was our way in and out. We reasoned it would be the least obvious exit.

Ebony informed us the invaders were searching the city building by building. They used advanced scanning equipment and were quick to open fire on whoever or whatever they found. One thing you could say for the Taxorians, they were thorough.

'I've found you a new location,' her voice resounded on the phone speaker. 'It's about three hundred miles west in the Rocky Mountains. The trip will be hazardous to say the least. The hunt for the resistance isn't restricted to only the cities anymore, though it is concentrated in the more heavily populated localities.'

We decided to cut our odds and split the group into individual trucks. They would leave the underground garage one by one, half an hour apart and all under cover of the darkness. Jonah, Nasheed and Aaliyah were in the second truck, Caleb, Kate and I in the fifth. Sly would stay till everyone else had left and drive the final pickup together with Logan.

'You all have a different route,' she continued. 'It will bring you halfway to your destination.'

The final location would be transmitted only after an airtight coded signal was received when we arrived at the stop point, just in case anyone was intercepted. We hoped everyone would make it there but had to plan for a worst-case scenario and keep the final coordinates under wraps. It brought home how extensive the invader's control was.

We waited with bated breath. The first pick up left the building an hour after midnight. There was radio silence, and we had no idea after they left the structure whether they would be okay, even Ebony was in the dark. Jonah, Nasheed and Aaliyah were next. We said our goodbyes and Jonah started the truck. The sound resonated loudly in the otherwise empty space. A shiver ran up my spine, surely the noise would alert someone, but it was unavoidable. They left in a slow assent to the surface.

We repeated the process another two times and finally it was our turn. Kate sat on the back seat while I took up a position in the passenger seat. Caleb drove. Sly slapped the side of the truck to indicate we should leave, and we were off. Caleb slowly circumvented the steep ramps up from the eighth level. I kept my eyes peeled, looking for anything out of the ordinary. We reached the fourth level without issues, and I started to breathe a bit. Prematurely, as it turned out.

A blue laser bolt narrowly missed us and slammed into the wall behind the truck, disintegrating the concrete and exploding shards everywhere.

'Lay down,' I screamed at Kate as the rear window shattered.

She quickly slipped off the seat onto the floor, hiding from sight and hopefully out of danger.

Caleb swerved for yet another beam which narrowly missed our vehicle. He floored the accelerator, and we sped up the ramp at neck-breaking speed. I peppered the area where the lasers had come from as we passed and was rewarded with a loud scream and the weapon losing its aim.

The truck wheels left the ground when we crashed out of the parking garage, hit the ground with a jolt and raced off down the access streets. More lasers attacked us from both sides as Caleb ploughed on into a grunt standing in the middle of the road aiming his weapon at us. The pure weight of the truck and the power behind the enhanced engine tossed him up into the air in a bundle of broken bones and flesh.

The truck swerved but caught its wheels again and we raced off into the night. Caleb cut the lights, and we descended into the deep darkness of the unlit city.

'What about the rest?' Kate's voice was full of the same worry I felt.

'They'll have heard the shots,' Caleb announced. 'Gone through one of the other exits.'

I sincerely hoped he was right. But we wouldn't know until we reached our final destination. The silence fell on us heavily. No one knew what to say, so we didn't try. We all searched the shadows in what little we could see of the streets and sped onwards.

Insurrection: Chapter Four

The halfway mark left us waiting under a copse of trees outside a small village. Like all other inhabited areas, street-lights were no longer lit, and the world was plunged into darkness.

I held onto Kate as she slept on the back seat of the pickup. The breakout had exhausted her, still unused to the adrenaline connected with a narrow escape. I softly stroked the hair from her face and thanked my lucky stars she was alright.

Caleb pulled the phone from his jacket and looked into the screen.

'We have coordinates,' he announced.

He moved to the truck and entered the coordinates into the sat nav. I looked over the backseat at the display and waited anxiously for the system to work out where we were headed.

A map finally covered the screen, and I saw we still had another hundred miles in an estimated ninety minutes to go. Caleb changed the route from the shortest option to a rural, more backroad one to keep us away from inhabited areas. That extended the trip with another forty miles and three hours. It would be worth it.

The night was quickly waning, and we decided to search for a place where we could hide until the next night. Driving around slowly we found a disused and abandoned barn. I dismounted from the car and carefully opened the broken doors wide enough for the truck to enter.

The barn's skeleton was completely constructed of rough, thick wooden posts. The dovetail connections between them were a work of art and I marvelled at the artistry. Thick wooden planks coated the roof and the sides. Some of them were missing and let fresh air into the musty area. Disused farm equipment and stacks of old hay balls were all we could find. I noticed traces of wild animals that had made the place their home but fled when we arrived.

A fire wasn't an option with all the flammable material and besides, we didn't want to alert anyone to our location. We pulled some of the hay bails out of the pile, broke the ropes and spread the contents out as a natural bedding. Caleb and I took turns on guard while the others slept reasonably comfortably in sleeping bags on top of the hay.

The weather had taken a turn for the worst, and it had poured down. Streams of cold water leaked through the holes in the roof, but it had the added benefit that it kept most people indoors. The incessant downpour receded later in the day, and we made plans to continue our trip. We shared a cold meal from our provisions before we left the barn at midnight.

The first part of the trip was uneventful. We stayed off the main roads and even occasionally took some dirt tracks. For the last thirty miles we left all civilisation behind and with it, good roads.

We decided to wait for sunrise before we tackled the more difficult trails up the lower mountains into the Rockies. The truck started to slip on the muddy trails, and we had some harrowing moments when the back wheels struggled for traction. Kate held on to my hand on one side and the door handle on the other. Her knuckles were white with the effort. She was terrified. I couldn't blame her. I was far from comfortable myself but trusted Caleb's driving skills. I squeezed her hand, and she offered me a half-hearted smile.

We made it up the mountain in one piece and the trail slowly flattened out. We started to breathe again and Kate's grip on my hand softened.

Caleb constantly checked the coordinates as we slowly continued our trip. I looked out of the window and marvelled at the beautiful scenery. The elevation on the mountain gave us a fantastic view over the vast forests that coated not only this mountain but the surrounding ones as well. The deep green of the fir trees were peppered with apple-green maple trees. Deep down in the valley, a river snaked through the gorge.

'It's beautiful,' Kate whispered beside me. I turned and smiled at the radiance on her face.

She was right. It was.

Caleb slowed the car and stopped on a large ledge where the track widened.

'I've lost the sat nav,' he announced.

I leant over the back of the passenger seat and observed the screen. It announced that we had arrived at our destination. That was alarming, because there was nothing there. I disembarked and walked to the edge of the ledge. From there I observed the area in more detail. Caleb and Kate joined me, and we all searched for any signs of a building or construction.

I couldn't see anything other than an endless forest and glanced at the others. They shook their heads.

'What do we do now?' Kate asked.

I didn't really have a clue. But we couldn't stay where we were, we were too visible.

'This could be another safety measure Ebony put in,' Caleb suggested. 'In case we were intercepted.'

'Sounds logical,' I answered. 'And she probably expects us to find it ourselves from here.'

'I think we should just continue on the trail,' Caleb continued. 'And see from there.'

We agreed, we didn't have any alternatives.

Back in the pickup we slowly made our way along the side of the mountain, descending with every turn.

An hour later the trail effectively stopped at the edge of the river we'd seen earlier. I could see it continued across the water. There was no bridge, and we couldn't really gauge the depth of the fast-running water.

'I'll get out and walk in front of the car,' I opted. 'Then at least we can see whether we can traverse it.'

'Why you?' Kate asked, her face lined with worry looking at the swift running water.

'I'm the strongest,' I answered. My Taxorian background was finally a bonus.

'We'll tie a rope to the front of the car as an extra security,' Caleb suggested, alleviating some of the concern in her features.

Ten minutes later I was up to my knees shivering in the cold mountain water. Progress was slow with me battling against the strong current. The car slowly followed me, keeping the rope around my waist slack so it wouldn't hinder me.

The river was only a foot and a half deep and we managed to cross it without issues. I rejoined the others, wringing out my socks and emptying the water from my boots. The heat of the car's interior was welcome, and I dried out quickly.

The only real option was to continue to follow the slowly disappearing track. Half an hour passed, and we entered a clearing losing the trail in the knee-high grass.

'Now what?'

I shrugged. I was out of ideas. Kate looked just as confused.

We scanned the clearing and the tree line beyond. Nothing.

I got out of the car and started to walk towards the centre of the open space. The warm rays of the sun were welcome on my still cold skin. My clothes were dry, but wading in the mountain water had chilled me to the bone. I estimated it to be almost mid-day, and the sun was almost at its zenith.

A movement to my right caught my eye and I swivelled, crouching down to minimise my target area.

I'd seen something from my peripheral vision but couldn't place what it was. I scrutinised the forest. Was there a movement?

In the trees to the right, I spotted a branch moving. Then another. I slowly made my way back to the truck; certain I wouldn't get to the cover before whatever it was came out. Maybe it was a bear, or a moose. Or worst-case scenario, an enemy.

Caleb had followed my gaze and pushed Kate back into the car where she once again lay on the floor of the vehicle behind the front seats. His gun was pointed at the movement between the trees.

We waited with bated breath.

Soft wind blew through the branches of the trees, birds called to each other, other than that it was silent. My hearts beat wildly in my ears, drowning out the natural sounds.

A figure materialised from the edge of the forest, then another and the tension seeped out of my muscles like the river we'd just crossed.

Jonah and Nasheed approached us with massive smiles on their faces.

I'd never been happier to see them.

We embraced and I turned to the car. Caleb and Kate had disembarked and were coming towards us. Kate rushed into Jonah's arms, and he enveloped her in his massive bear hug, lifting her off the ground. Caleb and Nasheed clasped arms and there were smiles all around.

'Good to see you all,' the big man declared.

'Same here,' I answered, my voice full of the relief that flooded my body.

Kate joined me and snaked her arm around my waist. I pulled her closer, my arm around her shoulder.

'Have the rest come in?' Caleb asked, the worry clear in his tense features.

Jonah shook his head. 'Not all of them yet,' he answered. His features softened as he acknowledged the intense nerves in Caleb's face.

'What happened?' Nasheed asked carefully, observing the damage to the car.

'We were attacked on the ramp driving up from the third floor,' I answered, choosing my words carefully. On the drive all our thoughts had been with the two teams still left in the underground garage when we escaped.

'Did the other teams make it to the halfway mark?' Caleb asked.

Nasheed glanced at Jonah. His worried look wasn't lost on Caleb and his brow creased even more.

'One of the teams called in,' the big man's announced, keeping an eye on Caleb's reaction.

'Do you know which one?'

He shook his head. 'No.'

Jonah clasped Caleb's shoulder in support. 'He'll be alright, Caleb. Ebony would have let us know if something had happened to him.'

Caleb attempted a smile; it didn't really work. He tried to nod. 'Yeah,' he acknowledged. 'The old man is hard to kill.'

We all chuckled at that. Sly did have a knack for getting out of tight situations.

The silence that followed was uncomfortable. We wanted to support Caleb, but there was nothing else we could do or say. Kate stroked his arm, and he covered her hand with his own in gratitude for the sentiment.

'You need to get you to camp,' Jonah announced. 'Get the car out of the open space. Nasheed will join you to show you the way.'

I nodded and turned to walk back to the car with Kate.

'You okay if I stay with you?' Caleb asked Jonah.

'Of course.'

Nasheed took the driver seat; I sat next to him with Kate behind me. We set off slowly to the edge of the clearing. Jonah and Caleb rearranged the grass behind us to hide our tracks.

I didn't envy Caleb. He was worried sick about his father. So were we, but his family bond was much closer. I hope he was right, that no one could kill him. Sly's stern and rough edges had grown on me, and he was a valued member of our strange and dysfunctional family.

Twenty minutes later we rounded yet another corner on the narrow trail and entered an area bordered with high cliffs on one side and deep dark forest on the other. The rock wall was almost sheer and towered up high above us with an overhang that initially made me nervous. It looked as though it could come down anytime. It also offered a natural cover for the caves and constructions that formed the camp, rendering it practically invisible from above. I understood the attraction the place had.

I stepped out of the pickup and looked up at the steep wall of rock. It was definitely impressive. There were caves on two levels, the upper ones accessible with rough wooden ladders made from local tree trunks and thick rope. I counted more than twenty openings at first glance. Some looked natural, but most I deemed man-made, their edges too regular and precise. The thirty metre by twenty metre area in front of the caves was flat. At the edge, under the foliage of the tall fir trees, I saw the four vehicles that left before us hidden under camouflage nets. Three more cars stood to their right, also covered with netting. Further on I spied a paddock with some horses, something I really hadn't expected.

'You made it,' Aaliyah's happy voice resounded, and I turned towards the sound. She approached us and hugged Kate—they got on like a house on fire—and then even did the same to me. I hugged her back; just as happy the family was coming together again.

'This place is amazing,' she voiced enthusiastically. 'The caves go on into the mountain and are very comfortable.'

'Was it already inhabited?' I asked, noticing some faces I didn't know.

'Yes, two families lived here. They've been very helpful and offered us a lot of information on how to live here.'

'How did they know about the caves?'

'Seems one of them was involved in the construction of what was supposed to be a shelter for the apocalypse. An eccentric millionaire owned the land, and he was convinced the end of the humanity was nearing,'

'Well, he wasn't far off.' I commented.

'No, but no one believed him.'

'Is he here?'

She shook her head. 'He died before the invasion. Built it all for nothing.'

'Well, good for us that he did.'

She nodded, her laughter warm and uplifting.

'Why did they welcome us?' I questioned, ever the pessimist.

'I think mostly because they're not warriors. They have no idea how to protect themselves, so our presence makes them feel safer. That and they just yearned for human contact.'

I raised an eyebrow. Aaliyah knew what I meant and shook her head slowly. Hmm, they weren't aware of our origins. Good idea to keep that secret. I resolved to tell Caleb and Kate to stay silent at the first possible option. The humans in our team were used to us being around and didn't really see us as aliens anymore, but I was under no illusion others would do the same. It was best to keep that piece of information to ourselves.

Grab your copy...
vinci-books.com/insurrection